Praise for *The Low End of Nowhere*

"The gumshoe private eye is back and his name is Streeter. Michael Stone has a great talent. *The Low End of Nowhere* is the way a mystery should be written."
— Clive Cussler

"Michael Stone brings a tongue-in-cheek update of the noir classics to the contemporary underbelly of Denver. *The Low End of Nowhere* has great imagery and snap-crackle-pop dialogue. For fans of hard-boiled, the old-fashioned way."
— Jeremiah Healy, author of *Act of God* and *Rescue*

"A sparkling debut . . . fast-paced and gritty, with more twists than a Twizzler. . . . If you think the days of tough-guy novels are over, then you need to meet Streeter."
— *Albuquerque Journal*

"The quintessential loner private eye . . . fans of the genre should eat it up."
— *The Denver Post*

"A fine first book that's sometimes just plain laugh-out-loud funny."
— *The Bloomsbury Review*

"*The Low End of Nowhere* is a high-end romp through the seamy side of Colorado that throws remarkably engaging characters and a gripping plot at the reader. It's written with the authority of someone who has been there and seen it all. In his first time to bat Stone has gone and hit one out of the park."
— Michael Connelly, author of *The Concrete Blonde*

"Stone . . . works the hard-boiled genre conventions with the insouciance of an old pro. . . . Streeter is an eye-catcher."
— *The New York Times*

"Exciting . . . a much-needed blast of fresh air to the private eye genre . . . non-stop action, clever plotting."
— *The Toronto Star*

PENGUIN CRIME FICTION

THE LOW END OF NOWHERE

Michael Stone, formerly a reporter for Wisconsin, Florida, and Colorado newspapers, including the *Rocky Mountain News*, and a correspondent for *The Dallas Morning News* and *San Francisco Examiner*, has been a private investigator in Denver for the past eleven years. Stone's second Streeter mystery, *A Long Reach*, is available from Viking.

The Low End of Nowhere

A STREETER MYSTERY

Michael Stone

PENGUIN BOOKS

PENGUIN BOOKS
Published by the Penguin Group
Penguin Books USA Inc., 375 Hudson Street, New York, New York 10014, U.S.A.
Penguin Books Ltd, 27 Wrights Lane, London W8 5TZ, England
Penguin Books Australia Ltd, Ringwood, Victoria, Australia
Penguin Books Canada Ltd, 10 Alcorn Avenue, Toronto, Ontario, Canada M4V 3B2
Penguin Books (N.Z.) Ltd, 182–190 Wairau Road, Auckland 10, New Zealand

Penguin Books Ltd, Registered Offices: Harmondsworth, Middlesex, England

First published in the United States of America by Viking Penguin,
a division of Penguin Books USA Inc. 1996
Published in Penguin Books 1997

1   3   5   7   9   10   8   6   4   2

PUBLISHER'S NOTE
This is a work of fiction. Names, characters, places, and incidents either are the product
of the author's imagination or are used fictitiously, and any resemblance to actual
persons, living or dead, events, or locales is entirely coincidental.

THE LIBRARY OF CONGRESS HAS CATALOGUED THE HARDCOVER AS FOLLOWS:
Stone, Michael.
The Low End of Nowhere: a Streeter mystery/Michael Stone.
p.   cm.
ISBN 0-670-86154-5 (hc.)
ISBN 0 14 02.4694 0 (pbk.)
I. Title.
PS3569.T64144B8   1996
813´.54—dc20   95–21208

Printed in the United States of America
Set in Minion
Designed by Virginia Norey

To Carla Madison,
for getting me going

The author would like to thank and acknowledge Rex Burns, Bob Diddlebock, Kitty Hirs, Irma Stone, and Danny and Shannon Dupler for their help and support. Also, a nod to Landmark Education.

The Low End
of Nowhere

1

Grundy Dopps, a sour-looking little pinch of white trash, waddled out of his trailer that morning somehow knowing it wasn't going to be his day. Unfortunately, this was one of those rare times that his intuition was right. His hay fever was killing him. An angry tumor of phlegm festered behind a nose that was rubbed so raw, it felt like he'd been wiping it with steel wool. The midday heat pushed the thermometer in his toolshed up past ninety-five. Everything was turned around. It wasn't supposed to be so hot this early in June, and the tree pollen wasn't supposed to be so thick this late in the season. Not in Colorado.

"Go figger it," he reasoned pitifully as he sneezed. "Very weird." More sneezes. "Everything's always so weird."

Then there was that call that woke him up earlier. The guy said he was an investigator for an attorney. Grundy had his doubts.

"My name is Soyko," the guy had informed him.

"You got a first name or is that it?" Grundy asked, holding a soggy handkerchief just inches in front of his nose.

"All you need to know is Soyko. We gotta talk, you and me."

It wasn't a request. "Man who hired me said we should go over your testimony. Make sure you get it right and all that."

Who does he think he is? Grundy wondered. Even Jesus Christ had two names. At least two. And what does he mean, "get it right and all that"? Grundy'd forgotten the attorney's name, but he had a good idea what was coming down.

"Is this about that maniac, what's his name?" he asked Soyko. "Fred Borders? Him and his murder trial?"

No answer at first and then a slow "That's it" slid out of the receiver.

"Ta-rrefic," Grundy mumbled and shook his head.

Tiny Fred Borders was a three-hundred-ten-pound bouncer at the Dangle, a biker-strip bar in Commerce City, just north of Denver. A sadistic lush who smelled like stale beef jerky, Tiny had all the charm of a buffalo with piles. One night a few months back, an investment banker wandered up to the Dangle for a little brush with life's underbelly and tested the big guy. He got stupid drunk and tried to stare down the bouncer.

"Nice bib overalls there, Gomer. Lose your way out of Green Acres or what?" the banker muttered in Tiny Fred's direction. Then he looked around the room, snickering at his own cleverness, and added in a loud voice, "What kind of loony breeding experiment produced a bloated moron like him?"

Truth, of course, was no defense in Tiny Fred's astoundingly limited mind. The bloated moron sucked in his enormous gut and simply went berserk. He threw the drunk, paisley tie and all, out into the parking lot. At that point, the banker shifted into some indignant mode and began cursing. The clown actually was going to put up a fight. Bad move. When Tiny Fred Borders decides to throw you a beating, about the best you can do is assume a fetal position until he gets winded or until his nominal attention span wanders. To call what happened next a fight is like calling what happens at a slaughterhouse a hunt. Still, when Fred finally stopped, the banker was able to totter to his feet, navigate to his BMW, and drive off. As he left the parking lot, he managed what proved to be the last gesture of a truly foolish man. He flipped off Tiny Fred.

Enraged, the bouncer jumped into his pickup and chased the doomed investment banker. About three miles to the south, he forced the BMW off the road and into a deserted parking lot. It was at that point that Tiny Fred, by virtue of one swift tire-iron blow to the head, made sure the uppity Yuppie would diss him no more. Grundy witnessed the fatal blow from the back porch of his welding shop, some thirty yards away. He recognized Tiny Fred standing in the headlights from his own numerous trips to the Dangle. Grundy saw the perspiring bouncer casually wipe blood from the tire iron onto the lifeless banker's pants and kick his stomach one final time. Then Borders farted passionately into the still night air, got back into the pickup, and drove away.

Wisely, Grundy shirked his civic duty and slipped out of town for a few days. He knew that calling the cops would put him on Tiny Fred's vast shit list. Just ask the banker what that felt like. But, alas, Grundy got drunk a couple of weeks later and started blabbing in a crowded bar. An undercover Denver cop overheard him and Tiny Fred was subsequently arrested.

"Listen up, you little turd," one of the investigating officers had admonished Grundy only the day before Soyko's call. "This trial starts in just four days, and if you even think of taking off again or if your memory goes lame on us, you'll walk into a shit storm so thick you'll never get out. You hear that, Dopps? We got us a dead white man here and we ain't gonna let nobody mess up our case. No way."

As he waited for Soyko, Grundy still wondered if he'd done the right thing by not splitting. Standing in the tepid shade of his shop awning, the welder idly ran one hand over his belly. He had an enormous gut and nose for such a short man with such a skinny face.

Suddenly a black El Camino in mint condition pulled up. The vehicle had a lone bumper sticker on the front proclaiming in green Day-Glo that "Disco Heals." It was Leo Soyko, with some guy in dark shades driving. They pulled around to the back, near the porch where Grundy stood when he saw the banker's murder and where he was now, more or less, poised. The car engine shut off, and the two men inside spoke to each other while staring straight ahead. Soyko then looked off as a narrow smile crimped his face. He had been at Tiny Fred's preliminary hearing. It was a joke. The welder up there on the witness stand all cotton-mouthed and twitchy, ratting out the big guy like that. Plain to see he'd rather be strung up by his toes than testifying.

Tiny's attorney knew that the state would have no case without Grundy but it had a virtual lock if a jury ever heard his story. Hence, Soyko was sent, cash in hand, to make sure that wouldn't happen. The lawyer specifically said he didn't want Grundy Dopps within a thousand miles of the courtroom come trial time.

"This is the damnedest thing I ever heard of," Soyko had told the attorney. "You want me to give this little punk three grand to cover his traveling expenses? Maybe I should kiss him good-bye, too."

The lawyer just glared and again told him to get Dopps out of town.

"You know, this screwing around makes no sense whatso-ever," Soyko now told his driver, Jacky Romp. "On three thou-sand like this, we could party serious. He wants me to just give it up like this guy's doing us a favor. It wasn't for him talking, Tiny wouldn't have all this grief. Just how do these jackoffs get through law school anyhow?"

"Beats me," Jacky Romp answered without actually moving his lips. He looked pained behind his shades. "No sense to it whatsoever, like you said. The whole thing makes me sick."

"This welder gives me any shit . . ." Soyko let the unfinished thought hang there in the midday heat. He sat for another min-ute, then got out of the car, still smiling.

What's so funny? Grundy wondered as Soyko moved toward him. Here the guy comes slouching up, dressed like James Dean just out of prison: blue jeans, white sleeveless T-shirt, dark motor-

cycle boots. His black hair was combed back in a casual pom-
padour, his sideburns were long and thick but closely trimmed.
He was squinting into the sun. Too macho for shades, Grundy
reasoned. When he got closer, Grundy noticed that his eyes were
small and incredibly dark: deeply intense but flat. Even with the
wide grin, there wasn't a sliver of warmth or humor in those
eyes.

Two other things about Soyko stood out. First was his wide
brown belt with the huge buckle. Second was his left arm. The
muscles were impressive enough, like rubber stretched over
chains. But high up on it there was a tattoo of a rattlesnake
wrapped in barbed wire, coiled and ready to strike. Above the
snake's head were two simple words: "Make Pain."

Damned Elvis impersonator on steroids, Grundy thought,
then quickly said, "You must be Soyko." He tried to sound calm.
"I'm the owner here. Grundy Dopps." He extended his hand.

Soyko kept coming slowly, looking around as he moved. He
was still fuming at the lawyer's strategy and he didn't answer at
first. Maybe he'd just handle this thing his way. Save the man
some money and crank up his own fee. And look at this goof
trying to act like he's in control of something. It was at that
point that Soyko decided to free-lance.

Grundy neither expected the kick nor saw it coming. Soyko
shot his right foot into the welder's unprotected groin so fast
out of his casual stride, and Grundy fell so quickly, that it looked
like the two men had rehearsed it. The air rushed from Grundy's
lungs, so that when his knees hit the ground he was sucking
hard. His hands instinctively shot downward to protect his ach-
ing balls, which had retreated inward in pain. He didn't fully
understand what happened but a look of terror swept over his
face. That was all Soyko needed to see. He swung his shoulders
a bit to the right, and as he came back he let the welder have a
solid backhand, two rings and all, to the side of his face. Grundy
let out a scream and Soyko knew that somewhere behind him
Jacky Romp was smiling.

"Let's us go over your testimony, pal," Soyko said. His thick smile remained despite what he'd just done. "We're not happy with it. Not at all. Guess you can understand that."

Tears gushed from Grundy's eyes as he struggled to get his breath back. The slap knocked him on his side on the filthy porch floor. He looked up at Soyko and squealed, "What the fuck you do that for?"

"If we're not happy, no way you're gonna be happy." Soyko waited a beat and then reached down and grabbed Grundy's neck with his left hand. "Let's get you up here."

There was just a trace of sympathy in his voice. His other hand snatched the front of Grundy's shirt as he guided him to a folding chair a few feet away. When Soyko got him situated on the chair, he stood over him. The smile was gone. His jaws clenched to indicate that maybe the worst was ahead.

Grundy felt blood rushing to his wounded crotch and he felt more blood flowing down his cheek. His nuts, along with the left side of his face, were swelling fast.

"I didn't want to tell them anything. Christ Awmighty, I didn't." Grundy's voice was shrill, tearful. His stomach was on fire. "They heard me say what I did about that Tiny guy and that was it. What am I supposed to do? Lie up there on the stand? They got me on record from that hearing. I change my story now, I'm totally screwed. Totally! They told me that already. You wouldn't believe the heat I'm getting from the cops. I can't lie up there on the stand."

The logic seemed highly reasonable to the welder as he spoke.

"No, we can't ask you to lie." Soyko sounded convinced, but he frowned. "You ain't getting up on no stand. That's guaranteed."

There was a finality in his voice that terrified Grundy even more. "I'm not?"

He was whimpering loudly now, and the sound infuriated Soyko. Little piece of garbage don't even know enough to protect his own balls and he thinks he's going to put Tiny Fred away, Soyko thought. Not in a million years.

"You're not. You're gonna be taking a long trip to somewhere very far away. Tomorrow night I'm coming back out here, and if you're still in this same time zone, I'll rip off your head and piss in your neck. You got that?"

A splinter of hope rushed through the man in the folding chair. Maybe there's a way out of this. He tried to focus. "I can't just leave, can I? I mean, I can't just . . ."

Soyko's jaw clenched harder. "You can if you want to keep your head attached to the rest of that lard-ass body. I'm not so sure I'm getting through to you. Take maybe two minutes to think about it. I'm going over to the car out there, and when I get back, let me know what you decide."

With that he turned and moved fluently back to the El Camino. He went to the driver's side and leaned in, his face close to Jacky's.

"I'm saving everybody three grand. This guy's so scared, he leaves town, it's with his own money."

"He giving you some grief?" Jacky never really moved his lips.

"A little. Probably too much. He's still asking all these stupid questions. Some guys're more dense than others. Maybe he's one of them."

"What next?" Jacky wanted to see if Soyko was done being nice.

"You're right." Soyko looked at Grundy as he spoke. He and Jacky had worked together for years and had been through enough jobs like this that they had their own shorthand down solid. "Done wasting my breath." Then he started back toward the porch.

Grundy was breathing almost normally, and his thoughts were clearing. Maybe this insane dude would let him go with just the warning. Could he leave town for the trial? The question rushed through him furiously. By now Soyko was again in front of him, and the welder didn't know what to say. He was about to learn that this was no time to improvise.

"You done with your travel plans yet?" Soyko was smiling again.

That alone made Grundy recoil slightly, his hands moving

automatically toward his groin. "I don't know. Those guys are gonna be really pissed when I get back. I miss the trial, they'll go ape shit on me."

The smile disappeared. "Let's us go inside and talk for a minute. You got any beer in there?" He nodded toward the shop door a few feet away.

Man wants a beer, Grundy thought. That's more reasonable. More like it. "Sure thing." He got up slowly and walked, huddled forward. When they got through the screen door, he turned to ask his visitor to sit down.

Soyko knew what had to be done, and he did it with few wasted motions. First, he grabbed the limping welder by the back of his neck. He squeezed so tight that Grundy couldn't see for a second and a harsh, gagging sound blurted from his throat. Soyko then reached down to his belt buckle and clutched it, moving his hand around. The welder was confused. Soyko shook his right hand, releasing the buckle head from the belt itself. It was a unique buckle, highly illegal. The head came loose from the leather, and when it did a four-inch blade slipped into view. Grundy could barely believe it. The blade must run behind the leather next to the buckle, hiding it.

Soyko lifted the blade to his chin level. Grundy felt warm urine flowing down his leg, but he had no idea where it came from. That was the last thing he ever felt, because Soyko thrust the pointed blade into his throat far too quickly for him to register any real pain. It cut his windpipe and slashed open an artery: either one could have killed him. A stream of blood shot out into the air for several inches, and Soyko knew Grundy was dead by the time he hit the floor. He'd seen it before.

"Tiny's trial is gonna go a whole lot easier from now on," he told Jacky Romp when he got back to the El Camino. "That's guaranteed."

2

Streeter knew that when you step into a lie, no matter whose lie, the same thing always sticks to your shoes. And what he was faced with now was nothing but pure, grade-A, designer crapola. From down the hall he could see the blonde take off her cervical collar and drop it next to her blood-burgundy, ever-so-stylish Prince gym bag. Then she grabbed her squash racquet and started bouncing it off her fingertips. Slow and relaxed, not even looking at it. Hot-shit boredom on her face, her hip cocked out like a naughty girl jock. She shot out her tongue for an instant, and the guy with her shook his head and laughed.

"Calvin, do you really want to beat up on a defenseless cripple like me?" She wore an innocent pout as she spoke. "But I guess I'm not supposed to say 'cripple' anymore, am I? Nowadays it's 'unabled' or 'differently capped' or 'structurally challenged.' Or whatever they call it so as not to make people feel like they're less than perfect. I can't even keep track of all the euphemisms we're supposed to call each other."

"Whatever they call it, I hardly think of the word 'defenseless' when I look at you," Calvin answered. "And that's even if you actually needed that collar."

With that, they both walked into the polished court.

Streeter touched the camera in his gym bag for assurance and headed down the hall. Clearly, the blonde hadn't seen him. The muffled smack of rubber balls on hardwood echoed around him. Subdued, almost eerie lighting engulfed the hallway. On both sides there were small doors with slit windows, like some kind of upscale prison in a Nike commercial.

He wanted to give the couple time to start their squash game, so he stopped in front of a tinted, one-way window looking into an empty aerobics room. Catching his reflection in the glass, he straightened his shoulders. Although he was pushing forty-two and he was just over six feet tall and weighed a solid two hundred ten pounds, Streeter still had the childhood habit of slouching. He also noticed that he should consider getting a trim. His thick brown hair was long and combed straight back. No sideburns. He kept his hair clean and combed. The ends fell nonchalantly far over the collar of his pale-blue Oxford shirt. He wore it long enough so as not to look corporate but still kept it neat. With his high, prominent cheekbones and clear, tan skin, he looked pleasantly rugged, but not pretty.

Hard digging and a little luck were about to pay off nicely. Streeter had been hired three weeks earlier by a nervous insurance-claims adjuster who asked him to dig up something on the little blonde.

"Show she ain't hurt nearly so bad, you know, like she claims in that bullshit lawsuit a hers," Swanson, the adjuster, had told him. "Do a real number on this chick—okay, Streeter? She's trying to make jerks out of us. No way in hell she got hurt with what happened to her." He opened a legal-sized file folder and read from it. "The jacket on her goes like this. Her name is Story Moffatt, if you can believe that. Looks great. Sort of beer-commercial cute." He pulled a photograph from the folder and slid it across his desk. "But she's savvy as hell in business. Runs her own successful ad agency, and she's all of maybe thirty-two."

He quit reading and looked up. "Then she gets into a two-car fender bender a few months ago. It's our guy's fault and now

she's suing for sixty grand. The old pain-and-suffering routine."
He emphasized his frustration with a prolonged shrug. "Claims
she's so bad off, most days she's lucky to hook up her damned
bra without screaming. Not much unusual about that, but our
guy was going all of four miles an hour when he hit her. More
like a burp than a collision. We fixed the damage with a tweezers
and nail polish, for Chrissake. Then she comes up with this crap.
Her lawyer knows a, shall we say, ethically limber orthopedic
surgeon, who diagnoses her: 'soft tissue injured, unspecified.' He
sends her to a chiropractor and pain clinic. Three treatments a
week at ninety bucks a pop, and now she's got enough medical
costs to sue."

Swanson had sniffed around on his own but came up empty.
So he called a friend who knew Streeter—a bounty hunter, of
all things. The adjuster didn't even know those guys still existed.
"Bounty hunter" sounded a tad theatrical, but Streeter made his
living tracking down people who posted bail and then couldn't
seem to find the courthouse at the appropriate time. He worked
alone, mostly for a bail bondsman with whom he shared a loose
business-and-housing arrangement. Because Colorado has no li-
censing for private eyes, from time to time Streeter also did re-
lated chores for lawyers and insurance companies. Chores like
witness interviewing and surveillances. Or skip tracing: locating
people who don't want to be found. As the bail bondsman put
it, "We're finders of lost assholes."

"You're gonna love this one, big man," Swanson said when
he gave Streeter the five-hundred-dollar retainer. "We're on the
righteous side here. No one gets hurt at that speed unless the
car runs over their head."

Streeter took the check and looked at the adjuster. Their mutual friend was a bookie Streeter had used for years. The bounty
hunter followed college football and basketball religiously and
wasn't above putting down a few bucks on games when he got
a stiff feeling about one of the teams. His feelings paid off with
remarkable frequency. Streeter had a keen eye for all manner of
team statistics and minute pregame detail. But that keen eye was

best utilized in his most passionate avocation: trivia. Annually, he fielded a team in The Knowledge Bowl, a trivia contest in Boulder, and Streeter had even made a two-day appearance on *Jeopardy* a couple of years ago. Pop culture and movies were his specialty. "I'll get right on it," he told Swanson as he stuffed the check in his shirt pocket.

It had started off badly, but Streeter didn't panic. He sat on Moffatt's house one Saturday morning and then tailed her late one Wednesday afternoon. Nothing. She was being careful, the cervical collar with her always. Story moved slowly, gingerly getting in and out of cars like she was wearing sandpaper panties. Strictly Oscar material. So much for deep distance and caution. The retainer was melting and his curiosity burned. That's when he decided to go face-to-face with the woman.

Getting people to talk was a strong suit. He had those safe, big brown eyes and that calm demeanor. He always listened intently, leaning in to people like nothing else in the whole world mattered except them. And usually he'd wait a few seconds after they spoke before responding. Just long enough to be noticed, but not so long as to be irritating. It let them know he was really considering what they just said. People responded to that, opened up. His size helped. Years of relentless weight lifting gave his shoulders mass without making him appear clumsy. Shoulders like a linebacker, which is what he was when he played the holy game of football in college. Linebacker intensity in the eyes, too.

People felt protected just being around him. Especially women. They liked Streeter and he liked them. Did he ever. Trouble was, his experiences in that department were consistently catastrophic. He'd already racked up four failed marriages, he'd been engaged another three times, and was at least nominally involved with more women than he could recall. They tended to own him. And it wasn't only that he couldn't say no to an attractive woman. Streeter couldn't say no to any woman with a pulse and at least a double-digit IQ. Take this Story Moffatt. He knew the first time he saw her smug beauty that she was trouble. Big trouble. If he ever fell for her, he'd be doing whatever it took to keep her around. Whatever. Good thing this was strictly business.

Story's advertising firm was located in Denver's eclectic Capitol Hill section, so named because it was a wide, low hill featuring the state capitol roughly in the middle of it. Her company consisted of five employees and a clientele that netted her nearly six figures annually. She was divorced, childless ("Who has time for a family?"), and overachieving in a business where nerve and style got you a hell of a lot further than an impressive résumé or real job skills. Streeter figured he could best get her attention by passing himself off as a prospective client. From his desk he dug out an old business card once belonging to Brad Tessmer, owner of the defunct Arapahoe Auto Body Shop. Then he set up an appointment with Story to get some four-color brochures made.

"That collar must really hurt you, Miss Moffatt," Streeter told her as they sat down in her office the following Tuesday afternoon. Collar or no, she looked sensational. Her hair, almost white-blond, was long but styled to accent the sensual roundness of her face. She wore a pinstriped pants suit, tailored to her body so closely that it easily avoided any trace of masculinity. "I bet that's slowing you up plenty, huh?"

"I manage," she said with little emotion and then flashed him a quick, obligatory grin. Even that forced, all-business smile had enough voltage to make Streeter blink. "But it certainly doesn't make life any easier. Please, call me Story."

"I had to wear something like that once. Hurt like a mother. How'd you get yours?"

"It's really not important." Her voice gave no openings. "Let's just say I earned it. A car accident, actually."

"Think that there might be a little payoff for you in all this? Hope you got yourself a good lawyer."

"Mr. Tessmer, I have a busy schedule this afternoon and I'm

sure a man like you has a million things to do as well. My neck will take care of itself, but this brochure will need our complete attention."

Her own deep-brown eyes—he had never seen such dark-brown eyes on a blonde before—returned his gaze. She used her best low-end client voice. A real pro. Not a trace of perfunctory flirting. She had a way of telling you to go pound sand that made it seem like it was your idea. Streeter pushed harder but got nowhere. Then, just as they were finishing up, she took a phone call. When she swiveled around in her chair to talk, he scanned everything on her desk. His prayers were answered in her open Daytimer. There it was, an entry for Friday morning. "Creekside SC—S. court. Match." Creekside Sports Club. It had to be. Combination meat market and high-tech gym, it was Denver's premier health club, located in fashionable Cherry Creek. "S. court. Match"—some kind of court game. Probably "S." for "squash."

When he left her office, he called the club to verify his hunch by pretending to be her confused opponent trying to nail down the correct time.

"Yeah," the guy at the front desk told him. "Story Moffatt. Eight-thirty on Friday morning. You got the date right. Court twelve." He said her name as though he knew her and liked her. That didn't surprise Streeter.

It put him just down the hall from court twelve at a little after eight. When Story and her friend had had time to get their game going, Streeter went to the court door and grabbed his camera. He let the gym bag slide to the floor. He noticed her cervical collar and he winced. Supposed to be for broken bodies, not for making quick cash. Streeter flashed on the man he'd killed long ago.

Killing someone with his bare hands drastically changed Streeter's life. It had a profound impact on Gary Van der Heyden as well. He was the twenty-year-old Streeter killed. It happened in the summer of 1974, between their sophomore and junior years at Western Michigan University. Streeter and Gary both played linebacker. The two never got along, and the animosity boiled over in a drunken fight at a preseason frat party. Insults were exchanged and they ended up on the frat house lawn, charging each other like a couple of demented rhinos. Finally, he gave Gary one good shot to the head. His massive forearm and elbow came up like a renegade piston, catching the smaller man just below the chin. Gary's head shot back, and his neck snapped like frozen vinyl. He died on the spot.

Streeter, who had been getting some attention from pro scouts after his standout sophomore year, never played football after that. He left Western Michigan without graduating. As close as he ever came to a four-year diploma was an associate accounting degree from a community college in his hometown of Denver. After that, he did bookkeeping by day and, because of his size and cool demeanor, he was a bouncer at country-and-western bars at night. That's where he met most of his wives and fiancées. That's also how he met Frank Dazzler. A veteran bail bondsman, Frank came to Mollie's Hitching Post back in the summer of 1985 looking for a jittery car thief who was partial to George Strait music and Old Milwaukee beer. He and Streeter got to talking about their respective jobs at the front door just before closing time.

"A bouncer and an accountant, huh? You like this kind of thing, big guy?" Frank asked, tossing his head to the side to indicate the bar. "You seem way too sharp to be checking IDs and throwing these phony cowboys around. Particularly at a shithole like Mollie's."

"Both jobs can get boring sometimes," Streeter conceded. "Especially keeping books. But this has its moments, if you can stand the music. It's really a pretty decent place."

Just then an announcement blared unceremoniously over the loudspeaker inside. "Last call for alcohol. Closing time. If you're not going to fuck the help, ya gotta leave."

Frank nodded thoughtfully. "Yeah, I see what you mean. Real classy. A regular Radio City Music Hall. But I'll bet it does have some payback, at that, what with the little cowgirlies and all. As for me, I'm way too old to chase these goofs around town day and night. Look, here's my card. You come by and see me sometime and I'll give you a job that's guaranteed never to bore you. You'll get to use your brains and your brawn. And there's some real money in it, too."

Three days later, Streeter walked into Frank's office and grabbed a pair of handcuffs, and he hadn't worked another bar or kept another book since.

Now, looking through the window slit into the squash court, he could see Story bent over, waiting for the serve. Bouncing easily up on the balls of her feet, she was ready. Kill-shot concentration. Her weight moved easily from cheek to cheek in a little round butt with dark shorts stretched over it tight as wallpaper. That butt had seen some serious gym time, Streeter noticed. Tanned legs flowed out of the bottom of the shorts without a sign of a wrinkle anywhere. The woman's entire life appeared to be so seamless. So smooth and nearly effortless.

He lifted the camera, and as he took the pictures, he knew he would be putting at least one major wrinkle in her day. He almost nodded to her out there on the court. You know: Good try, lady. She made a strong run at easy insurance money. But thanks to him she'd be coming up short. She had some real brass to her, still Streeter sensed that the line between brass and bitch was so slender, at times it almost disappeared. When he was done shooting, he took one last look as she scooped low to backhand a stinger off the front wall. Not a hint of pain or stiffness anywhere. He just wished he could be there when her lawyer showed her the pictures.

3

Max Herman sat squirming across the desk from his lawyer. Max had already had his shot in life. Clearly, he'd blown it. Here he was, all of forty-three, and he'd pissed away more than most men ever have. Ten years earlier, the American dream was his. A beautiful wife, two daughters, a plumbing-supply business that grossed him nearly a hundred and a half a year, and a cool one-ninety-four bowling average. Within a few years, it was sliding fast, and by the time he was forty it was gone. In its place was a cocaine Jones that cost over a grand a week, a twenty-three-year-old Mexican girlfriend with a prison teardrop tattoo, and his two daughters in therapy—neither of whom would talk to a daddy who was over a year behind in his support payments.

"Oh, hell yeah. I know I got troubles." Max bent forward to crush out yet another Camel Light. He coughed savagely, spraying ashes across the otherwise immaculate desktop. "That's obvious, counselor. Everybody seems to want a chunk oudda my tail. But there's gotta be a way oudda all this mess. There's always a way, ain't that the truth?"

"Of course there is," the lawyer offered unenthusiastically.

The attorney, Thomas Hardy Cooper, looked at his client and

wondered how well he was hiding his disgust. If it weren't for the twenty-two-thousand-dollar retainer, already cashed and spent, Cooper wouldn't give this guy the sweat off his socks. Cooper, who was five years older than Max, couldn't imagine ever looking that rough.

Amazingly, Max had managed to gain about fifty pounds of extra blubber while using cocaine daily. "I thought this shit's supposed to melt the fat off," he would tell himself angrily as his stomach grew larger by the week. Add in his chain-smoker's rasp and top it off with the thinning blond hair wilting sadly over his shoulders, and it was obvious that he'd torched his prime. Here he is talking about some "group of heavy hitters" he's putting together for a townhouse development in the foothills west of Denver, near Golden. Yeah, right. He's facing up to twenty years for possession of cocaine with intent to deliver, a few more tacked on for a weapons violation, and a whole bunch more thrown in for allegedly threatening a police officer. Top it all off with some forty-three thousand dollars in back child support and Max is basically screwed.

Only thing is, he was way too far gone to realize it. His brain was so incinerated from his many vicious habits that he'd become prone to monumental lapses from reality. Like three weeks ago, after he was served with a temporary restraining order to keep him away from his ex and the two girls. There was a ten-thirty court hearing set for a week later. Max showed up, all right. Made quite an appearance. He waltzed into court just out of bed, wearing a ratty plaid bathrobe and a vile-looking pair of slippers. But the real *coup de maître* was that he had an open plastic bottle of Aunt Jemima pancake syrup sticking out of one pocket.

Cooper thought how if he had half this yahoo's troubles he'd save the legal fees, make one more big coke run, and then take off for someplace warm and unknown. Instead, the lawyer focused on his assistant and unofficial paralegal. He couldn't forget the skirt she wore that morning. So tight, he recalled, he could practically count her pubic hairs. That is, if she didn't regularly shave "that particular stretch of paradise," as he referred to it. Streetwise, sexy beyond belief, and precisely half Cooper's age, Rhonda "Ronnie" Taggert was his sweetest dream come true.

Cooper was pretty much of a full-fledged dorker himself until law school and a rigid program of self-improvement made him presentable. With a clientele consisting of Max Herman types, he came off as almost classy. But he had never experienced anything like Ronnie. The first time she came into his office, she was with a guy who rivaled Max for sheer, brazen stupidity. She had these bee-stung lips and this porno-queen attitude the lawyer found irresistible. Cooper took on the guy's rather winnable auto-theft case, along with a seventeen-thousand-dollar retainer, and then did everything humanly possible to see that the poor schlep got double digits in the state prison at Cañon City.

Coincidentally, that left the precocious if pouty Ms. Taggert unencumbered, uncertain about her future, and open to all offers. The one Cooper made was that she come to work in his office, get her GED, and generally clean up her act to make herself palatable to the lower echelons of Denver's legal community.

"We get a little participation from the people up there on the Jefferson County Board and this project should come together real nice," Max was saying intensely. "I get the whole entire contract for pipes and fixtures, which makes me very well, thank you. Financially speaking, that is. We take care of this bullshit holding charge and all that other crap and get Charlene and the kids off my back, and things'll look just about right."

Christ, Cooper thought. The only pipe Max had touched since he lost his plumbing shop back about six years ago was loaded with crack cocaine. And where did he get this "bullshit holding charge" from? Even if Cooper gave it his best shot, which he certainly wouldn't, Mr. Herman would be spending what was left of his middle age—not to mention a good chunk of his golden years—behind bars.

"That's a fabulous attitude, Maxwell." Cooper beamed, but Max seemed puzzled by the use of his full first name. "I feel we have an excellent chance of getting most of their evidence disposed of at the suppression hearing. Actually, I was *exceedingly* amazed that we even got bound over for trial. I did not believe that the judge was too impressed with their evidence. It seems more of a political gesture, their continuing this travesty. I'm convinced that, once we get in front of a jury, we shall get the results we desire and so justly deserve."

Not too impressed? Cooper almost laughed. The judge nearly sentenced Max right at the preliminary hearing. And if any juror in his right mind takes one look at this pathetic load and the evidence against him, the DA gets a standing ovation.

"You know, I've been working overtime on this matter," he continued. "On all of your various troubles. You've had an incredible run of bad luck, Maxwell."

"Fuckin' A, I have." Max nodded wildly. "Incredible, like you said. Who could believe all this shit?"

"Taken individually, these matters are quite manageable. However, in the aggregate, they are indeed formidable. We have almost exhausted your retainer and secondary monies. I will require another payment of precisely fifteen thousand dollars by the weekend in order to proceed."

When Max heard the number he rolled his eyes and made a sour frown, like he was suppressing a fart. "Fuckin' A, fifteen large. What are you doing, burning the money I give you? Hell, Cooper, that might take some doing."

"I understand. But you have to understand that keeping you out of Cañon City for twenty years plus will take some doing as well." Cooper was getting irritated. This was the first time Max had even hesitated about coming up with money. "Trial preparation is no easy matter. There's expert-witness fees, process serving, a million details to work out. For God's sake, Maxwell, I and my staff will be holed up here for most of the weekend working on your suppression hearing."

Fat chance. Cooper and Ronnie had reservations at a bed-and-breakfast near Vail for the weekend. Neither he nor his "staff" would be within a hundred miles of the office or Max's files.

"I'm not saying I won't come up," Max said bitterly as he looked away. "Just it's a lot of money, is all. Okay. I want the best shot you got. You and your guys here. Balls to the wall on this one, counselor. Nothing less. You fuckin' hear me?"

Max had never seen anyone except, as he put it, "that sexy bimbo Cooper was always drooling over" and "that fat spade chick"—the former being Ronnie, and the latter being the receptionist, who snarled at him whenever he came to the office. But, based on Cooper's incessant pep talks, Max assumed that he had several partners and an eager support staff.

"But of course. That's precisely what you'll be getting, Maxwell." Cooper decided to tack on another hour just because of the hard time he was having. He reasoned that it was bad enough he had to go through this phony tap dance without having to hear a ton of shit in the bargain. "Right after this money situation is properly addressed."

Cooper, if not a class act from birth, was by no means stupid. He had worked himself up in life through basic determination, grit, and greed. First as a private investigator. After going back and finishing college at thirty, he created a résumé from sheer nerve and imagination that boasted of his "five years of experience as a trained legal investigator," and hunted up work. But he soon grew tired of chasing lawyers for forty dollars an hour in fees and decided to chase clients for one hundred forty dollars an hour. He went to the University of Denver Law School, where he realized that lawyering wasn't that hard. Not if you're willing to trim the edges. Life was simply too short for jumping through all those silly hoops. Like doing this tedious grunt work that Max's case required and actually logging all those hours he was billing. A man'd have to be totally insane to do that.

Cooper's way made sense. Stall his client for a few weeks and ignore the DA's offer. And a pretty good offer it was. Plead to the drug charges and they'd drop the threatening business, which was weak anyway. Also plead to the weapons charge and the two sentences would run concurrently. The DA would sit quietly at sentencing and Max would get maybe eight to ten years. He'd be out in four or five if he behaved himself and didn't get his throat slashed.

Cooper tabled the offer and told Max that the DA was being a real hard-nose. Then, after they got clobbered at the suppression hearing, he'd let the poor slug know how much trouble he was really in and how the judge was a total maniac on drug dealers. Scare the hell out of Max with the possibility of twenty years for sure. Finally, a couple of days before the trial, he'd lay out the DA's deal like he had just fought to the death for it. Max pleads out, thinking Cooper saved his ever-expanding butt. Everyone's happy. Especially Cooper.

"Awright, Chrissake, awright." Max wanted to end the discussion, too. "You'll have the fifteen by the weekend. I think I'll get trucking now, so you can get down to work. You give it your best there, counselor. Right?"

"You have my word." Cooper nodded and leaned forward with enough insincere humility to win office. "I will keep after the district attorney's office and see if we can get some concessions on these matters. However, judging by the way they're being so stubborn, I believe we will end up going to trial as scheduled. They simply do not want to bend. They're coming after you hard, Maxwell."

When Max left, Cooper focused on the problem that had nagged him since he read his morning newspaper. On the lower half of the metro page was a twelve-inch story about the murder of a Commerce City man, Merrill Dopps, aka Grundy. The story said that Dopps was the victim of an apparent robbery, because the cash drawer in his welding shop had been rifled. That sadistic bastard Soyko clearly had gone too far, the lawyer pondered as he read. Cooper had only wanted the welder out of town, not out of body. So this jerk goes and kills the guy. But, more important, what happened to that three grand he gave Soyko for traveling expenses? Cooper wanted answers and he wanted them now.

"Ronnie, get in here," he yelled toward the door.

He didn't have to wait long. When Ronnie saw Max leave, she

fluffed up her bleached hair and put on a seasoned pout that showed she was ready for business or pleasure. Cooper was no killer in the looks department, but, then, Ronnie never thought she'd have an attorney courting her. This guy would probably never make the Supreme Court. Still, he generated solid revenues and he paid his gold card on time. She'd be his secretary, his mistress, his *whatever*, until he produced a diamond and walked her down the aisle. She grabbed her notepad—not that she had ever taken one word of dictation. But she'd seen secretaries do that in a million old movies and so she'd acquired the habit.

When she walked into his office, Cooper looked up and tried to act serious. It was a real stretch, because just the sight of her in that red dress aroused him to giddy distraction. The longer he knew Ronnie, the more he realized that he was falling for her. Falling hard. At first, she was just this terrific lay. Given his luck with women, any lay was terrific, which put Ronnie completely off the charts. But as time went by, he noticed that he liked her for more than sex. She was really quite bright, and she came up with ways to work a client he never imagined.

For her part, Ronnie felt a certain fondness for the lawyer. With his choppy Beatle bangs, uneven, gaunt mustache, and doughy body, he had a certain harmless appeal. She'd had her fill of disturbed bad boys, thank you. All danger and excitement. All pain and disappointment. Like the cretin she married when she was sixteen. That crazy biker used to jam the barrel of his thirty-eight against her forehead and threaten her repeatedly. When he died in a motorcycle accident a year or so later, she was still so afraid she almost didn't go to the funeral.

"You see what that nut case Soyko did with our little problem in the Borders trial?" Cooper looked her over. He always felt the urge to impress her, let her know what a take-charge kind of man he was. He continually used the malicious and emotionally erratic duo of Soyko and Romp, in part just to show Ronnie that he could play hardball and hold his own with the two marginally psychotic "investigators." Cooper mistook her warnings against them for interest. "I better have a talk with that guy.

Tighten him up a few notches. Both he and his partner. This is really way the hell out there. Totally unacceptable."

He tried to sound cocky, but he couldn't pull it off. Actually, nobody on earth could tighten Soyko up. He was so toxic that even the criminal-justice system didn't want him. He'd been up on felony charges seven times, some of them serious. But except for periodic and brief county-jail time, he'd never seen the inside of a prison.

"I told you this guy could get out of control. I knew it the first time I ever met him." Ronnie casually smoothed out the front of her dress with one hand as she spoke. She never missed an opportunity to showcase her body to Cooper. "He reminds me of too many of those creeps I used to date. Mean as a snake with a hangover, and you never know what they'll do next."

"You mean 'the first time I met him,' honey," Cooper corrected her. "When you said 'the first time I ever met him,' it's redundant." He couldn't resist the constant urge to correct, improve, and refine Ronnie. It reinforced his notion that she needed him: that he was her best hope for a better life. He also knew the value of Soyko's services. "Look, your instincts were right about him, but don't forget the good work he's done for us. One conversation with that man gets more results than twenty restraining orders or depositions."

"Come on, Thomas Hardy. I know they've muscled some good results for you, but this is murder." She always called him that when she thought he was acting naïve or stupid. "I'd say that qualifies as something beyond 'totally unacceptable,' for God's sake. You just like all this heavy crap because it makes you feel like a regular gangsta. You better grow up if you plan on growing old."

Cooper leaned back in his chair and mustered all his nonchalance. "That is not correct, Rhonda." He used her formal name when he wanted to put her in her place and let her know the discussion was over. "Leo Soyko's propensity for violence and the so-called gangster mode do not factor into my hiring the man. He gets results. It's just that simple." He wished he believed it.

Jacky Romp picked up the phone on the first ring. "So talk," he said through clenched jaws.

Cooper was surprised by the rancor in his voice. "Uh, is Soyko there?"

Jacky knew it was Cooper, so he didn't say anything for a minute. Then, "Why?"

The attorney regained his composure and put some authority in his voice. "Because I asked you, that's why. Kindly put him on."

Kindly take a flying fuck, Romp thought. But he just smiled, knowing he had riled the man at the other end of the line. He waited before nodding to Soyko, who was sitting on the couch nearby.

Soyko guessed who it was by the way Jacky spoke. "Counselor," he said when he took the phone. He sounded relaxed, moderately amused. "What's to it?"

Cooper didn't like that. The crazy bastard ignores his orders, kills a man, and doesn't feel a bit defensive.

"I read about our welder this morning. That was not what I requested."

"The way I remember it, you just wanted to make sure the little prick didn't go to court," Soyko said slowly. "Even if they do get him there now, a corpse ain't gonna hurt you. Did my job, the way I see it."

Cooper had to admit Soyko took care of the Dopps problem. It would be just a matter of time before the charges against Tiny Fred would be dropped.

"Look, I'm not going to quibble over semantics. Suffice it to say that I did not order an execution. What about the three grand I gave you for his traveling money? I take it you'll return that to me."

"I don't know squat about semadics, but, the way I see it, you asked for this. You're the one sent me up there to deal with this crumb fuck. Do it your way, it's like he just won on *Wheel of Fortune*. The guy's ratting your client out and you want me to help him pack for a vacation. That three grand, the way I see it, I saved the money from being pissed down a rat hole. I should get it. That's just part of the cost of taking care of this particular piece of business."

Cooper could see there was no point in arguing about the killing. That was history. But the money definitely was not history.

"How about if we split it? Call it a misunderstanding or a tip or whatever. Fifteen hundred each." He could see Ronnie rolling her eyes slightly.

There was a pause on Soyko's end. Then, "That maybe sounds fair."

A done deal. Cooper moved on. "You can bring it by the next time we get together. I'd like to see you over the next couple of days. There's a certain woman I may need you to interview. Could be some money in it for both of us."

"I'm listening," Soyko said. "Who we talking about?"

Ronnie gave Cooper a hard look and mouthed, "No." It was way too soon to think about using this lunatic for Story Moffatt. Cooper just held up his hand, palm toward her, as if to indicate, "Don't worry."

"A nobody. But I might need you," he shot back to Soyko. Then his voice softened. "So how do you intend for us to split up the money you took from this Dopps' cash register?"

4

The red neon "Jesus Saves" cross that hung out over the front door hadn't worked in years, but it still demanded attention. "Jesus" ran horizontally and the "Saves" came down vertically. The first "S" in "Jesus" was the first "S" in "Saves," with a star above it to complete the cross. Streeter called it Bible Deco, and he kept it up there more as a novelty than as a statement of faith.

"They tell me that thing busted down about the same time Humphrey Bogart died, back in '57," Frank explained the cross to Streeter when they took possession of the brick church five years ago. "Could be some deeper meaning there. I'll tell you one thing, that man could eat up the screen. Bogey, that is. Not Jesus. No one like that around no more. Bogey, that is. At the time, this place was the Temple of Faith—a charismatic church, I'm told. That was the last religious go-round. It was St. Teresa Catholic Church when it opened back in the twenties and then, sometime right before the Korean War, it became Jesus the Redeemer. That's of the Methodist African Episcopal denomination. Whatever *that* is."

Streeter told Frank that he wasn't much interested and he just wanted help moving his furniture into the loft space above the rectory. Now that he and Frank owned the two-story church and his fourth divorce was just about final, he planned on living there.

"In good time, buddy," Frank told him. "You got to know what you're moving into first. Now, it stopped being a church in the early seventies. That's about when I moved my bail-bonds office into the old Sunday-school rooms. People told me I was nuts, being so far away from the jail downtown. But I told them, with all the housing projects sprouting up around here, I'd have more customers within spitting distance than I'd ever know what to do with. I was right, too."

Streeter and the aging Frank Dazzler took ownership of the place when the previous owner s son made an untimely run for the border, leaving behind a huge surety bond secured with the old church. Under a creative agreement with the father, Streeter went down to Mexico and brought the three-time armed robber back. He and Frank then took possession of the building. The robber's old man had plenty of property, and at the time an abandoned church in a then-decaying neighborhood wasn't seen as much of a prize.

Frank's office and small apartment shared the first floor with the garage and, later, a feminist survival-defense school forbiddingly named the Womyn's Workout Space. At first, Frank was delighted with the idea of his new tenants.

"I thought it'd be one of those aerobics places and they were just being cute with the name," he told Streeter when the gym first opened. "I expected some spandex jiggle show where the gals stretch wide, and sweat and bounce around to that loud music that's so popular nowadays. You know, that rap shit or whatever they call it. But then it turns out to be mostly a bunch of feminist maniacs in flannel shirts practicing kung fu so's they can castrate men. Gives me the creeps."

He was overstating the school's mission, but when they put signs in the window like "Mao was gender neutral, are you?"

Frank, a decorated Korean War infantryman and ex–sheriff's deputy, got more uneasy. Then, to everyone's utter amazement, the gym's normally stern founder took a shine to the gruff bondsman. The two of them had been carrying on a creaky romance in the nearly four years since.

The church was located on the fringes of Denver's rapidly Yuppifying "Lower Downtown." The Colorado Rockies' baseball stadium—Coors Field—was sprouting up a half-mile away, and the old warehouse district to the west was being converted into lofts and brew pubs to accommodate fans. To the north were the last remnants of the Old West, bucket-of-blood bars that had so excited Jack Kerouac when he passed through town some forty years earlier. Although the church was built without a steeple, its pitched, metal roof and dramatically arched stained-glass windows throughout gave it a definite cathedral look. But it also was as sturdy and defensible as a medieval fortress. Streeter—being in a business where angry and deranged bail jumpers came with the paycheck—particularly liked that. Actually, it looked a little like an armory, so he dubbed it Fort God.

Story Moffatt parked her Audi in front of the church and double-checked the address for Dazzler's Bail Bonds. Then she spotted the small "Bail Bonds" sign right below the nonfunctioning electric cross. When she and her lawyer saw the squash photos, they had no choice but to take the insurance company's offer of twenty-seven hundred dollars. The only concession she got from that weasel Swanson was that he told her the name and work address of the man who took the pictures.

She walked toward the church and noticed the Womyn's Workout Space. There was a window display featuring T-shirts imprinted, "Potential Rape Survivor," for fifteen dollars. Just to the right of the display, at the main church entrance, a man in a rumpled linen suit slouched against the wall genially taking in the neighborhood. She placed him just over sixty, but he had a quick smile and there was a hard liveliness in his blue eyes. This one had plenty of good years left in him, Story decided.

"Tell me you're not here to join the nutcracker sweets over there, darlin'." Frank straightened up and nodded toward the window display. "You look too tender for that crowd."

Story glanced back at the Womyn's gym. "Seems a little paranoid, and they could use a spelling lesson," she answered. The man appeared to be a borderline mouth-breather but he had a gentle lilt to his western twang that made him seem both smart and kind. His face had the warmth of age, like an old wooden desktop. Yet his features were sharp. She could tell he could be an ass kicker if he had to be. "You wouldn't happen to know where Mr. Streeter is by any chance, would you?"

He looked at her for a moment and then shook his head. "Who wants to know?"

"Obviously, I do."

"And you are?" His voice stayed gentle, even.

"Story Moffatt." She stepped forward and held out her hand.

He shook it carefully. "Frank Dazzler. Your friend in the bail-bonds business, darlin'."

At that moment, Streeter walked out the front door into the June sunshine. Story saw him come from behind Frank and immediately recognized him as Brad Tessmer. A smug grin took over her face, like she just stomped him at Yahtzee.

"And is this my friend in the bounty-hunting business or in the auto-body business?" she asked.

Streeter's eyes widened, but only for a second. "Well, well." He smiled broadly. "Squash, anyone?"

She was disappointed that he stayed so calm. She wanted to see some remorse, or at least a hint of surprise. Big guys always seem so cocky. "You work in a church. I suppose that makes you the insurance company's savior."

"You two kids know each other?" Frank moved away from the wall, looking back and forth at them. "Am I missing something here?"

Streeter looked at him and said, "It's a long story, Frank, but she's not about bonds. She's that deal I did for Swannie."

"Yeah, Frank." Story's face hardened. "I'm *that* deal. I don't know, maybe I came to the wrong place."

"That's possible," Streeter said. "Why are you here?"

"Is there somewhere we can talk in private?" she asked.

Frank shot both hands into his pants pockets and he rattled his car keys. "Use my office. I gotta head over to the jail. Go on and grab the office. It looks like you two kids got things to discuss."

Streeter shifted to the side of the church door and held out his left arm, indicating that Story should come inside. She walked up the steps and into the building. The large foyer for the main church had two doors inside. One went straight ahead, into the church itself, which was now used by the Womyn for their self-defense studio. The altar overlooked the workout gym and served as a combination lectern and reference library. The second foyer door, the one on the right, opened into a short hallway that led to the old Sunday school and assorted smaller rooms. That's where Frank's office was, with his apartment behind it farther down the hall in the old rectory. The office itself had the weird atmosphere of a combination holy place and government work space. There was thick, flowered carpeting, and rich mahogany cabinets and beams, yet the desk and the few other furnishings were strictly state-issued. Pale Formica and painted metal.

"I love what you've done with this room." Story glanced around. "It looks like a parochial mental hospital."

"Somehow, I knew you were the type to have opinions on everything." Streeter nodded for her to take a chair in front of the desk.

"I'm not a type, opinionated or otherwise." She sat down.

"What brings you to our humble little parish?" He moved slowly behind the desk and sat down in Frank's overstuffed chair.

"Mr. Dazzler is your partner?"

"Basically. It's a loose arrangement. Why?"

"He seems a little rough around the edges. All that darlin' stuff. Maybe a little patronizing to women."

"Astounding. You spend two minutes with the man and you've already got him pegged. Look, Frank's from the old school. He calls women darling because he always has and because he likes them. He's just trying to be friendly. And you'd be rough around the edges, too, if you ran a bail-bonds business. Frank Dazzler got me started in this racket and he's a decent man. Honest, beyond question. And he'll do anything for you once he likes you. Anything."

"I didn't mean to criticize, Streeter. By the way, what's your full name?"

"Streeter's full enough."

She just shrugged, obviously not amused. "Well, Streeter whatever, you caused me problems and you cost me money."

He hoped she hadn't come just to complain. "That's what they hired me to do. How'd you find out who I am and where to get a hold of me?"

"Your friend Mr. Swanson provided me with that. He told me you work with Frank Dazzler, so I just came here on a hunch. Do you live around here?"

He didn't answer and instead made a mental note not to work for the adjuster again. Streeter was highly secretive about where he lived. He was protective of his entire life. There were precious few ways to track him. No credit cards, no insurance of any kind. He subscribed to no magazines or newspapers, and belonged to no organizations. Streeter banked through Frank, so he had no accounts in his name; his two cars were registered and insured under Frank's name. His driver's license was under the name of someone he knew who more or less matched his description and had died years ago. Even his half-ownership of the church was a side arrangement with the bondsman, so his name appeared on no city property-tax rolls or utility records. Because he dealt almost exclusively in cash and barter, the IRS barely knew how to reach him. Streeter told no one his address and he never got mail. His friends got hold of him through Frank's business number, and his ex-wives never called. He had no children or siblings.

"So now you're here to tell me to go to hell or what?" he finally said. "If you want money, you're out of luck."

"Actually, I'm here to give you some money. You'll have to earn it, of course. But when someone does good work, I can appreciate that. Even if it causes me problems. You did good work, Mr. Streeter. As you know, I may have been somewhat less than totally candid with my insurance claim. I was pretty careful, but you got through all that. Now I want to see if you can help me. Show me that getting those pictures wasn't a fluke. I need someone like you, so I thought, rather than getting someone like you, I may as well get the real thing."

"I've been called worse, Ms. Moffatt." What's with this "fluke" crap?

"Please, you can call me Story. How would you like to get three thousand dollars up front for your time and have a chance to make a lot more down the road if we get what we're after? By the way, how much did you get for those squash pictures?"

"That sounds promising, in answer to your first question. None of your business, in answer to your second. Tell me about this three-thousand-dollar proposition."

"Fair enough." She settled back into her chair. "Basically, I want you to find money. Do you do that kind of work?"

"An assets search? You mean find out someone's net worth."

"Not exactly. I'm talking about finding money that I think exists. It's probably cash. It would have been left by someone who died a couple months ago. April 5 to be exact."

"An estate?" Streeter frowned.

"You might say. I just know that Doug—the man who died —left valuables around, and I want to find them. I've tried everything I could think of with no results, so now it's time to hire a professional. I'm told you do skip tracing. I figured if you can locate people then you can find things as well. I suppose I could get a private investigator, but, judging by what you did in my insurance case, I think you'll do just fine."

"I take it you were close enough to this Doug so you have a legal claim to his estate."

"Definitely. I'm really the only beneficiary in his will. We lived together for the better part of the past three years. We were even thinking about getting married. Actually, we were thinking about it less as time went by." She cocked her head to the side just a shade as she spoke. Cute but a little too affected. "We weren't very close at the end, but he didn't have any heirs and he was barely on speaking terms with his family."

"How much are we talking about?"

"I don't know. I never actually saw it but I'm estimating as high as six figures. Could be a couple hundred thousand. Maybe more. Certainly enough to make all this worthwhile." She waved her hand in the air to indicate her being there discussing it with him. "Doug was a realtor and he also used to dabble in selling cocaine. I think he made a ton of money at both in the eighties in Boulder. Being a realtor up there, he knew a lot of the fast-trackers. To be honest, I think he did better at real estate than at cocaine, but he made out fine with both commodities. He dealt drugs until things got too hot for him there. You know, police poking around, his suppliers making threats. Just hassles in general. So he bailed out of the business about four years ago. At least he said he did. He moved to Denver and sold real estate here. He did pretty well, and then, about seven months ago, he got popped for possession with intent to sell. Major trouble, and it was the last thing our relationship needed. I had no idea he was still dealing."

Streeter nodded like he believed her, but he kept thinking, Is she lying about not knowing or just stupid? Generally, drug dealers are about as subtle as a Madonna concert.

"Anyhow," she continued, "we were just about to come apart at the seams when he totaled his Porsche one night. He was very drunk and going about a hundred out on the I-25."

"And now he's dead," Streeter finished. "What makes you think he kept money around?"

"Well, for one thing, there were times when we needed quick cash and he always just went out and got it. And we're talking about a couple of grand each time. Sometimes quite a bit more.

He'd leave and then come back in an hour or less with the money."

"You never questioned that? I take it you're not a very inquisitive person."

She frowned but continued. "Never look a gift horse in the mouth, Streeter. As I was saying, he also told me that when he was dealing up in Boulder he used to keep a large amount of cash in his house in case of a robbery. Drug dealers are easy marks for robbers. He called it 'go-away money.' Ready cash to make the robbers just go away. He considered it part of his operating costs."

"If it was go-away money," Streeter said, "why didn't he keep it at your house? It wouldn't do any good if there was a robbery and the money was sitting in a bank somewhere."

"You're right." Story studied his face. "But I don't think he was afraid of being ripped off anymore. I think it was just force of habit that he liked to have cash on hand."

Streeter looked off for a moment. Then, "What about his personal belongings? I assume you went through all of them."

"Many times. I couldn't find anything, but you're welcome to look. I went through the car some. Checked the inside, the underside. There wasn't anything left of the engine compartment. Then I went through his office, the house. As I told you, he left everything to me. I get his half of the equity in our townhouse, some insurance money, and his personal belongings. He left this really nice clock, but not much else of value. I was thinking maybe he kept money in a safe-deposit box. Secure, but difficult to trace."

"That's possible," Streeter said. "Could be he kept the key on his key chain or in his glove box."

"Well, if he did, it won't do us any good." Story shifted in her seat. "That part of the car was demolished. The Porsche was very badly burned."

"I suppose I could do a sweep of every bank within, say, a ten-mile radius of your house for a safe-deposit box. Where do you live?"

"Cherry Creek. You know, Creekside."

"Yeah." He automatically flashed on her in her gym clothes at the Creekside. He'd done that more than once over the past couple of weeks. "I'd need a letter that gives me authorization to find out if Doug had a box. What was his last name?"

"Shelton. Doug Shelton."

"For three thousand, there's plenty I can do. But this could easily take a hell of a lot of time." His voice betrayed little, although he had raging doubts about this advertising woman who thought nothing of being "somewhat less than totally candid" with insurance companies and who so dispassionately hunted for a dead boyfriend's money. Still, if she had cash up front, there was a challenge to working for her that intrigued him. Streeter's last divorce had been final shortly after he moved into the church, and his last engagement was two years ago. He'd been keeping women at arm's length ever since. This would be a chance for him to see if he could hold his own with someone like Story without acting like a hormone-crazed teenager.

"You said something about me having a shot at making more money."

"It's a little treasure-hunt incentive. If you find whatever we're after, I'm willing to give you a quarter of it. That could add up if it's what I think it is."

"Why all the extra?"

"To keep you motivated. Do you think that'll keep you motivated?"

Streeter leaned forward, skeptical but interested. "This could end up being a total waste of time. I hate wasting my time, but more than that I hate not getting paid for wasting my time. Usually, I work just for Frank, bringing in bail jumpers. Sometimes I free-lance, like with Swanson. And sometimes I do skip traces for friends. Mostly, I deal in cash, and that's how it'd have to be with us. I'll need five thousand to get started and you'll just have to trust that I'm working for it. You don't get any invoices or written reports. If I think I've worked my way through the five grand, I'll ask for more and you can decide if you want to stay with me. And when we find this pot of gold, I get a third. Not a quarter. Your story has enough holes to read the newspaper through, and, if you'll pardon my bluntness, it's hard to believe anyone can be as dense about their boyfriend as you say you are about old Doug. But for five grand and a third of the action, I'm willing to work for someone that dense."

Story stared at him for a long time. "It's going to be a real pleasure working with you. I didn't know what to expect from a bounty hunter, but I guess good manners and class don't come with the territory."

"Lady, with some of the vicious clowns I track down, manners and class are not a plus. Besides, how much class does it take to fake a neck injury for insurance money? I do this work because I'm good at it and there's money to be made. And, to be absolutely honest, because my cooperative skills stink I have to work alone. Don't let the church fool you. This isn't missionary work. I get fed more horse manure in a week than most people hear in twenty years. But if the money's good enough I can live with the manure. Farmers do it all the time."

"My, aren't we the cynic." Her voice was as flat as her expression, but she had flushed visibly when he made the crack about the insurance fraud. "You're sweeping me off my feet, Streeter."

"Really? That wasn't my intent. You must be easily swept."

"As you get to know me better, you'll find out that I'm not easily anything. You don't think I'm telling the truth?"

"For three thousand, I'm not sure. For five thousand, it becomes less important. Listen, you'll tell me what you tell me. But the more you hold back, the longer it'll take me to find anything."

She finally nodded. "You'll do, Streeter. We've got a deal. I'll have your money for you in about two days."

"Then I'll start working in about three days. I can do the safe-deposit box check, but I have my doubts. I'll want to look through his personal belongings, talk to his family and friends, and then work my way out."

"You won't find zilch with his family. They hadn't talked to each other much in years. His mother's some sort of religious-fundamentalist nut up in Wyoming, and he has a retarded, I mean mentally disabled, brother who lives with her. The mother almost disowned Doug because of the drug arrest. She only briefly came to the funeral, and even then she treated me like I was trash."

"What did you expect? You're the jaded broad living with her son the coke dealer. Out of wedlock, no less. She probably figured you led him astray. It's easy for mothers to get into denial and blame other people for their children's problems. Maybe I'll save her for later. Did he have any hobbies?"

"He golfed some and played a little racquetball." She thought for a moment. "It was strange. Doug was pretty superficial for the most part. Certainly not an intellectual. But he did go to the Denver Art Museum from time to time. I guess he had an eye for beauty."

Streeter could see that, but at what cost? "Did you ever go with him?"

"No. I'm not big on art galleries. They seem so dead to me. He'd never talk about it, either. It was just kind of an interest of his. He liked to fix things, too. Or at least try. He liked to take things apart and see how they worked. Mechanical things, like toasters and VCRs. Trouble is, he wasn't very good at it. Half the time he'd take apart what was broken and then end up calling a repairman or we'd have to go get a new one. That happened with the disposal and the stereo."

Her eyes widened for just a second. "But not that Porsche of his. It was his baby. He put a lot of himself in that car. There was only one mechanic in town he'd let work on it. Hell, he'd barely let people ride in it with him, and he would never let anyone in the back seat. He was very tiresome about it."

"Some guys do that," Streeter said. He hesitated a moment. "There's one other thing. You said you two were on the outs. Is there any chance he had a girlfriend on the side?"

"Doug was a very good-looking man. He had this jet-black

hair. Great butt, great smile. Women liked being with him. He probably did have someone on the side. Our sex life was non-existent those last few months. It wouldn't surprise me if he had one or two tucked away. Men seemed drawn to him, too."

"Men? You mean he might go both ways?"

"I'm not sure which 'ways' he went. Let's just say that he had a lot of charisma and sex appeal and he said things sometimes that led me to believe bisexuality was a possibility. I didn't want to think about it, because of AIDS and all that."

"I'd say you two weren't close. I'm surprised you even noticed that he died."

Story stiffened. "You know, buster, you'll be getting a lot of money in your pocket soon. If you want it to stay there, you might keep in mind whose money it is. I don't need all these judgments."

"If it's in my pocket, I know whose money it is. Mine. And the name's not 'buster.' " Streeter leaned back. "But I'll certainly keep that in mind. Just remember, I warned you that my co-operative skills stink."

She gave one eyebrow an I-give-a-shit lift and moved on. "Look, I didn't press Doug about other women, *or men*, because secretly I hoped he had someone, and I just let it take its course. That would make it easier for us to break up. His car wreck did what neither of us had the energy or the strength to do."

"If he kept money with a girlfriend, we may as well kiss it goodbye," he said casually. "We'll never be able to pry it away."

"Probably not. But if you do find someone, I'll still want to talk to her."

"We'll see what we can work out. Let's not worry about girl-friends right now. Just get that letter for the banks ready and organize his stuff for me. There may be something you missed. I have to get going. Is there anything else?"

Story inhaled theatrically Another gesture he didn't like. Why do so many attractive women have all these drama-queen man-nerisms?

"Doug had this attorney I never liked the guy and I don't

trust him. He was at the funeral and he's called me a couple of times since then to see how I'm doing. The last time we talked, about a week ago, he hinted that Doug still owed him a lot of money. That's nonsense, because the guy hardly did any work. Hell, the charges against Doug were even dropped. There was some trouble with the evidence, and the case was thrown out shortly after the preliminary hearing. But this lawyer made it sound like I might be on the hook to pay him. Do you know about financial obligations Doug's estate might have if he owed money?"

Streeter shrugged. "Do you have a lawyer?"

"Of course. For my business."

"Ask him."

"Her."

"Ask her. I'll ask around, too. Who was Doug's lawyer? Maybe I know him. Assuming it was a him."

"His name is Tom Cooper."

Streeter knew the name. He had heard about Cooper and it wasn't flattering, but he couldn't remember what it was. Something in the paper a couple of years ago. The details were long-forgotten. He frowned.

"I take it you know him," Story said.

"Maybe. When you get my money you can just leave it with Frank if I'm not here."

5

Streeter glanced at his coffee maker and wondered why, no matter what type of expensive blend he put in the basket, the final product always tasted like ground water from Love Canal. He carried his cup into the living area of his loft. The place was enormous, taking up most of the entire second floor of the church. But it had an offbeat warmth to it thanks to huge throw rugs, overstuffed chairs and couches, and numerous bookshelves displaying more than a dozen sets of garage-sale encyclopedias and well over two hundred resource books. Twenty-seven framed movie posters helped give the room a light feel. His favorite was of the torrid beach scene from Lina Wertmuller's *Swept Away*. A tinny-sounding stereo, circa 1981, stood off to the side of the open kitchen area. He had little interest in music, since he was tired of sixties and seventies "Classic Rock" and anything remotely current struck him as redundant, not to mention aggravating, noise. "I can't tell U2 from R2-D2," as he put it.

He set down his cup and picked up a small address book containing the phone numbers of friends and professional contacts. He had his own network of sources scattered around the front range of Colorado, north up through Wyoming, and south into New Mexico. It was necessary. If he had to drive or fly everywhere to check out small leads and tips on bail jumpers or other people he was investigating, he couldn't get half his work done. Plus, many of his sources had access to information he couldn't touch. Before he did anything else, Streeter wanted to check out the cast of characters he was dealing with regarding Doug Shelton. He wanted more information on Doug as well as on Story Moffatt. While he was at it, he decided to find out about Thomas Cooper.

His first call was to a computer information source located in Castle Rock, a mall-and-golf community about twenty miles south of Denver. Stevey was the man's name and he was a world-class propeller head. Anything on record in any data bank was at his fingertips. He was invaluable for skip tracing and court searches, the latter of which Streeter ordered for Shelton, Moffatt, and Cooper. Stevey could do a statewide court sweep and get a printout of the case summaries. He got right on it, and about a half-hour later called the bounty hunter back.

"Let's see here." Stevey obviously was reading his screen while he talked. "Mr. Shelton was the plaintiff in a collections case in Boulder in 1983 and another one in 1986. He was awarded a small judgment both times. Then he got arrested for possession of a controlled substance in 1988 up there, too. Got probation. He was arrested again in 1993 in Denver for possession with intent to sell. The charges were dropped.

"Story Moffatt. Is that name for real? She likes to sue people, too. And she likes to win. I've got six collections cases where she was the plaintiff. All between 1987 and 1994. All in Denver. She won judgments in five. The sixth is still pending.

"And Thomas Hardy Cooper. He's either a lawyer or a doctor. Sounds like a real gem. He's been sued twice for malpractice. Both cases still pending. Looks like he was charged with assault in 1983 in Jefferson County. The case was later dismissed."

"Quite a crew, huh?" Streeter asked. "Thanks for the quick

turnaround, Stevey. Drop the printouts in the mail, okay? I want a closer look."

His next call was to a close friend, one of the few lawyers he would work for from time to time. "How you doing, Bill?"

The voice at the other end came back relaxed. "Not bad. Yourself?"

William Wesley McLean usually sounded relaxed. A former district attorney in Arapahoe County, just south of Denver, Bill McLean had a reputation for being cool but tough. The man would rather lose an eye than take an ounce of trash from anyone. He and Streeter had been tight since they had lived next door to each other during Streeter's last marriage. As with his first three marriages, Streeter and Beth lasted only two years. But during those two years, he and McLean got close, and their friendship continued to grow even after the divorce. He was one of the few people the bounty hunter let call him by the shorthand nickname of Street.

"How's Darcy?" he asked Bill.

"Excellent, as ever." Bill and Darcy had been married nineteen years. She was a successful psychologist. "She's working at the clinic. Thursdays she works family counseling. There's so much child abuse out there, it makes you sick."

"Tell me about child abuse. My father drank and my mother made me take accordion lessons."

"I'll bet you were a natural, Street." Bill, pushing sixty, was almost six feet six inches tall and had a full head of white hair. It gave him a distinguished credibility that helped greatly in court.

"Listen, I've got a quick legal question," Streeter said. "There's this lady I'm doing a little work for and it looks like she's going to be hassled by a lawyer. She's the executrix and main beneficiary of her boyfriend's estate and the lawyer claims the guy died owing him money. Does she have any legal obligation for his bills?"

"Depends. Did they ever tell people they were married? Were they engaged?"

"She says no."

"Then it's unlikely that his claim'll hold up. Who's the lawyer?"

"A spastic named Tom Cooper."

Bill grunted on the other end of the receiver.

"Guy with an office downtown? Yeah, I seem to remember him from back in my last days with the county. He was just getting into practice. Real nervous and tried to cover it up with a kind of swagger. Couldn't pull it off too well. Thought he was a real lady killer, too. But he couldn't pull that off, either."

"If he comes after her, will you represent her?"

"Sure. Who is she? You usually don't take private clients like this. Why the change for this one?"

"Interesting case, lots of cash up front, gorgeous client."

"Gorgeous, huh? Look, Street, you better be careful if you try to mix business with pleasure. What's that old saying about not slamming your dick in the cash register? You don't want to do that."

"That's very eloquent. And you're right, I don't. Catch you later."

Streeter hung up and then called Carl Shorts, a Boulder private investigator he used occasionally. A great many people in the Denver area knew Carl, if not for his legendary drinking habits and relentless womanizing, then at least for his nickname: Pokey. Try being ignored with Pokey Shorts for a handle. Rumor had it that he got the nickname because, as a newspaper reporter, he was slow at deadline time.

"How you doing, Poke man?" Streeter greeted him.

"Hey, Tarzan. Long time no see," Pokey shot back. Although just a shade past fifty and married with two sons, Pokey drank and caroused like he was just out of college. But when it came to investigating, he knew the secrets of every soul in Boulder County, and his drive for digging up dirt was even greater than his love of the bar scene.

"Too long. But this is more business than pleasure." Streeter told Pokey about Story Moffatt and her late boyfriend, emphasizing the part about his living in Boulder and dealing drugs.

"So now you need to find out about Mr. Shelton," Pokey said.

"You got it."

"The name sounds sort of familiar. I think he ran with Marcus Greenberg and that crowd over at Potter's and Quinn's. Some of those Pearl Street Mall watering holes. Let me look into it and I'll give you a holler back. I'm also thinking we should get together for a couple hundred beers one of these days."

"That sounds fine to me."

Streeter's last call was to Detective Bob Carey of the Denver Police Department. Carey was his only real source on the department, but one source like him was plenty. Carey had twenty-three years on the job and he played cards with Streeter and some friends every other week. They'd been doing it for just over ten years, and Carey had walked away a winner maybe five times.

"Robert, Streeter here."

"Robert?" There was a pause. "That means you want something."

"Right. Do you know anything about a Doug Shelton? A coke dealer who died in a car wreck a few months ago."

"Should I?"

"I'm just asking."

"Don't mean nothing to me. I'll check around, though."

"How about a drug lawyer named Tom Cooper?"

"Now, that name I do know. A regular certified shithead. You're not working for him, are you?"

"No. Against him probably."

"I don't think you want to work for him or against him. What you hear next, you didn't hear from me. We were looking into this Cooper jackass and so were the guys up in Adams County. Seems they had a homicide up there a while back. Some little welder who was supposed to testify in a murder trial ends up with his throat slit. Cooper was the defense lawyer in the aforementioned murder trial, and he has this investigator named Psycho or some damned thing that everyone is very interested in.

Psycho is right. Totally nasty fucker. Looks like the sergeant at arms at a Teamsters meeting, from what I hear. So far, he's clean. But Cooper and his friends are bad people. You be careful. You got half my pay for the last ten years at the poker table and I want a shot at winning it back."

"With all your stinking luck, you still never give up. I don't know if that's persistent or pathetic."

Carey coughed into the receiver. "Bad luck's like a marriage, Streeter. Sooner or later they both gotta end. You should know all about that."

6

As Jacky Romp watched Cooper walk across the parking lot, a shadow of amusement twitched across his face. Actually, Jacky never looked totally amused or totally happy or totally anything you might call pleasant. His features were delicate, not unattractive, but at the same time he projected an overriding meanness. There was a strange menace to his entire being, like barbed wire covered with pale skin.

Watching Cooper shuffle toward the diner, he smiled and looked across the table at Soyko, who was stirring his coffee. Jacky glanced back out at the lot and muttered, "Goofy fuck-wad," seemingly without moving his jaw.

Soyko nodded. He was so used to his partner's not using full sentences that he just glanced at the scurrying lawyer and understood. Leo couldn't really disagree. Romp and Soyko had done numerous jobs for Cooper over the years, making a good chunk of change from the hard-assed collection shakedowns and intimidating interviews. The work had increased in both volume and scale lately—as Cooper's practice grew and intensified—to a point where it was now Soyko and Romp's main source of income. "That jerk's a regular cash cow," as he put it to Jacky not long ago. But if anything, Leo's regard for the attorney decreased with time. Now, watching him in the lot, Soyko could only think, What a clown the lawyer is. Cooper always sort of shuffled along bent forward, as if he couldn't get where he was going fast enough. Or maybe he couldn't get away from where he'd just been fast enough. Either way, it appeared awkward and panicked to Leo.

Cooper had asked Soyko to meet him at The Full Belli Deli in the sprawling suburb of Aurora, immediately east of Denver. It was their usual spot. He didn't like Soyko coming to his office, and because he also lived downtown Cooper didn't want to meet in the city, where they could be recognized. The Full Belli was just fine. Soyko lived nearby and Cooper liked the coffee and the service. What he didn't like was Jacky Romp, and his features hardened as he entered the restaurant and saw him sitting there. Not that it surprised him. Soyko and Romp were inseparable. Still, the attorney's dislike for Jacky was monumental.

The feeling was eagerly reciprocated. Romp generally considered anyone who wore a suit to be "pure Yuppie rat shit," and Cooper specifically to be a phony stooge. The attorney sensed that hatred immediately and viewed Jacky as a highly repugnant loose cannon with the added liability of not being necessary. When he hired Soyko, he always felt like he was paying a little extra for Jacky even though Leo could do the job just as well by himself.

"There he is." Cooper smiled and approached the booth, looking straight at Soyko. "The most persuasive investigator in town. How you doing, my man?"

My man this, Soyko thought, looking back impassively. This jerk really thinks "my man" is some sort of hip street jive. "Yeah, my man." He looked over to Jacky and nodded. "Sit down, Mr. Cooper." There was no warmth in the invitation.

Cooper slid into the booth next to Soyko, still deliberately avoiding eye contact with the man across the table. Usually he barely acknowledged Jacky's presence and spoke to him only when necessary. For his part, Jacky seldom talked to anyone but

Soyko anyway, and the few words he directed at Cooper were mocking or vaguely obscene.

The waitress came and Cooper ordered coffee. Then, for the first time, he looked directly at Jacky, and his venom rekindled. Soyko had the blocky muscles and thick, strong hands of a foundry worker. Basically, he scared the hell out of Cooper. But Jacky Romp seemed too frail to be intimidating, so Cooper frequently took shots at him. The lawyer looked intently back at Soyko and in the deepest voice he could muster he asked, "Do you have to always bring this malignant piece of shit with you?"

Soyko had no idea what "malignant" meant, but the "piece of shit" part was clear. He rolled his eyes for a second and looked out the window. The constant friction between the two men bored him. "All right, ladies." He looked back with no emotion on his face. "Let's cut the 'malignant' bullshit here and get down to business." He glanced toward his lap and slid an envelope along the booth seat at Cooper. It contained fifteen hundred dollars in wrinkled bills. "Like we said on the phone, for the thing with Tiny. And now no more about it." His voice indicated that this was the end of the subject. Absolutely the end. "What's next? Something about a girl you want me to talk to?"

"That'll come in good time." Cooper looked down at the envelope and pushed it back at Soyko. "But first, I want you to gather information on a former client of mine. I'll want some real digging on this guy. Keep the money to cover your efforts."

"Who we talking about?" Soyko said in his slow, can-do tone.

Cooper lowered his voice slightly. "You know anyone named Doug Shelton? Greaseball handsome guy, always dressed to kill. Sort of a low-end player with the blow and the ladies. Hung around places like El Chapultepec, the jazz bar, and the Wynkoop poolroom."

The two investigators looked at each other for a long time, like they were having a telepathic conference. Then Jacky simply said, "Porsche prick," through his closed mouth.

Soyko nodded and looked back at Cooper. "I think I know who you mean. Guy about thirty-five maybe. Little older than me. Waved a lot of cash around but wouldn't even shoot you pool for fifty cents. I know he deals. Drives a red Porsche and acts like he's hot shit, too. Ain't seen him in a long time."

Cooper smiled, once again amazed at the broad range of people that his investigator knew. "Nor are you likely to see him in the future. He died a few months ago. He'd been arrested late last year for possession of several ounces of flake, excellent quality. Had a short rap sheet from here and there and he was facing some state time. Most judges have big erections for drug dealers these days. Like they think that putting them away for a few months to play tennis in medium security somehow protects society. It's a joke. But what the hell? It keeps me supplied with clients.

"At any rate, our Douglas was basically screwed because it was a hand-to-hand sale. Then something very unusual happened. A couple weeks after his preliminary hearing, I received a call from the prosecutor telling me they were going to dismiss everything. Seems the cocaine had inexplicably disappeared from the police-evidence locker. Other physical evidence disappeared as well. As we hadn't had a chance to test the coke yet, the charges were dropped and Douglas was free."

Soyko frowned. "Too bad he died." Then his face brightened slightly. "Normally, that means he's out of the picture, but I'm sure, if there's any way to get something out of a dead guy, you'll think of it. He owed you money?"

Cooper frowned in pained sincerity. Doug Shelton had paid him over nineteen thousand dollars in two quick cash installments. That basically covered his meager legal efforts about five times over. If anything, Cooper owed the estate a refund, but no one, least of all Soyko and his crazy partner, needed to know that. "A considerable sum, and I certainly don't intend to wipe out the debt without trying to collect," Cooper said severely. "I put in long hours on this man's case and I'm entitled to the appropriate payment."

Soyko studied his face. "I tell you this, it would break my heart to see you take it in the shorts like that. But don't you usually collect a shitload of money up front before you even budge on a case?"

Cooper inhaled deeply and spoke with a forced patience. "That is not at all an accurate characterization of my practice. Typically, I do like to get a decent retainer. That's just prudent business. But I provide all my clients with the best legal assistance possible regardless of their ability to pay in advance. I also do a considerable amount of work pro bono—that is, without receiving a penny. It's the least I can do."

Thomas Hardy Cooper was more likely to get pregnant and deliver twins than do one hour of pro-bono work and everyone at the table knew it. Jacky Romp spit out a laugh and turned away.

Soyko just shrugged. "Whatever you say. But if this guy was such a slow pay, what makes you think he had any money to go after?"

"I've handled a great many drug defenses these past few years and I can tell when a dealer has money. Theoretically, they all should have plenty, because their profit margin is so obscenely vast. Christ, just last month I had these two post-office guys, letter carriers, come to hire me. A couple of coons, no less. They had been arrested dealing eight balls to their fellow employees. They come to me and they're dressed about a notch above Goodwill. I tell them I'll need ten thousand in cash just for starters, figuring that would turn them away. One says to me, 'Okay, but I gotta get the money from the credit union.' He says it like it's hysterical. Then he reaches into one of his socks and pulls out a wad of cash the size of his dick and counts out the ten grand. I'm sitting there just about creaming my pants and thinking, Why didn't I ask for more?

"But drug dealers, like so many of us, fail to handle their money properly. Sadly, a good many of them are addicted themselves, so they piss their money away. Our Mr. Shelton was not like that. He also had a good real-estate income. He was always well turned out. You know, the car, the clothes. Plus, this evidence theft took some doing. It seems obvious to me that Douglas arranged it. He had to have someone on the inside, on the force. That costs plenty. He damned near told me that he arranged it, and he implied it was no big deal, money-wise. That man had assets, no doubt about it."

"He had a way of flashing it around, I'll give you that," Soyko interrupted. "Had a nice-looking blonde chick with him sometimes. Great ass and legs. His wife?"

"I'm not certain," Cooper answered, uncomfortable that Soyko knew about Story. "He implied that it might have been a common-law situation."

The three sat in silence for a couple of minutes. Finally, Jacky spoke up. "We supposed to be reading your mind or what?"

Cooper glanced at him for a second and then turned back to Soyko. "I want you to find out everything you can about Douglas. I think he kept women on the side, and I'm dead solid certain he stashed money. He used to brag about the financial reserves he kept hidden from his lady. Gentlemen, if this is anything like what Douglas led me to believe it is, there could be close to half a million in it for us. Or whoever has the balls to go get it. I'd say it's definitely worth a little looking into, wouldn't you?"

For the first time since he'd known them, Jacky and Soyko seemed impressed.

"And the girlfriend doesn't have it?" Soyko asked.

"Maybe a little sliver of it, but he used to brag about keeping her in the dark. We've got to dig into this. If I intend to collect from his wife or whatever she is, I'd like to know that she can pay. If he was keeping a woman, you may have to talk to her. But no more of that Grundy Dopps cowboy nonsense."

Anger flared across Soyko's face. "I don't want to hear about that."

Cooper backed off fast. "Well, just see what you can find out about Mr. Shelton." With that, the attorney stood up, pulled a twenty from his wallet, and dropped it on the table. He turned and walked out of the diner without another word.

Jacky Romp watched him leave and then, to no one in particular, he snarled again, "Goofy fuckwad."

Ronnie Taggert lived in a garden-level apartment on the city's predominantly Hispanic near West Side. The rent was a reasonable three hundred twenty-five dollars a month for a spacious two-bedroom, with a laundry next door and free cable. She had gotten used to living in that part of town from her days as a party-animal waitress at a rock-and-roll bar located there. Her apartment wasn't a prestige address, but the building was clean and she liked the nearby Mexican restaurants. Cooper hated visiting her there, because he intensely disliked all minorities. He always felt as though he were taking a giant step down the social ladder when he crossed the viaduct over the Valley Highway, just north of Mile High Stadium, into "their neighborhoods." Besides, in his book, "garden-level" was nothing more than a euphemism for "half-assed basement apartment."

He knocked on her door and smiled when she answered in just a silk slip. "Hi, baby," he said.

"Come on in." She kissed him on the cheek as he walked past her. "How did your meeting with those two deranged Nazis go?"

"You should stop referring to my investigative staff as Nazis. Even in jest."

"I'll keep that in mind." She lit a cigarette and turned her back to him.

"We had an interesting strategy discussion. You know I'm looking for a payoff from Doug Shelton's estate. This Story woman doesn't have a clue about what he paid me. She didn't know about his dealing coke, nor about his womanizing on the side. She's just some harmless, artificial advertising person."

"Yeah?" Ronnie turned to face him. "You sure?"

"Indeed. I've developed a twofold plan. First, I've retained Mr. Soyko to kick around under some rocks at the bars and hangouts that Doug frequented. If he had a girlfriend, I want to meet her. The second part calls for us to draw up one hell of a bill for

Story Moffatt. I'm figuring around forty thousand. This will have to be some of our best work, but if I can establish that they held themselves out as man and wife, I think I have a real shot at getting the court to order her to pay. Hell, I can probably just finesse it out of her without even having to go to court."

Ronnie thought in silence. "Developed a twofold plan." She hated the way he tried to make everything sound so formal. "Don't be so sure about his girlfriend. My hunch is that she's tougher than she looks. She held up pretty well at the funeral and she runs her own advertising agency. That's a tough racket, advertising. You really think you're going to stick a bill in her face, start screaming about court, and she'll just hand over forty thousand?"

Cooper walked to the kitchenette just off the living room where the refrigerator was and grabbed a beer. He knew it would be a long shot trying to talk Story out of money. She'd have to be nuts to just fold up and pay. But there was money for the taking, and he hated the condescending attitude she gave him at the funeral. Maybe she is tough, but she's never dealt with anyone like Soyko, he reasoned.

When he returned to the living room, he smiled at Ronnie. "Well, we shall just see what evolves. What's the worst that can happen?"

"Tom, with the way you practice law, damned near anything can happen."

7

Story sent Streeter an authorization letter, and the following week he hit a dozen banks during a two-day stretch. Doug Shelton had no accounts or safe-deposit boxes at any of them. Then the bounty hunter got bored. One of the reasons he never went into law enforcement is that he didn't have patience for repetitive, detail work. If the police were doing this search, they'd check every bank in the city. But Streeter liked to go on his instincts and his ability to read people and situations rather than relying on "procedures." Also, the more he thought about it, the less likely it seemed that Shelton kept a stash in a bank. As he told Frank after the two days, "Banks have short hours, which would be a definite drawback to a free-lance guy like Dougy."

"What about ATMs?" the bondsman asked. "They're open day and night."

"Yeah, they're always open, but you can only get a couple hundred dollars a day. That's nowhere near what we're talking about. Besides, ATMs and safe-deposit boxes can be traced."

He decided to check out Doug's court file. The criminal complaint would tell him a lot, like where he was arrested and if there were codefendants. He went to the basement of the Denver

Courthouse, room thirty-eight, and got the complete file on Douglas Lawrence Shelton's arrest of November 10: case number CR 94 1083. Although inactive, it was still over an inch thick.

Streeter copied every page and took it back to the church to read it. Most of it revealed nothing of value. The complaint and the arresting officer's report primarily interested him. There were no codefendants: Doug was arrested alone. He was popped selling almost one pound of cocaine to a Denver undercover officer behind a bar just off the touristy Larimer Square. That translated to close to sixty thousand dollars in street value, about half for Doug at wholesale. Tax-free.

The buy was made shortly before midnight, and the primary arresting officer's name was Detective Arthur Ernest Kovacs. Obviously, the name of the undercover narc who set up the buy did not appear. Doug apparently walked to the bar, because there was no mention of officers' finding or searching his Porsche. He also must have known the narc fairly well, because Doug was unarmed, and it mentioned several times that the two men had an ongoing relationship. There was a list of prospective witnesses, most of whom sounded like other Denver police officers or lab technicians. It appeared that no fewer than fourteen people were needed to bring down Douglas Shelton.

Streeter was disappointed when he finished. Nothing seemed to pertain to his search. He decided to call Detective Kovacs and fish around. Kovacs' work number was listed in the report, and the detective picked up on the second ring.

"Kovacs here," he answered abruptly, like he was just on his way to lunch or, more important to a man with his bowel miseries, to the restroom. Streeter explained who he was, that he was working for the estate of Doug Shelton, and that the survivors were curious about the arrest. Kovacs made it clear that Doug's estate was of no concern to him.

"No offense there—Mr. Streeter, was it? Yeah. But I give a good rat's ass if any of them ever find more money." Kovacs now sounded bored, like he was reading junk mail out loud. "This bum made his money from selling drugs, and in case you haven't heard, that's against the law. Hell, if we knew he had any cash laying around, we'd have grabbed it for the state. We can do that, you know. Your client's just lucky we didn't go after their house and stuff like that—attach all the assets from illegal activities. That's the way we used to do it in Detroit, back when I worked out there. Now, if that's it, I'll be saying goodbye. Maybe you should try the girl. You might have better luck with her than we did."

"His fiancée? That's who I'm working for. Story Moffatt."

"I ain't talking about any Story. Or any poem or any book, for that matter. I'm talking about the broad at the bar. The fuck's her name? It was on the witness list."

Streeter shuffled through the papers on his desk and found the last page of Kovacs' report, with the witness list. He started reading all of the women's names out loud.

"Nora Lewinski?"

"No, she's over at the lab. Keep going."

"Shannon Mays?"

"Bingo. There you go, Mike Hammer. She was the one that was waiting for him over at Marlowe's. He told our guy about her just before we popped him. We sent a couple uniforms over to talk to her after the arrest. We'd a loved to pop her, too. Smug little bitch."

"Why didn't you?"

"Possession of a wine spritzer ain't a crime in this state, ace. Least not that I ever heard of. Anyhow, we found her just sitting there having a drink. Happy as a pig in shit, if you pardon my French. A real cool customer. We tell her that her boyfriend just got nailed and she acts like we read her the weather report for Poland or something. But we had no cause for an arrest."

"Why wasn't she listed in the report itself?"

"Cause she didn't mean nothing to the investigation."

"Then why is she on the witness list?"

"No reason really. Just to bust her chops a little. Maybe shake her up some. Damned coke whore."

"Do you have an address on her? A phone number?"

Kovacs grunted something bitter-sounding at the other end but then said he'd check. A couple of minutes later, he came back on the line.

"I couldn't find no phone. She told us she lives at a joint, some high-rise, in Capitol Hill. Seven forty Pennsylvania. Number nine oh three. But I doubt she's going to be much help to you."

"Was she that uncooperative?"

"You might say so." Kovacs honked out a thick grunt indicating amusement. "I think you'll find her—how would I put it?—very tight-lipped. Anything else, ace?"

"No. That'll do it. And, Kovacs, it's been a real pleasure."

Former Detroit cop, Streeter thought as he hung up. An FBI agent he knew once told him that Detroit cops were world-class scammers and shakedown artists. He said that the Detroit FBI office was the only one in the entire country where the bureau specifically told its agents to share nothing with local police officers. He said so many of them were on the take there was no way of knowing whom to trust.

Just from his attitude, Streeter could picture Kovacs rutting around Motown, "kiting the coloreds out of a few bucks, ace," and generally being a useless imbecile. We'll see who's tight-lipped, the bounty hunter thought. Just because this Shannon Mays wouldn't talk to a clown like Kovacs didn't mean she wouldn't talk to him.

At his end, Kovacs could feel a decided twinge of activity in his lower intestine when he hung up. Pushing fifty-five, randomly flatulent, and constipated as a cement block, the detective was chugging into retirement some three months away. He subsisted primarily on cut-rate bourbon, Maalox, and your basic bran cereals smothered in prunes. Any inquiries into the whole Shelton business were about as welcome as another bowel obstruction. He decided to make a call up north for a little input on the matter. This bounty hunter probably didn't know his ass from a rearview mirror, but Kovacs had heard of Story Moffatt.

What he heard was, you don't want to underestimate her. He'd make the call later. First, he grabbed the *Sports Illustrated* off his desk and headed for the john, determined yet realistically glum. A weary veteran, he knew he was in for another long and at best moderately productive siege.

Shannon's building, imperiously named Penwood Heights, was a concrete high-rise built in the mid-1960s near the governor's mansion. The on-site manager was an aging, painted beauty who wore perfume so foul it could drop a wasp at ten feet. She was the kind of maintenance day drinker who was never really drunk, yet never fully sober. Streeter was surprised that a nice building would have such a rank manager. Fortunately, she was incredibly high-strung and talkative.

"My name is Nancy," she said when she buzzed him into her office just off the lobby. "Who did you say you're looking for, dear?"

She wore orange polyester slacks tight enough to render her childless and stood in the doorway with a cigarette in her right hand, the elbow braced against her side. Her left forearm ran across her waist in front, with that hand holding the right elbow for support. She looked fragile, like one solid belch would cause her to fall apart.

"Shannon Mays. I was told she lives in nine oh three, but the name on the register out there is Viveney. I buzzed up and they said Shannon doesn't live here anymore. I was wondering if you might have a forwarding address. She witnessed an accident and we need her help."

He'd used that witness story a thousand times. It made landlords feel safe in giving out forwarding addresses.

"Oh my." Nancy's ashen face flashed a sharp crimson. "Well, we don't have, I mean, there is no forwarding address. Shannon's dead. She died some, uhm, some, I don't know, maybe three months ago. Or so."

Streeter froze. His first lead and here she was dead. That bozo Kovacs knew it, too. Tight-lipped is right.

"Just a few months ago?" At first he asked it because he couldn't think of anything else to say, but then he realized the timing was curious.

"Yes, well, something like that, dear." Nancy seemed genuinely saddened by having to relate the grim news. Her erratic speech was due equally to Scoresby's Scotch and actual distress. "My goodness, yes. It was so sad. Such an attractive woman."

"Do you know what happened?" he asked.

"Car wreck. It was, oh my, a big car accident. Out on the freeway. Well, I don't mean there were big cars or anything." Nancy paused to suck in a deep breath. Then she hacked out a phlegmy cough that sounded like part of her throat came up with it. "It's just that, uhm, it was a big collision. Two people died. Shannon and her boyfriend, I think it was. Only one car, we heard later."

Doug died in a one-car accident. "Was the boyfriend's name Doug Shelton?"

"That was it. Yes. Very nice-looking young man."

Streeter felt his stomach twitch and his skin got suddenly warm. Obviously, Story knew about this. "Is Shannon buried here in Denver? Was her family from here?"

"I believe they were from, uh, let me see, California." Nancy took a deep drag from her cigarette and then looked around for her ashtray. "That other woman was here from, ah, from the lawyer, from the lawyer's office, asking a lot of questions, too. Maybe she's working on the same thing you are, dear."

"What woman? When?" He snapped the words out.

Nancy seemed upset by his tone—almost guilty, like she had done something wrong. "I'm sorry, dear. Let me, uh, think for a minute. I still have her card. No, it was the card for the lawyer. She, let's think, she had a very strange name. Like a man. She was just here about a week ago."

The manager's forehead went into spasms of concern. She pulled a stack of business cards out of a desk drawer and started rifling through it. The card she sought was near the top. She studied it and then handed it to him. That done, she appeared deeply relieved. It was Tom Cooper's card.

"Did the woman give you her title?"

Nancy frowned again. "She was a, uhm, what do they call it? Something legal."

"Paralegal?"

"That's it. Funny name she, uh, had. A man's name. Donnie. Ronnie. Something like that. I think, yes, it was Ronnie. Cute little thing. Very serious, though."

It figured that a greedy ambulance chaser like Cooper would be on the trail of the money, Streeter thought. And the lawyer easily would have known about Shannon. Streeter's only surprise was that it took Cooper a couple of months to get over here. The bounty hunter knew he had to get together with Story to talk about it. He was angry at her for not telling him about Shannon, but far more angry at himself for being so careless and not asking for details. Still, why the hell would she not let him know all about the accident? He had asked her if Doug had any girlfriends, and it was doubtful that Story believed Mays was just Doug's pal. It could turn out to be an insignificant detail, but it didn't do much for his trust level with his new client. He wondered what else Story neglected to tell him. He definitely wanted to talk to her, but for right now he mainly wanted a drink. That and to get out of range of Nancy's hideous perfume

8

Story didn't liked Streeter's attitude on the phone when they set up the meeting. He sounded surly, sarcastic. She did not need grief from the hired help. However, she did want a progress report. Also, she wanted to talk to him about that dipshit Cooper's latest ploy. Sometimes Story wondered why men didn't simply shut up and get with the program. Just because they didn't menstruate, they seemed to think they ran everything.

And what was with this Thomas Cooper? He calls a meeting with her to discuss "Doug's outstanding balance," as if it were any of her concern. She didn't know specific numbers, but Doug had told her more than once that he dished out a huge amount of money to his attorney right after the arrest. Now Cooper was going to try and browbeat her into paying his phony bills. That kind of grief was something else she did not need. If he kept pushing her, he'd find out that hassling Story Moffatt could be about as pleasant as attempting foreplay with a cornered razorback.

But Mr. Streeter concerned her more right now. Even though he ruined her lawsuit and he was crabby on the phone, she liked the guy. He was probably no genius, but he was street smart and he had a gentle way about him without losing his masculine edge. As if someone with forearms and shoulders like his could ever lose his masculinity. They planned to meet at the Pearl Street Grill, an upscale, quasi-British pub in south-central Denver. She liked the Grill's secluded patio. The meeting was set for eight o'clock Friday night, and he was calmly nursing a Beck's Dark when she walked in a little before nine.

"Sorry to keep you waiting, Streeter." Her smile was barely noticeable as she walked to the back patio, where he was waiting for her at the far end, near the lighted garden. "Business, you know."

"It's okay with me. In my line of work you get used to waiting. Plus, it's your money we're pissing away here. I'll wait until closing time if you want to screw around like this."

She hesitated for an instant and then sat down. Streeter could tell he'd riled her. She had a way of letting you know she wasn't pleased with a quick, pinched-up smile. The waitress came and Story ordered a club soda. Then she turned back to the bounty hunter and gave him an intense stare. "So, how are we doing with our little search?"

"We?" He hesitated before continuing. "Nothing on the bank-vault idea. I've checked a bunch of them and come up with zip." He paused again. "Why didn't you tell me Doug wasn't alone when he died?"

So that was it, she thought. Poor little boy must feel excluded. The waitress brought the club soda, which gave Story a chance to think. She took a long sip and carefully put her glass down, deliberately wiping the corners her mouth with a linen napkin.

"Shannon doesn't have anything for us," she said as she settled back in the black cast-iron patio chair.

"That's really not the point." Streeter didn't like her lack of reaction. "If I'm going to do this job, you'll have to tell me everything that relates to the man. You had to know something like that was important, or at least it might be important. This hunt's going to be difficult enough. I don't have time to screw around. And how can you possibly know she doesn't have anything for us?"

"I spoke to her family and . . ." She shrugged, holding her palms out innocently.

"So what? You think they're going to come out and tell you. 'Hey, we found, oh, about seventy-five thousand bucks on top of Shannon's refrigerator. It must be yours. After all, she *was* screwing your fiancé. Here, take it.' Is that what you think?"

"If you'll let me finish. I also went through her apartment."

"How the hell did you manage that?" He leaned forward.

"Look, I may have been somewhat less than totally candid with you the other day. I knew about his affair with Shannon. All about it, including where she lived. Streeter, this hasn't been a picnic for me." Her voice softened and a trace of genuine pain spread over her eyes. It softened them nicely, he thought. "Telling you all about Doug's problems and the troubles he and I were having was very difficult for me. The drugs, the women, the lying. I just got tired of going into all the gory details." Then her voice stiffened slightly. "At any rate, I went over to Shannon's shortly after the accident and talked the weekend manager into letting me in. I told him I was her sister and he bought it. I went over every inch of the place and there was nothing."

Streeter didn't say anything for a moment and they sat in silence. Finally, he spoke. "You've got this annoying little habit of being 'somewhat less than totally candid.' Just keep it up and we'll be somewhat less than totally successful finding Doug's money. You're quite an operator there, Ms. Moffatt. Your fiancé isn't even cold in the ground yet and you're going through his mistress's apartment looking for his money. Sounds like an adult sitcom."

"Hell, our life together was a sitcom. Doug probably had several 'hobbies' like Shannon Mays. Let me tell you a little about us. I tried to make it work but he never really let me close. In public he could be very aloof and uncaring. And in private, well, let's just say Doug made love like he did everything else. Quickly.

To get done with it, and with as little hassle as possible. Half the time he was either so drunk or in such a big hurry, it was almost comical. We must have looked like the Special Olympics of sex, for God's sake. He'd put in a little showmanship along the way, but never with any real feeling. I endured a lot from him. If he left anything, I'm entitled to it and I'm going after it. It's my inheritance we're talking about. Maybe I should have told you about Shannon. I didn't and I apologize. But now let's get on with it."

Streeter shrugged. "You really don't have to tell me anything you don't want to, but if you keep holding back it'll just slow things up. I wasted a lot of my time, not to mention your money, finding out something you could have told me about last week. I got paid up front, so, if you want me to keep flushing it away, keep doing that."

They both sat in silence again until Streeter spoke. "Did you know that Tom Cooper is looking into this, too?"

Story blushed for a second. "I, uh . . . No, I didn't. Into what? How do you know?"

"I assume he's looking into Doug's affairs, if you'll pardon the pun. When I went to Shannon's apartment building, the day manager told me about it. It wasn't Cooper but some girl from his office. Ronnie or Donnie or something like that. She was there last week asking if Shannon had left any of her stuff."

"That jerk. That mother . . . I think I know who you're talking about. I met his secretary with him at Doug's funeral. She had some butch name like that. Kind of cheap-looking, and I got the impression Cooper and her had a thing together." She took a sip of her club soda. "He called me yesterday and we set up a meeting for next Wednesday. He wants to discuss a bill that Doug supposedly owed him. Can you believe the gonads on that schmuck? He's going to try and bully me into paying for what Doug already paid. I probably deserve a refund!"

"You have any invoices, receipts? Documentation?"

"No, but Doug told me he paid a bundle to Cooper right after his arrest and he was worried that Cooper wasn't doing much to earn it. I'm sure Doug didn't owe him anything. By the way, did you ever find out if I might be liable for his debts?"

"I talked to a lawyer friend of mine. He told me that, unless you two were calling yourselves husband and wife, telling everyone you were married, then Cooper probably doesn't have much of a chance. But he can still make the claim, and it could cost you a bundle to defend yourself."

"I've been thinking about that. When you start in with the lawyers, it always costs." She sat silent. "Will your friend work for me on this?"

"He said he would. His name is William McLean. He was the DA in Arapahoe County for a whole lot of years. Every lawyer in town knows him and knows how good he is."

Story nodded. She stared at her club soda, running her finger around the lip of the glass. The patio seemed almost dead except for some rustling in the trees that formed a green awning over part of it. At a nearby table, three androgynous Generation X'ers sat mumbling to each other, apparently lost in deep conversation. They all had the standard ponytails, baseball caps worn backward, pierced faces, and vacant, vaguely obtuse expressions. Story glanced at them for a moment. They seemed indistinguishable from one another. A warm breeze swept the whole area, causing the leaves to rustle much louder. Pronounced yet soothing, like soft, muffled chimes. She looked up, her face set like Charles Barkley's when he was charging the basket.

"Maybe I can cut Cooper off before he gets started," she said. "How's this for an idea? We'll draw up a demand letter saying that Doug told me he paid, hell, I don't know, thirty thousand dollars or something major like that for a retainer. We'll say he told me that only a small part of the money was earned by Cooper when the case was dismissed. I'll ask him for a breakdown of how the money was spent and demand about half of it back. We'll put it on McLean's letterhead. If his rep is as good as you say, Cooper might just fold up like a cheap telescope when he reads it "

Streeter considered the plan. "That'll sure give him something to think about. It couldn't hurt to put him on the defensive."

"Precisely. I'll run it all by McLean to make sure we don't cross the line. Nothing illegal. I just want to cut this guy off at the knees so hard and so clean that he'll go away for good. Plus, if he's tracking down Doug's money, this might get him off that trail. My hunch is he doesn't have the stomach for a fight."

Streeter thought about what Carey told him about Cooper's trial in Adams County, but he said nothing.

"It's important to show this joker that I'm no pushover," she concluded.

"That might do it, but don t underestimate Cooper. Is this how you run your business?"

"Advertising is like being at war half the time. You have to strike hard and fast. First impressions, appearances, they can mean everything. These guys I pitch to wouldn't take me seriously for a minute if I couldn't show right up front that I mean business. Don't tell me that in your line of work you never shovel a little crap or take a few shortcuts to fake someone out."

"True. I remember my first job for Frank. I found a bail jumper—a confidence man, of all things—up in Salt Lake City, staying at his sister's house. Frank wanted me to have him come back here on his own money so we could save the airfare cost. I sure as hell couldn't call him up and ask him politely to come home. So I decided to play on his greed. I sent him a cheap clock radio, like he's won a contest back here in Denver. I also sent with it a registered letter saying he's won the grand prize— a Town Car, I think it was; even put a Lincoln brochure in with the mailing. But the real clincher is, I sent him a one-way ticket to Denver. Told him he had to claim his prize in person. A lot cheaper than paying all that extra airfare for me and him. Course, I was taking a chance the guy didn't just keep the radio and cash out the plane ticket. Luckily, he was as greedy as I thought. Not to mention as stupid. I went out to the old Stapleton International the night his flight's due in, and sure enough the slob got off the plane looking every bit like he was expecting Vanna White to meet him. You should have seen his expression when I put the cuffs on him."

"You're kidding. That's fantastic. I knew there was something about you I liked."

"Coming from you, I'm not so sure that's a compliment."

Her smile stayed in place. "I suppose it's that kind of cleverness that got you on *Jeopardy*?"

The question surprised him. "How'd you find out about that?"

"When I gave your name to my secretary, she said she remembered seeing you on the show a couple of years ago. Memories of the big, bad bounty hunter from Denver stuck with her. She said you won the night she watched. You were pretty sharp with the facts, she told me. How'd you get interested in that?"

He shrugged. "It's all in the family. My parents and I used to toss trivia around while we ate dinner." Streeter didn't want to tell her the whole saga, but his parents—both pretty smart— liked to show off. They used their knowledge to outdo each other. Some families called it arguing, but his mother referred to it as a "lively exchange of ideas." "Trivia's a hard habit to break, I guess."

By now it was dark, and she asked him to walk her to her car. "I parked across the street, behind that office building. I know I'm not supposed to, but it's so hard to find an open spot around here. I'll show you my baby, too."

"Your baby?"

"Corky. He's my wheaten terrier. He's a good little dog but he's so cute, all white and fluffy, that I spoil him rotten."

They paid for their drinks and left. As they crossed the street they heard a faint jingling from down the block. Story seemed confused.

"That's Corky's bell collar. How'd he get out of the car?"

The sound grew louder as it came quickly toward them. Corky was about a half-block away when they spotted him in the streetlights. There was a bright-red streak along his side, and when Story saw that she screamed. "Corky!"

The dog didn't seem to be hurt as he ran toward his mistress. When he got to her, she and Streeter could see that someone had sprayed red paint on his back and down his right side. The dog was oblivious to the paint and clearly delighted to see Story. As she bent down to check him out, he jumped up and licked her face like it was smeared with lamb chops.

"Who did this to you, Corky?" Then she looked up at Streeter. "My car!"

They quickly walked around behind the two-story brick building to where she had parked. Corky had made out much better than the Audi did. Someone had slashed all four tires and sprayed red paint on the left side of the steel-gray sedan. The driver's door was jimmied open and they could see in the glow of the inside overhead light that someone had sprayed the dashboard with more of the paint.

"Oh my God," Story yelled when she saw the damage. "What the hell's going on, Streeter?"

He walked up to the car and noticed a crumpled piece of paper lying on the front seat. "Someone left a calling card." He picked up the paper and read it. The two simple words "back off" were scrawled in blue ink on the stiff white paper. He turned and showed it to Story. "Very subtle. It looks like someone wants you to stop doing something."

She took the paper between two fingers like Corky had just gone to the bathroom on it. "Who? What do they mean?"

Streeter again thought about his friend Detective Carey's warning on Cooper. "Maybe Doug's lawyer is sending you a message. Is there anything else you're doing that someone might want you to stop?"

"This is crazy." She dropped the note and walked slowly around the car, carrying her dog, who wiggled with excitement without knowing why. "They could have killed Corky. Is Cooper really that nuts?"

"Who knows? It's unlikely that he would pull something like this right after he sets up that meeting for Wednesday, but who the hell knows? Is there anyone else who might know about Doug and what we're doing?"

"It's hard to say." She was regaining her composure. "Doug knew so many people. So many nut cases. He probably dealt drugs with a lot of weirdos. Could be one of them found out about what we're up to."

"Well, it was either Cooper or someone else."

She stopped and looked right at him for the first time since they got to the car. "Now, that was profound, Streeter."

They inspected the damage for a minute and then she turned to him again. "Is there anything we can do before I call the police to make out a report?"

"Let's knock on a few doors across the alley and ask if anyone saw anything."

They talked to several neighbors. People in the first two houses noticed nothing, but at the third backyard from the entrance to the alley, they saw a man go into the back door. Streeter hurried up and knocked. A balding man maybe ten years younger than the bounty hunter answered. He was wearing just a pair of shorts and sandals and carried a half-empty quart bottle of Budweiser. Presumably, no one with such a swollen white stomach would leave his yard without a shirt.

"Excuse me," Streeter said. "My friend's car got vandalized sometime over the last hour and a half. It was parked in the lot of that office building." He nodded toward the end of the alley. "You didn't happen to see anything over there, did you?"

The man frowned in wild confusion as he listened, but when he answered he sounded basically lucid. "I thought I saw someone coming out of there about twenty minutes ago. I didn't get much of a look, but he left his car sitting still idling in the alley while he got out for a while and headed to the parking lot. Then he got in his car again and backed out and drove off. I couldn't see much of anything from my backyard and I didn't know what he was up to but I'll tell you this, he looked really pissed off. Major pissed off. I got a decent look at his license plate and I caught the three letters and the first number. B-J-J-3 something or other."

"That'll help. Thanks a lot." He walked back to Story and told her. They tried a few more neighbors, but no one else saw anything, so they went back to the car.

"I'll call the police," she told him when they got together again.

"Now, *that's* profound," Streeter said.

As they waited for the police, Streeter realized there was something familiar about the partial plate number, but he couldn't quite place it.

9

Soyko was all of eleven years old when his stepfather started kicking the hell out of him regularly. The old man, a bitter ex–professional middleweight, called each beating a "boxing lesson." They lived next to their junkyard on Chicago's near North Side, a couple of grimy miles from the city's Loop. Soyko, who seldom used his first name of Leo because he hated it, absorbed the beatings until he was big enough to fight back.

And finally, one day shortly after his seventeenth birthday, in the back lot of the junkyard, he put an end to it. Business at the yard had been going south lately, and the old man was in a particularly toxic mood. It was cold out, midwestern bitter-damp, with the sky so low you could scrape it with a pool cue, when the old man wanted to administer another lesson.

The fight was as short and violent as it was one-sided. Soyko got in the first punch and never really gave the old man a chance. He delivered the final blows with a ball-peen hammer. The coroner's report later said that the old man suffered massive internal bleeding and had seven cracked ribs, a splintered vertebra, four broken fingers, and several smashed facial bones. The kid even managed to break both bones in the elder Soyko's left forearm.

When it was over, Leo went back into the house, grabbed a few clothes, and left Chicago forever. Incredibly, the old man hung on for five days and then died without coming out of a deep coma. In the years that followed, Soyko often wondered if he'd actually meant to kill his stepfather. But he never wondered about his reaction to it. He was glad it happened.

"We'll divide this up," Soyko instructed Jacky in their search for Doug's money. "I'll take the strip joints and you check out the pool halls. The bars, places like that. I'll see if he had any girl-friends and you just try and get a handle on anyone at all who knew the guy."

He didn't want to let Jacky get too near women. Soyko was bad enough in that department, but Jacky was pretty much out of control. Neither man appeared to really like women, and they never had girlfriends. But Jacky seemed to genuinely hate the gender. Women knew it, too. The only ones he was ever with sexually were hookers, and even then he had to pay a premium for his bent desires. Not that Soyko was much better. His idea of romance consisted of a drunken, doggy-style roll on the couch with some dim-witted trailer-park bimbo. He'd usually keep his shirt and socks on, and he never spent the night. But at least he could talk to a woman without scaring the hell out of her.

He also wanted to work the strip joints because he sensed that Doug Shelton would have leaned toward that kind of thing. To a good-looking, fancy coke dealer, strip clubs would be a natural turf. Soyko started with the upscale strip bars, like the Diamond Cabaret and the Mile Hi Saloon. They were more like bizarre, X-rated aerobics classes with bars and restaurants attached. Horny professionals and free-spending construction workers couldn't seem to get enough of those places. Soyko talked to most of the dancers and waitresses at both bars and found nothing. He then went to the mid-range strip joints, like P.T.'s and Shotgun Willie's. Less flashy but still attracting a somewhat sane crowd. Again, no one remembered Doug Shelton, or at least admitted it.

But Soyko was not the type to get discouraged. He figured the further down the skin ladder he went the more he could relate to the dead realtor. And the bottom rung was a ragged joint near the city's Performing Arts Complex, appropriately named Art's Performing Complex. The dancers were mainly sad, sagging biker chicks with a blank toughness in their eyes. Their bodies were freckled with tattoos and laced with stretch marks. But the lighting was low enough and the show raunchy enough for the place to bring in a good buck. Art's was so murky that it didn't appear to have actual interior walls, but, rather, it was surrounded by a muddy darkness from which people drifted in and out.

Soyko hit paydirt when he talked to an off-duty waitress who said she'd "sort of dated" Shelton over the past couple of years. She told him her name was Chantel. She had naturally blond hair but her breasts stood at attention just a shade too well to be original equipment. Her face had broad, country-girl features, pretty if not overly distinctive.

"I'm not from here," she said. "Originally, I mean. I was born in Marshfield. That's a little-bitty town way up in the middle of Wisconsin." She was chewing gum, smoking, and drinking, all with a determined ferocity that let Soyko know she was pretty coked up. "It's the string-cheese capital of the world, you know," she added with a childish pride.

Of course, he thought. Who the hell doesn't know that? "That's really something. Lotta women up there named Chantel, are there?"

She stopped chewing for a minute and studied his face. Then she must have decided he was genuinely curious, because she started chewing again. "That's not my real name, actually. It's sort of a stage name I hung on to from when I danced here. It's not good to let these creeps know your real name."

"Can't be too careful, huh?"

"Boy, you said a mouthful right there." Her eyes widened. "You would not believe the maniacs we get in here sometimes.

Bikers, molesters, all sorts of weird ones. You look safe, though. I can always tell."

Soyko decided she must be a lot younger than she looked. "How'd you meet my buddy Doug? He a regular here?"

Chantel frowned. "You really friends with Doug? He never mentioned you."

He stared hard at her. "We ain't blood brothers or nothing, but we hang out together. I buy product from him, sometimes."

At that, her face lit up. A girl can never know enough men with cocaine. She looked around the room. "It's so noisy in here. You think you might be interested in maybe going somewhere to party a little?"

"Like where?"

"I could get us a room. There's a place I know out on Colfax that gives good rates."

"How much this party gonna cost me?"

"Well, you catch the room. Maybe thirty for that. Then"— she smiled and tried to twitch her shoulders like a little girl— "I'm thinking some nose candy for me would be a nice idea, too."

"And sex?"

"I'm not a pro. The sex is free." Then she lowered her voice, which was now anything but childlike. "But I practice safe sex and I keep skins in my purse. They'll cost you seventy-five each."

Seventy-five bucks for this clod, Soyko thought in disgust. "Those prices, maybe I bring my own rubbers."

"Not to my party you don't. You want me, you use my rubbers." There was a sudden edge in her voice that she didn't pick up in any string-cheese capital.

"Let's go." He stood up.

They drove to a dump on West Colfax Avenue with a name Soyko promptly forgot. It's the kind of place where they try to wash away the filth with industrial-strength antiseptic cleaners. It ends up smelling like a third-world hospital and has about the same overall charm as one, too. When they got to the room,

Chantel started bragging about how good she was in bed. It was supposed to turn him on, but it merely annoyed Soyko.

"I fuck like a Michael Jordan plays basketball," she said, "I mean, I get into some sort of hot zone and I'm a pure pleasure machine."

By now, Soyko was really losing his patience. Princess Condom here was getting dumber by the minute, and he had no intention of having sex with her. Not to mention that maybe she didn't know a thing about Doug. He decided to find out. He grabbed her in the middle of her left bicep and squeezed hard. Chantel's arm scrunched up like a water balloon. She let out a quick, shocked squeak, her eyes bulging in terror.

"Keep it down, Miss String Cheese," he snarled as he let go of her arm and shoved her into a chair with one hand. "I'm done listening to your bullshit and I wouldn't fuck you if you were paying me seventy-five a pop. Now, you're going to tell me everything you know about Dougy Shelton. If you convince me you're on the level, you might make it out of here."

Chantel just stared at him. Her eyes began to tear up at the corners. He pulled the dagger out of his belt, slammed the blade point down into the wooden dresser, and let it go. It sort of quivered there for a second and then stood still.

"Let's talk and maybe I don't have to use that."

She nodded her head so fast that she didn't even notice when her gum shot out of her mouth and dribbled down the front of her blouse.

"What do you want to find out?" Her voice was lifeless and hoarse.

"Mainly everything." He smiled back, knowing he was in complete control. "How long you known him?"

"Not quite two years. Maybe. He sold coke and I know he got busted for it last year. I remember that he got the living shit beat out of him right afterward. He said the cops did it. Who knows? Look, I only went out with him a few times. He'd come on like this big lady-killer and flash the money around. He had the car and all the good clothes. But he was different once you got to know him."

"Yeah? How?"

"Well, like he wasn't much of a stud. The way he looked, I expected him to jungle-fuck me into a coma, but with all the blow he put up his nose he couldn't cut it much. Half the time we went to bed, he'd get coke dick and we'd just sit around talking. Not that I was missing much anyhow. I mean, the guy was pretty small in the old pecker department. If you follow me. But it never seemed to bother him much. Sometimes I even thought he might be more into guys. Like maybe he was bi."

"You're kidding?" Soyko considered that. "Why'd he keep whoring around if he liked guys and he couldn't get his sorry little thing up?"

She thought for a second, getting a little more composed as the conversation went on. "Lots of reasons, I guess. He thought coke dealers were supposed to be lady-killers. It was all part of this front he was putting on. I think he was mostly just sad. He was living with some woman, but she couldn't do much for him."

Soyko thought about the blonde. "What was with them?"

Chantel shrugged and looked like she was going to cry. "He told me about her once." She shrugged again and smiled weakly. "But I was pretty wasted then, too, and I don't remember much. She was really kind of a bitch, from what he said. Looked good but had ice in her veins."

Figures. "He get coke dick with her, too?"

"How would I know? Probably. If I can't get 'em hard, who can?" She smiled, then glanced at the knife again, and the smile disappeared. "This is the same stuff that cop asked me when he came to Art's. He wanted to know all about Doug."

Soyko frowned. "Cop? When? What cop?"

"I don't remember the name. It was just a few days ago. All of a sudden everyone's so interested in Dougy."

"A uniform cop?"

"No, a detective. An old guy. He must have been over forty. A real meany, too. A bully. He scared me. I didn't tell him Jack shit. Course, he didn't pull any knife on me, either."

Soyko filed it away. "Did Doug ever talk about money much? You know, like he had a lot?"

She frowned. "Seems he told me a couple of times he was real rich. Sounded like more coke talk. He told me he was a good lover, too, but look what kind of shit that turned out to be."

Soyko pondered what she said, lit a cigarette, and didn't say anything for a while. Chantel kept quiet. He finally broke the silence. "Did he keep much cash on him?"

"He had it but he didn't spread it around much. If he went out for a night on the town with three hundred in his pocket, he'd go home with two ninety-five. You know what I mean? He was good about giving away coke sometimes, but the cash he held on to pretty much."

There was a whiny twang to her voice now that bugged him, so he slapped his open palm down on the dresser, next to his knife. It sounded like an explosion and Chantel jumped about four inches in her chair.

"Look," she said, "the guy was loud and showy and deep down he was cheap and scared or something. Maybe even a queer, I don't know. But just so he kept the coke coming, I didn't ask questions. I'll tell you this much. Whatever he did with his money, he didn't let it get too far out of his sight. He watched it closer than anyone I ever saw."

"He move much product?"

"Some, I guess. He could move a good amount of coke when he had to."

Soyko could see how scared she was. He believed her but, more to the point, he was tired of listening to her. He pulled his buckle blade out of the table and looked at it as he slowly turned it. Then he put it back in his belt.

That made Chantel feel more comfortable. She sat up for the first time. "Mind if I have a cigarette?"

"What do I care?"

She took a Kool out of her purse and lit it, studying his face as she did. "You think Dougy has money for you?"

"What do you care?"

"Maybe I can help you with something. I know a lot of people around town. I ain't seen Dougy in a long time, though."

"Neither have I. You know where I can maybe find him?"

She shrugged childishly, the string-cheese capital coming out again. "If I see him, should I let you know?"

"You and me friends now or something?"

"I just thought maybe I could give you a hand. And if I do you'd remember me if you got any money out of it."

Soyko had to smile at that. Coke whores. He shook his head. Here she is, scared for her life two minutes ago, and now she's trying to turn a buck.

"Just forget you ever saw me and I'll forget I ever saw you. No yakking to this detective about me. If anyone gives me grief about our little talk here, you'll be the one in trouble. I'll come looking right for you. You getting all this?"

Chantel thought about back at the bar, when she told him he looked safe. "I hear you. We'll never see each other again. I mean that."

"Nothing would make me happier. Or you. That's guaranteed. Have a nice walk home."

10

First thing Wednesday morning, Thomas Hardy Cooper put on his sharpest power suit. It was a double-breasted, deep-navy-blue number that cost him a ton.

"That faggot salesman at Neiman Marcus made it sound like only a blue-collar cretin would hesitate to spend eighteen hundred on a suit," he had told Ronnie the day before. "But I have to admit, I cut a pretty impressive figure in that thing. And I want you to wear something black. Something conservative. None of those thigh slits and come-fuck-me neckline plunges tomorrow."

He only hoped she owned such a garment. Then he called in Dwayne Koslaski, his part-time paralegal, short on experience and ambition, "but a beefy two hundred thirty pounds of ugly Polack," as he put it. He wanted Dwayne to attend the meeting with Story to help set the right mood. He hoped to present a united front, strong and solemn, when he hit her with a bill for unpaid for services in behalf of Douglas Shelton. He figured he'd sit at his desk with the large window behind him. He'd keep the shades wide open, so Story had to squint to see him. Cooper in his massive swivel chair, the enormous paralegal on his right, and a devoted Ronnie on his left.

Doug's invoice itself was a cleverly crafted bit of fiction totaling just over twenty-six thousand dollars. It was less than Cooper originally projected. But it had a more credible sound to it. He and Ronnie spent most of Tuesday afternoon creating it, and they were both justly proud. Unless Doug had been telling Story about his finances all along, the invoice should appear genuine. If she challenged it, Cooper could easily present it in court with a straight face.

"Straight face, hell," he told Ronnie when they finished. "I'm so impressed with this thing, I'm almost looking forward to showing it to a judge. All this legal research, pretrial motions, client conferences. Not to mention conferences with the district attorney, paralegal fees, and endless investigation by Soyko at sixty an hour. When I look at this I'm not so sure I didn't actually earn the money."

Ronnie, of course, was sure he hadn't. She said only, "You half-earned it just by making it up, honey."

"Here's the way we'll do it tomorrow," he told her. "I figure I'll hit her with the invoice before she even has time to settle into her chair. Feed her some crap about how much I hate to do it, seeing as how she must still be grieving over her loss and all. But I busted my hump for her Douglas and all I have to show for my Herculean efforts is that paltry thirty-five-hundred-dollar retainer. I've even dummied up a receipt copy for that amount. I dated it right after Doug's arrest.

"I want to shove this invoice into that flawless, condescending face and ask her how she'd like to arrange the payments. I expect she'll counter with a few tears and maybe bitch about not being liable for Doug's debts. But tears do not mean a thing. Not when we're pulling a number like this. We'll be in the red zone, Ronnie, with a nice piece of change just a couple of yards away. We get this close, we can't let a few tears sidetrack us.

"I figure that when she stops blubbering I'll hit her with the threat of a suit. Then I'll lighten up a little by offering to knock fifteen—no, make that ten—percent off if she pays within thirty days. Let her know I'm not heartless. But I don't want there to be any mistake by her about my intentions here. No bullshit. If she really puts up a fuss, I've got a little surprise waiting for her in the other room."

But the next day, before the meeting was two minutes old, Cooper sniffed the foul odor of calamity in the air. First of all, Story showed up almost forty minutes late. Second, she brought along this side of beef named Streeter who made Dwayne look like a puffy blob. Then things got worse.

"Please be seated, Miss Moffatt, Mr. Streeter," Cooper said, a little more quickly than he intended. "Traffic bad or something?"

Story didn't answer and Streeter just moved his eyes slowly between the lawyer and his two assistants.

"Streeter? May I call you by your first name?" Cooper continued, not liking the vibe he was getting from across his desk.

"Streeter's fine."

"I believe I have heard about you. You are a bounty hunter employed by Frank Dazzler, the bondsman, are you not?"

"I know Frank," was all Streeter would acknowledge.

Cooper went through the Rolodex in his mind, struggling to recall what he knew about Streeter. He had a solid reputation in the legal community as a savvy skip tracer and bounty hunter. He never abused the people he was tracking. But he never gave up or took any guff, either. Cooper could feel the desired mood slipping away. Even the sky was against him: the cloud cover all but erased any sun glare on Story.

"Why, may I ask, do you feel the need for this burly assistant?" Cooper turned his attention back to Story.

"Why, may I ask, do you feel the need to paint my car?" Story had decided to throw out one quick accusation about her Audi to see if he'd bite.

He didn't. In fact, he seemed genuinely puzzled. "Is that supposed to be a joke?"

"Forget it. What is it you wanted to see me about?"

"This is not a particularly pleasant subject," he began, holding out his hand for Ronnie to give him the invoice. She fumbled with her papers, so Story jumped in. He had barely finished his sentence when Story slid an angry-looking document across his desk, pushing it gingerly with one finger.

"Well, this is a particularly pleasant subject for me," she said. "I like it when people owe me money and they pay up. Doug kept me posted on the financial arrangements he made with you. According to my calculations, based on numbers he supplied me, his estate should be getting money back from you. It's all spelled out in there. Take your time. I'm sure you're familiar with demand letters. But there can be no dispute that you didn't earn all the money for that little work you did. I've retained William McLean, as you can see. If you have any problems with the numbers, I suggest you speak directly to Mr. McLean."

So much for her crying, Cooper thought. Now he could really feel his plan sliding into the toilet. McLean, of all people. Ronnie finally handed him his invoice. Suddenly it looked feeble next to the demand letter, which he started skimming. Story was looking for fifteen thousand and change, saying Doug had paid thirty thousand up front. The numbers were off, so he knew she was guessing. Still, she was in the ballpark and he was in for a fight.

Streeter kept looking at Cooper and his crew. The attorney had one of those chunky bodies that made even an expensive suit look like it came off the rack at Kmart. Story's letter apparently had had the desired effect. Cooper looked like he was reading a death threat from the Ayatollah. The blonde next to him wasn't quite as cheap-looking as Story had described. Sort of sexy, but with a definite air of intelligence. Quite sexy, actually, and obviously pissed. She was glaring at Cooper and she seemed to be shaking her head. And the bovine paralegal with the hideous posture merely seemed confused. He looked like all he wanted in the whole world was to leave the room.

Cooper looked up when he got the gist of the letter. "You're kidding," was about the best he could do. "You can't be serious. I've got an itemized invoice here documenting far more than the sum of this fictitious retainer to which you allude. Hell, all Doug came up with was thirty-five hundred. I've got the receipt right here."

He nodded to Ronnie, who didn't budge.

"Speaking of fictitious," Story said, glaring back, "I'd like to see that invoice. Talk about fairy tales. Listen, Cooper, you've got my letter. Give me your invoice. We'll let a judge settle this. There's no point in us arguing about it now."

That really hit Cooper. His final trump card was Jacky Romp waiting in the next room to serve her with a summons and complaint in a collections action. But if she had William McLean ready to go to court, the suit sure as hell wouldn't shake her. Chalk one up for Ronnie. She had read Story a lot better than he had. But he'd come this far, might as well play out the string. He leaned over to Ronnie and told her to get the process server. She was watching their two visitors across the desk, thinking what a bitch Story was and how the big bounty hunter had nice forearms and such a gentle face. He can hunt my bounty any day, flashed through Ronnie's mind. Then she turned and looked hard at Cooper and seemed about to speak. Instead, she merely got up and left the room.

"In anticipation of your response, I've formalized my grievance in the lawsuit that is forthcoming," Cooper said without much enthusiasm.

The door opened and Jacky Romp entered. His eyes darted around until he saw Story. He broke into his patented lizard smile and strolled toward her.

"This would be for you, lady," he said with his mouth shut. He looked over at Streeter and his smile faded. Then he turned and left the room.

Streeter shifted in his seat and pulled some sort of document from his back pocket. He looked at Story. She nodded. Then he leaned across the desk and chucked the papers toward Cooper.

"In anticipation of your chicken-shit response, Mr. McLean drew this up." Story smiled. "It's a summons and complaint all of your own. We'll see you in court. And another thing." She glanced at Ronnie, who had returned to her chair. "Tell Hot Stuff there to quit looking into Doug's past. I know she was over at Shannon Mays' place and I can only guess what else she's doing. And if anything more happens to my car, I'll hold you personally responsible."

Cooper's mouth dropped open in genuine shock. Papers flying at him from every direction and now all this cryptic talk about cars and Shannon somebody. Ronnie stayed cool, glaring at Story but not saying anything. "Shannon's? I don't . . ." Cooper quickly regained his composure. "The activities of my staff are none of your concern."

"From the looks of it, they're not much of your concern, either," Story shot back. "Just don't pry into Doug's life. A judge'll settle this."

With that, she and Streeter got up and left.

Soyko had just rounded the corner next to the elevators when he saw Doug Shelton's girlfriend and some guy coming out of Cooper's office. He was surprised, because Cooper had told him the meeting would be long over by then. The couple didn't seem to notice him as they passed in the hallway. When they walked by, he turned to admire Story, or more specifically her bottom, heading for the elevators. He also noticed the size of the guy with her and wondered if her new boyfriend had any fight in him. In Soyko's world, it was performance that counted. Bulging muscles without a killer instinct meant nothing. Just more meat to put down.

A frowning Dwayne Koslaski came out of Cooper's office, and Jacky was sitting in the waiting area. He was ignoring the receptionist, who was ignoring him. When Soyko walked in, she switched into high gear and ignored both of them. Jacky gave him a quick nod toward Cooper's office and rolled his eyes. Soyko walked slowly over and sat next to him.

"That clown gets more worthless all the time," Jacky fumed.

"Tried to lean on the little blonde, and I gather she handed him his ass. She had some meatball with her."

"I saw them out in the hallway. She wasn't going for any of his bullshit lawyer bills? Some move, huh?"

Jacky grunted through his teeth.

"How you know what happened in there?" Soyko asked.

"When the fat guy walked out of the office, he left the door open. Mr. Shit-for-Brains Lawyer was yelling at the broad that works for him, Mrs. Shit-for-Brains. Something about her sticking her nose into something or other. She looked like she wanted to kick his butt. Probably could. Anyhow, he started whining about how the other broad might be more trouble than she's worth. Looks like another Cooper fuckup in the making."

Soyko nodded. He stared at Cooper's office door. "Let's find out what's going on." When they walked into his office, the receptionist didn't even look up from her crossword puzzle.

"Jesus, all I need is you free-lancing," Cooper was yelling at Ronnie. They stood in the middle of the room, about a foot apart, glaring at each other. Neither seemed to notice when Soyko and Romp walked in. "Every idiot in town is looking for that money! What the hell were you doing, going over to her apartment like that?"

"Somebody better get real on finding that money," Ronnie hurled back. "If you think these two dildos are going to locate anything"—she threw her arm out in Soyko's direction—"maybe you should find another line of work. Like sorting apples."

Cooper noticed them for the first time. He straightened his tie, went behind his desk, and threw himself into his chair. "That will be all for now." He looked back at Ronnie, trying to put as much authority into his voice as he could. No one in the room bought it.

She studied him. "We'll talk later." With that she left.

"See what happens when you spoil a woman?" He looked at Soyko.

"I see. She nosing around in your business, counselor?"

Cooper's face got red. "Everyone's nosing around in my business. And it appears that everyone has the same idea about Mr. Shelton's cash reserves. That goddamned girlfriend of his is out looking for it. You're looking for it. I'm looking for it. That one out there is looking for it." He nodded toward the door. "What the hell is going on around here?"

"Looks like you're having one miserable morning."

"It would appear so." Cooper was now more reflective than depressed. "And then that Story woman practically accused me of trashing her car. I'm not sure I know what she was implying. Either of you two been screwing around with her?"

Soyko frowned. "Hell no. What for? Tell me what happened and we'll see what we can come up with." He sat down across from the attorney and Jacky flopped onto the couch.

Cooper stared at Soyko for a long time before he spoke. "My meeting with Moffatt went like shit. Not only is she contesting my invoices, but she's fighting back. Here I thought she'd be glad to take a discount just to make it right with me. That bastard Doug must have told her something about our arrangement, because she has a pretty good handle on the money end of it.

"As though that weren't enough, she's hired William McLean to represent her. Even getting her served"—he nodded quickly to Jacky—"didn't faze her. She brought some muscle-head with her to glare at me. That miserable Koslaski damn near wet his pants. He tells us his name is Streeter. So I asked his first name. He sits there like Buddha and says to me, 'Streeter's fine.'

"Then comes the grand finale." Cooper's eyes got wide as he scanned the room. "My own secretary is out there looking for Doug's money without even telling me. Jesus, who can you trust? This thing's beginning to look like one monumental foul-up. Maybe I should just dump the whole effort."

Soyko nodded. "Who can you trust, is right." He made a

mental note to have a little chat with Taggert. He wouldn't tell Cooper about that, because he would get all protective. The lawyer acted like Ronnie was the only woman on the face of the planet. He could never understand Cooper's loyalty toward her. Any woman of mine starts messing in my business, Soyko reasoned, she gets the belt.

"Don't get too discouraged," he advised the attorney. "Just give it a shot against this McLean guy. You already served the papers. Can't stop that train once it's left the station."

Cooper knew he was right. He doubted if Moffatt could get any money out of him. He might as well take his chances in court. See if he could squeeze something out of her in front of a judge. If she had money to hire McLean, she had money to pay for Doug.

"About the rest of it," Soyko continued, "just don't worry so much. I got an idea there's something to all this hunting around. I talked to a couple of people who knew Doug and it seems he did move a fair amount of blow. I just know that he had some serious money—of the six-figure variety, like you said. My own theory is that he wasn't hiding it with no girlfriend. This Story doesn't have it, why should some other broad? I'm thinking maybe he tucked it away somewhere else. And don't worry about her goon. He gives you too much grief, you let me know."

The prospect of Soyko's going up against Streeter intrigued Cooper. "I might just do that."

"Your little girlfriend there isn't the only surprise person nosing around into this business, either."

Cooper stiffened. "What do you mean. Who else?"

"Some cop's been sniffing around the last few days. My hunch is, this Story asked the cops some questions and that got them interested in Doug all over again. By the way, did Dougy get into a fight last fall? Maybe around the time he got busted?"

"I'd hardly call it a fight. Someone beat the snot out of him shortly after his incarceration. He wouldn't tell me who did it. I never understood all that happened last fall with him. The beating, the charges being dropped. Not that I was paying much attention. This cop worries me more. You really think Story got them worked up again?"

"Who knows. But this may not be bad news. It seems to me that, the more attention this guy's estate gets, the more likely it is he left some serious money behind. And we're the ones gonna find it. That's guaranteed."

11

"So, how did we make out with the opprobrious Mr. Cooper this morning?" Bill McLean asked. Streeter had called him when he got back to the church just before dark.

"I'll have to get back to you on the opprobrious part," Streeter answered, "but we sure put the fear of God into him. This guy's in a league of his own. I can understand trying to shave the corners a little to get a few extra bucks. But what corks me is that he acted indignant when we nailed him on it. Amazing. He tried to intimidate Story and she ended up crushing him. When he got that demand letter and then the complaint, I thought he was going to pass out. To top it off, his own secretary is out looking for Doug's money and he didn't even know about it."

"He may be a fool," McLean said, "but you have to admit that he has a pair a pumpkins on him. Serving Story like that. I'm looking forward to getting into court with this guy. I'd love to have seen his face when you served him. I bet they could hear his butt clamp shut all the way up and down 17th Avenue. Legally, I think we're in good shape, and I've got a few ideas how we can speed things up. I don't want this to drag out and let Cooper think he's got a shot."

"Story'll like that. Speaking of which, someone trashed out her car, spray-painted her dog, and left her a cute little message. They want her to back off. They apparently meant our treasure hunt. It could be one of Cooper's associates. I heard he has some dangerous friends."

"I've heard stories myself. Between his secretary and his investigators, he'll be spending half his time watching his own backside. We can assume that the secretary's looking for what you're looking for. And we can further assume that, if Mr. Cooper wasn't looking for that before today, he is now. That means you better be very careful. As Story's attorney, my main concern is keeping Tom Cooper's hands off whatever Doug left her that she already has. I'll try to get a quick hearing on this. Tell Story I'll call her when we have a court date."

When he hung up, Streeter called his client. He gave her McLean's message and then he filled her in on something else. "I've got a meeting tomorrow afternoon up in Boulder with a guy named Carl Shorts. He's plugged into the whole county up there and he's got a line on an old girlfriend of Doug's. It sounds like she might have something for us."

"Who is it? Do you have a name for the woman?"

"He didn't tell me on the phone. You think you might know some of his friends from when he lived up there?"

"No, but I might have heard the name before. Let me know what you find out."

"You got it."

Frank walked into the office shortly after Story hung up. "Working late, are we?" he asked.

"Just wrapping up some calls. What's to it, Frank?"

"Same old. I take it you're still busy with that lady from the other week."

"Busy with her problem. It's getting weirder all the time. Maybe you can give me a hand. Someone messed up her car last

Friday night. Spray-painted the side—along with her dog, if you can believe that. Left her a bad note that made me think it might be this lawyer we're dealing with. But the guy who lives across the alley from where she was parked got a partial on the plate of the car the painter was driving. I'm trying to think of why it rings a bell with me. The guy got B-J-J-3 clear but he couldn't see the rest. That mean anything to you?"

Frank frowned and flicked his thumb against his ear a couple of times. It was his way of letting you know he was thinking. "It means you might have a cop on your case. That's what it means to me. As I recall from my days with the Sheriff's Department, all the plates for Denver unmarked police cars start either with B-J-J or J-B-J. They're the only ones who get those prefixes. No wonder it sounded familiar. I probably told you that back when you started with me. If that's the car that did it, your friend's got at least one cop trying to tell her something. What the hell's this little lady done to make the police want to paint her doggy?"

"Beats me. Maybe she's got some unpaid parking tickets and they just wanted her attention. Maybe she wouldn't buy raffle tickets. You could write several long books on what I don't know about her."

"Well, we can sit here and crack wise all night, but if the cops are behind this you've got some serious trouble. I'm surprised, though. The Denver police may not be a bunch of geniuses or Eagle Scouts but this just ain't their style. I've dealt with these guys for thirty years and I know that's true. Listen, I'm hungry. Let's you and me go get pizza or some other big hit of garlic."

"Sounds good to me."

When they got back to the church after eating, Streeter read a little and then went to bed at eleven o'clock. But Frank's revelation about the police car wouldn't let him sleep. Finally, shortly after midnight, he got dressed and went to his weight room to think. Since he'd been a teenager, he had found solace and comfort in lifting weights. Growing up in a home with an alcoholic father, he used to retreat to the basement gym. It was his sanctuary where he could escape the endless arguments between his parents upstairs. He liked being alone with the cold iron, the smell of chalk dust and cold grease. There was a huge mirror on one wall, and a rusting bench dominated the middle. He would go through hours of repetitive sets, feeling strength and, more important, a sense of order in his chaotic and angry house. When he moved into the church, he immediately built a weight room off to one side of the garage.

He warmed up with five sets of fifty push-ups, his feet elevated a couple feet off the ground to give him more range and stretch. Then he did six fierce sets of bench presses, working up to two hundred forty-five pounds for a set of five. It was an easy weight for him. Next he moved on to curls, doing slow sets of six with a hefty one hundred eighty pounds. His biceps bulged and the veins shot out like someone had injected blue fluid in his arms.

Streeter knew he was biting into trouble when he and Story took on Cooper. But he never figured anyone else was in the picture. Much less a cop. Or cops. He had no idea how many there were, who they were, or what they were after. Nor did he know how far they'd go.

The most logical theory he'd been toying with was that the same cop who heisted the evidence against Shelton somehow heard that he and Story were looking into Doug's business. Obviously, that cop wouldn't want anyone nosing around. He was sure the cop thought that any possible problems died with Doug. All snooping now was to be discouraged. Before he and Frank went out to eat, Streeter had put in a call to Carey. He hadn't heard back yet. He'd ask his friend to sniff around the department and see if there ever were any suspects in that evidence theft.

His other theory was more disturbing. What if the cop or cops got wind that Doug left a bundle and they jumped into the hunt? Because of Doug's arrest, the police might have the inside track.

Who knows what Doug told them? He tried to think of who the renegade officer could be. Frank had a point. This isn't the way Denver cops usually behave. Still, you wave enough money in front of anyone and they can turn sour. Then he thought of Arthur Kovacs. This had to be the best suspect. The guy was right in the middle of Doug's case and he had been a Detroit cop. Streeter knew about them. Spray-painting foreign cars and dogs could be a hiring requirement in Detroit, for all he knew. Kovacs gave him that stupid tip about Shannon Mays and he made it clear what he thought of Story and Doug's family. He'd ask Carey specifically about Kovacs while he was at it.

Streeter got so deep into thought that his lifting was getting sloppy. He decided to call it a night at about one-thirty. No lights were on when he came out into the garage. His dumpy brown 1979 Buick Belvedere, a mule of a car that fit in with most of the neighborhoods he worked, sat illuminated by a streetlight through the huge stained-glass windows. Streeter's concern about how far the cops would go was about to get some illumination of its own.

The gunshots were loud but sounded distant. Streeter guessed a three fifty-seven or maybe a forty-four. He could almost swear that he saw the two bullets go through one of the high garage windows. He heard one of the bullets ricochet about twenty feet from him and it sounded like it ended up hitting the Buick.

He had dropped to his stomach when he first heard the rounds. After a minute or so, he got up and ran to the small side door. He opened it and stuck his head outside. No one was in sight. He figured that whoever did it was not firing at him. Not at that hour in the dark. Rather, they just wanted to send a couple more messages into the church.

One message was clear: I know where you live. The second was implied: Back way off.

Frank came slugging around the side of the building a couple minutes later. He held a large flashlight and he looked furious.

"That son of a bitch," he hissed. "I looked all over and he's gone. How the hell we gonna get a new window? Stained glass and all. I'm starting to wish that little lady friend of yours never found this place."

Streeter was thinking the same thing.

12

Rhonda Taggert, aka Ronnie, stubbed out yet another cigarette, then quickly grabbed the pack. Even though it was empty, she stirred her finger through it for quite a while. Then she crumpled it and tossed it on the table, wondering if she should go out for more. Better not. Her lungs already felt cooked and her warm breath was shallow. She'd gone through well over a pack that day, mostly since their ridiculous meeting with Story Moffatt.

The whole day was pretty much of a bust. The meeting soaked up most of the morning, and then she spent the rest of the day convincing Cooper that she'd done nothing wrong. Nothing disloyal. She'd never seen him that mad. It took a stream of tears and some quick sex on his desk to calm him down. But she had to admit the look on his face when Moffatt mentioned her being at Shannon's almost made it worthwhile. She thought he was going to blow breakfast right in his chair, and he looked pretty queasy for the rest of the day. Seeing the big bounty hunter helped make it worthwhile, too, she noted. He had an aura of competence about him and yet he wasn't pushy about it. He seemed stable but there was something unpredictable and exciting about him.

"Really, Tom, I wasn't actually looking for that money for myself," she had explained breathlessly to her employer. "All I was really trying to do is keep an eye on those two bozos you hired. I don't trust them, and you shouldn't, either. I think you're nuts to be using them all the time. Plus, honey, I wanted to surprise you. I wanted to show I've got a little initiative of my own. Maybe you can use me for some investigations from now on. Man, I can't believe you don't trust me after all we've been through. After all the love that's between us."

That seemed to satisfy him. Somewhat. Then, after he came off the ceiling from the blow job, she got down to some world-class ball busting.

"I told you this Story chick was no pushover," she laid into him. "She's got a pair of stones on her. A blind man can see that. You underestimated her and now you're looking down the barrel of a lawsuit. You could easily get your ass handed to you in court by this William McLean, whoever the hell he is. Keep going like you are and you'll end up paying her. Good day's work, Thomas Hardy. And you think I was a bimbo for snooping around into this mistress stuff. At least I didn't shove my tit into the old wringer like you did."

"You should have told me what you were doing," came his feeble response. Clearly, he was a beaten man. Overwhelmed on all sides. Then he added for emphasis, "You just should have told me, is all."

By the time she left, Cooper was so fed up with the whole pathetic soap opera he just wanted to go home, knock back some Scotch, and hit the rack. Pretend the day never happened. That was fine with Ronnie. She needed some downtime by herself to think of her next move. She knew the day could have gone worse. Much worse. What if, she pondered, Cooper had found out the truth about her and Doug Shelton? That was the kind of thing that got you tossed out of the job for starters and maybe netted you a conversation with Soyko and his lunatic partner. It would be a one-way conversation that might be your last.

Ronnie met Doug in the office a couple weeks after his drug

bust. He was feeling his old cocky self again and he was taken
with Ronnie's street smarts, not to mention her MTV sexuality.
For her part, Ronnie liked his looks and his constant patter. Too
bad he couldn't produce in the bedroom. Like they say on the
rodeo circuit back home, "Built like a Brahma, hung like a
mama."

When Cooper started all this talk about the missing money,
she thought she might have a little edge because of some of the
things Doug had told her. She decided to give it a ride on her
own. Hence, the trip to Shannon Mays' apartment. But so far
she'd come up with nothing.

She walked to her desk and pulled out a small pad where
she kept some rough notes about the deceased realtor. "Sex a
D-minus. Definitely fucked up about women. Talked about himself and money constantly. Big surprise! Talked about his mother
and darling brother up in Montana or somewhere. Acted like
his car was made out of gold. He wouldn't let me stay in it alone
when he went into liquor store. Said he didn't think I would be
safe there by myself. Bullshit. Probably afraid the little whore
would pee in the ashtray. Remember what Bobby said. Stingy
with just about everything. Claimed to have tons of money but
I never saw much. Lots of BS about how money sticks to him
and he'll never worry about it again. Sure right about the 'sticks
to him' part."

There was a knock on her door. Ronnie put the notebook
back and went to answer it. Initially she hoped it wasn't Cooper,
but when she opened it she instantly wished it was. Out in the
hallway, leaning against her door frame, was a supremely relaxed
Leo Soyko. His smile was thin and humorless. Ronnie sucked
for air, startled but concealing it pretty well. How did this maniac
find out where I live? She felt utterly unprotected, like when she
was little and her mother's nameless lovers, with whisky and
decay on their breath, would touch her all over. She was terrified,
because she knew that the man at her door could do worse than
that. His eyes, dead and furious at the same time, took in every-

thing. Those eyes could see right through a concrete wall, she thought.

"I bet you're surprised I'm here." He widened his smile and thought how Ronnie didn't look nearly scared enough. "You're not going to ask me to come in?"

"Why would I want to do that?"

"That's not very nice." He pretended to be offended, something they both knew was impossible.

"All right. Why are you here? Did Cooper send you?"

"Don't I get to come in?" He said it with enough sting this time that she knew letting him in was her only move.

"So please do," she said as she stepped aside, giving him plenty of room. He had a faint body odor. Not dirty, more like he never used deodorant.

"You gonna offer me a drink?"

Ronnie hated the look of her place with him in it. She knew she couldn't force him out, but she doubted that he had come to hurt her. Her best shot was to hear what he wanted and get him out fast. Don't want him feeling at home here. Not ever. "You're not going to drink, you're not even going to sit down." She put as much spine in it as she could without sounding shrill. "Why don't you tell me why you're here, so then you don't have to be for very long."

Soyko studied her face. She kept even eye contact and didn't budge. His eyes said nothing, but when he spoke again his voice softened just a trace.

"Cooper could use your nerve, Goldilocks. Probably your brains, too. And, no, he didn't send me. The counselor doesn't know I'm here and I want it to stay like that. This visit's strictly my idea."

Ronnie acknowledged nothing. "What do you want?"

"What do I want?" he repeated as he leaned his butt against the dining-room table. His way of settling in. Show her he had all the time in the world. "I'm sitting there in Cooper's office today thinking, Why's Goldilocks out there looking for this money? And I'm wondering, What's she finding out? One thing's a dead-sure cinch. Perry Mason there won't be getting much out of you. I figure, you show him some snatch, he'll believe damned near anything you dish out. So whatever you told him today was either pure horseshit or only about a tenth of what you know."

Again there was silence. Then, finally, Ronnie spoke. "You figured that out, did you?"

"Yeah, I did. And here's what else I figured out. I figured I don't give a rip if someone beats me to that money. I'll just take it away from them and all they get out of it is hurt. But if someone was to help me get there first, why, hell, I'd be in a very generous mood. Wouldn't want to hurt a friend like that. Might even want to give them a little something for their trouble."

"You might, huh?"

"I might."

"Someone could get hurt, huh?"

"Oh yeah. That's guaranteed. Guy named Grundy Dopps would verify what I'm saying but he's not talking much these days."

Grundy's name drew blood. Ronnie looked away. This guy wasn't fooling around. He wouldn't mention Grundy if he wasn't certain she knew about that little number. This was his way of telling her to play ball or else end up in the same condition as the welder.

Ronnie'd been squeezed like this before and she had always worked her way out of it. When she was fifteen, a boyfriend had left her out in Ohio with these crazy drug dealers. She was the insurance on a big cocaine buy. If the boyfriend didn't produce the cocaine, Ronnie would get shot. Simple as that. The boyfriend didn't produce, but Ronnie came out okay. She had managed to get on the good side of one of the guys who were holding her. She was so young, but she could turn on the Marilyn Monroe so heavy the guy let her live. She became his sex slave for a couple weeks until she found an opening, and then she split.

But Soyko made those dealers look like Jerry's Kids. He

wouldn't get thrown off the track by a little action. No sir, this guy was after blood. Always. He never let up. That was her read. He was pure Robomaniac, with only maybe a nodding interest in sex and absolutely no interest in mercy. She decided to take the practical path. Feed him a little shit and stall him.

"I think you pegged Tom Cooper about right." Her voice softened but not too much. "He doesn't get it half the time. See, he's playing by some set of rules he must have learned at college or someplace weird like that."

"I'm not learning anything new here."

"Listen, I like your idea. There's no point in us both doing the same things without the other one knowing about it. I'll tell you what I know, which isn't all that much, and you tell me where we go from here."

"Then I tell you where we go from here," he repeated more to himself. "Say you don't know much, huh?"

"This is on the level. I didn't find nothing from the girlfriend's apartment. They wouldn't even let me in. But I'll tell you something you didn't know. I sort of went out with Dougy. Not really a date and no sex or nothing, but he met me for a drink one night. It was a few weeks after he got busted. We went over to some stupid theme bar in Aurora. The Jolly Douche Bag or something. Had a few beers and he loosened up a little. He told me that he wasn't close with his wife or whatever she was. Moffatt. You want my advice, you might look where he goes and no one else goes. I'd go through that car of his, maybe, for starters. He guarded that thing pretty damned close, if you ask me. It was really nuts."

"Didn't someone already do that?" Soyko sounded less sure of himself.

"I don't know. The man treated that thing like it was a woman, that's all I know. There must be other places to check, too. For instance, it might be nice to go through his townhouse. Another thing. There was something really strange about him and his mother. Seemed that way to me. She lives up in Wyoming or Utah or some damned place. Doug seemed really afraid of her but he talked a lot about her. Maybe they had some sort of deal going. He spent a lot of time talking about her—to me, of all people. Like I could give a rip."

"That sounds sick. What do you mean, some sort of deal going?"

"I'm not talking about sex. More like they had this connection that seemed important to him. It's hard to explain and I think it's a long shot. But you wanted to know what I know."

"I'll keep that in mind. Why didn't you do any of those things? Why didn't you try to check on all that?"

"I just got started. Plus, I've never done any of this before."

"Why'd you meet him out at that bar? You liked this guy?"

"He was kind of cute, but when we talked for a while he bored the hell out of me. About the only topic seemed to interest him was him. Boring with a capital B-O-R-E."

"What else do you know?"

"Nothing really. But I can be some good to you. You could use eyes and ears inside Cooper's office. My eyes and ears. You'd know what's going on everywhere."

"It could work, at that." Soyko sounded almost pleasant. "I just might like to know what's really up with that guy. Here's the deal, Goldilocks. You keep those eyes and ears open, let me know anything important. I get the money, I'll see you're taken care of. But if I find out you're holding back on me or you tell Cooper, then I come back here. And I bring Jacky. You know him, he's more than a little off the fucking wall. Like me. We come back out here, you wish you'd never heard of us."

She already wished that. "You won't ever have to come back here. You got my word on that."

13

Pokey Shorts stared at the woman across the table from him and thought, What a waste. What a horrible waste. Here she is, still relatively young, body by Hooters, and a face as sweet as sin. Susanne Skiles was built to party, and for most of her first three decades she did just that. Then, one week shy of her thirty-third birthday, everything changed. She woke up yet another morning when even her eyelashes ached from the previous night's indulgences. She looked in the mirror and her pretty face was puffy and contorted from toxins her liver could no longer process adequately and she could see how she would look at fifty. Sick and tired of being sick and tired, she made her way to a noon AA meeting. From then on it was twelve steps to happiness. She even quit smoking after a few months. Caffeine was her new drug of choice, celibacy the order of the day, and if she stayed out past ten she was living on the edge.

Susanne looked back at Carl Shorts and thought, What a waste. What a horrible waste. Look at him, she thought. We've been here all of a half-hour and he's slamming down his second beer and sizing up a shot of Jack Daniel's. And can't he give his lungs a rest? He must smoke at least three hundred cigarettes a day. He wouldn't be a bad-looking man if he'd quit trying to kill himself and act the fifty or however many years old he is.

"Yeah, Carl, those were the days," she said with little conviction. "Hot tubs, hash pipes, and dry red wine. I loved it. But times change and you start thinking about the future and what you might want to do with yourself. Hangovers can eat up a lot of precious time. Like we say in AA, 'Life is what happens to other people while you're waiting on a barstool.' "

"Tell me about it." Pokey's voice sounded sincere, but recovery talk bored him senseless, and her hot-tub comment set off a fantasy sequence that distracted him. He looked fondly at his beer. "I suppose I should taper off a little, but to be honest I've been at it so long I'm starting to enjoy the stuff."

Susanne pressed on. "Well, 'your ass was built for a barstool,' like we say in AA. That seems to be the case with you, all right. But if you ever give any serious thought to quitting, Carl, just let me know. Honestly. I can take you to a meeting. It's not that hard to quit. It totally changed my life, and I cherish my sobriety above everything else."

Pokey's eyes glazed over when she said "sobriety." The concept was unfathomable, but he appreciated her sincerity. "I'll keep that in mind. Yes, I will."

The sight of Streeter walking toward them gave Pokey a good reason to change the subject. They were sitting just off Boulder's Pearl Street Mall at a garden-level bar and restaurant called the Walrus. Pokey chose the place because it would have a mid-sized happy-hour crowd, perfect for secluded conversation. It was also one of the last places in town where he could have a cigarette without hearing a load of crap about the dubious hazards of secondary smoke.

About thirty freeway miles northwest of Denver and snuggled in the rolling foothills of the Rocky Mountains, Boulder was a place Streeter liked to visit. But not too often and not for long. The town itself was beautiful, but there were too many holistic fanatics who considered pyramid power to be perfectly reasonable and tie-dye to be hip and high art. It's a place where the local Birkenstockers dabbled in colonic irrigation and yet were mortified at the thought of eating red meat. He quickly tired of all the pious, new-age self-absorption and the naïve, Woodstock-driven politics.

"Street man, over here," Pokey yelled. Then, quietly to Susanne, "Here's the guy I told you about. He's a good man. You can trust him. I use him to track down people in Denver for me and he always comes through."

Susanne nodded serenely. In her sobriety, she relied so heavily on spirituality that human deception became almost irrelevant.

"When you trust your higher power, Carl, everything else falls into place. Like we say at the meetings, 'Let go and let God.' "

"I'll keep that in mind, Susanne." Why, he wondered, does she always have to talk like she's going for her black belt in recovery?

Pokey introduced her to Streeter. He thought she was attractive, but she seemed to work a little too hard at being relaxed. And he didn't like the look she gave him when he ordered a beer and bummed a cigarette off Pokey. Although Streeter stayed fit, he liked to kick back with a few beers and have a smoke from time to time. And there was something about doing it in Boulder, where he could tick off the sanctimonious locals, that made it even more inviting.

"How's my old friend William McLean?" Pokey asked.

"Great. He says hello," Streeter said. "You know he's helping me with this."

"So you said," Pokey responded. Then he turned to Susanne. "Bill's a lawyer down in Denver. Used to be a DA. Great guy. Intelligent. Excellent attorney. Harvard Law School and all that. But he's sort of crazy at the same time. He's always up to something provocative. Always slightly perverse. He's the type of guy who farts in a crowded elevator just to stir things up."

"He sounds charming," she said flatly.

Pokey stared off for a minute, smiling, as he contemplated Bill. "Well, let's get down to business. I know you have to leave soon, so why don't you tell Streeter what you told me."

She turned to the bounty hunter. "Carl tells me that you work for Doug's widow? Is that right?"

"Something like that."

"She's probably heavily codependent, what with Doug's substance-abuse problems. Tell her to call me if she's looking for a Codependents Anonymous group. I go to an excellent CODA session on Thursdays." Then, after some thought, "Carl tells me she's trying to find out if he salted some money away?"

"That's right." Streeter was put off slightly by the twelve-step talk. A few years ago, when he was concerned about his own increasing drinking, he went to a few AA meetings. He found that the concept of group support and confronting your problems was solid, but the relentless guilt, drama, and depression of the meetings, along with the religious overlay, put him off. He quit drinking for a few months. Then he decided he was tired of not having any fun, so he started nailing back a couple of beers from time to time and an occasional glass of wine with dinner.

"I didn't even know he was married. Actually, I haven't seen Doug for quite a while. Probably about four years or more. It was before I got sober, I know that. That poor man could have used some intervention and a spiritual program himself. He was wrestling with so many demons all the time. I understand he was very drunk when he died."

"I don't know about that. I hear different things about his partying."

"That's because he usually went through different phases," she said. "Sometimes he would hit the coke pretty hard, and then other times he would just drink. Sometimes both, sometimes neither. He would go through dry-drunk spells where he wouldn't do anything except sit around and be grouchy. Then he'd go off and become Captain Party for a while."

"When exactly were you with him?" Pokey asked. "I mean, how long?"

"Let's see. I met him in about '86. We lived together for a couple of years. Maybe more, maybe less."

"Was he dealing?" Streeter asked.

"Hell yes. He was dealing everything. The real-estate market was picking up, and he was moving a fair amount of coke, too. He bought a big house on Mapleton Hill. I think that's where a lot of his money went. He sold it a couple of years later and I think he lost some on that, if you can imagine losing money in the eighties."

"Tell him about the nickname," Pokey interrupted.

"I gave it to him back when we lived together. I called him Squirrel. Some of his friends used it, too. We came up with that because he had this habit of squirreling things away, all around town. Coke and cash, mostly."

"Did you ever see any of these places?" Streeter leaned in to her.

"No. Nobody else did, either."

"Did he ever talk about them?"

"No. But this happened a bunch of times. We would go out and someone who knew him would come up and ask to buy coke. It would just be kind of spontaneous, but Doug always managed to go score. He'd leave me at a party at midnight and go out for twenty minutes, maybe half an hour, and come back with flake. And usually it was a good-sized amount.

"I remember once he sold these bartenders at the old Pelican Pete's an ounce at closing time. The deal came up at the last minute and he had no way to know in advance that he would need it. No matter where we were in town, he could get cocaine or cash real quick. The only thing I could figure out was that he stashed it all over town. The guy was a genius that way."

Streeter thought about what she was telling him and tried to reconcile that with what Story had told him. It all fit. "Did you ever go with him?"

"He always went alone." She shook her head seriously. "I think he got a kick out of the squirrel thing. It was sort of his little specialty."

"Do you think he went to his supplier's place?" Pokey asked. "Maybe his source was close enough to handle all the last-minute orders."

"No. His supplier lived in the mountains somewhere. About an hour away. There wouldn't have been enough time. Plus, he couldn't count on his supplier being there all the time, and Doug never came back empty-handed. Listen, I have to take off in a second. I don't know if that helps you much. But I'd be real surprised if Doug left money or anything valuable with anyone. He didn't trust people. And if he was still hiding things, you'll have one tough job finding them. He was a very clever man who protected what he owned."

"Thanks." Streeter smiled. "Here's my card. If you remember anything else, give me a call at that number. A guy named Frank will probably answer, but he'll get a message to me. Anything. Patterns or similarities or information about how he did it. Will you do that?"

"Sure. By the way, I heard he got busted just a few months before he died. Is that true?"

"Something like that. He was arrested, and he was separating from my client. He got beat up around that time, too. Then the car wreck. He was on a real losing streak."

Susanne considered that for a moment. "Like we say in AA, 'Life doesn't come with any instructions and there's no guarantees. Shit happens.' "

14

Tom Cooper figured that day in his office with Story easily ranked as one of the five worst in his legal career. But what happened to him before District Court Judge Manuel Herrera eight days later went off the high end of the shit meter altogether. In addition to ruling against him, His Honor insulted him repeatedly from the bench. All Cooper could do was stand there and take it. That and watch Moffatt and McLean gloat, which royally tore his ass.

As usual, Cooper had no one to blame but himself. When he sued Story as administrator of the estate, he had the nerve to file an attachment on her and Doug's townhouse for the amount he sought. That enabled McLean to request a hearing and get a fast court date. That, in turn, meant both sides would go before a judge and be allowed to offer testimony on the merits of Cooper's claim. And that, finally, resulted in Judge Herrera's pitching his specious claim out the window. If only, Cooper chided himself later, he hadn't gone after the real estate. At least that way the case would have dragged on and given Story something to think about for a few months. Who knows, maybe she would have folded by then.

McLean and Story were delighted. They called Streeter from her office, not far from the courthouse, shortly after the hearing ended.

"I don't think Mr. Cooper will be much of a problem from now on," McLean told him. "Herrera spanked him and sent him home. You should have seen it. We couldn't have written a better script if we'd been on the bench with him. Cooper has his book-keeper or whatever she was up there giving this convoluted BS about how they arrived at the numbers. And then Story takes the stand and relays everything Doug told her about the fees. The judge tied into Cooper like nothing I've ever seen before. Then, to top it all off, Herrera rather cordially invited us to request attorney's fees and court costs. He damned near came out and said if we file he'll sign the order. And that's not to mention we still have a claim in county court for a refund on Doug's retainer. All and all, it was not a bad day's work."

"That's great, Bill. I suppose your client's ecstatic."

"She sure is. I'm in her office right now. She wants you to come by here at—what? When did you want him here?" He put his hand over the receiver and looked at Story.

"One-thirty would be fine."

"She said one-thirty today. Can you make it?"

"Sure." Streeter wanted to talk to her about the unmarked police car, and the gunshots into the church the week before. He'd hoped to meet with Carey beforehand, but the detective was out of town for a few days' vacation. She needed to know about the new danger, and he couldn't wait to huddle up with her. "Tell her I'll be there. And good going, Bill."

"Thanks. I'd really like to be done with this Cooper jerk, but then something else came up yesterday."

"Yeah, what was that?"

"Out of the blue, I received a call from Max something-or-other. Max Herman. He's facing serious trouble on a cocaine charge, among other things. It seems his lawyer—or former lawyer—is none other than Mr. Thomas Hardy Cooper. Max did a little snooping around with people he knows in the DA's office and he finds out that he's been offered a pretty good deal. However, our man Cooper hasn't even told him about it yet, just so he can run up the legal fees. Well, now, Max is about ready to clobber his former legal team. He wants me to take his case and also wants to sue Cooper for malpractice."

"You going to do it?"

"I haven't decided yet. I'm meeting with him first thing Monday morning. In a way, it might be fun to keep after Cooper for a while."

"Sounds like you can make a decent living just beating up on him. Anyhow, I really appreciate what you did for Story."

"That's what I'm hired to do."

Story's offices suited her, Streeter remembered when he walked in that afternoon. Tasteful and impressive. She was on the second floor of an impeccably restored mansion that she shared with an architectural firm and two attorneys. The place was on the Denver tour of historic homes. Her suite had turn-of-the-century elegance with hardwood floors yet all the modern touches, including a built-in microwave.

"Sounds like you had a little fun this morning," he said as she showed him in.

"William was just phenomenal." She pointed for him to sit down across the desk from her. "He had that dope so confused and scared, I almost felt embarrassed for him. Almost. You should have seen Cooper. He stammered and stuttered and in the end he just took his beating from the judge. He looked like his diapers needed changing and he hoped no one noticed the smell. When we were leaving court, he just glared at me. I thought he'd explode."

"Are you going after a refund?"

"I considered it, but then I decided it would be such a hassle and I really don't know how much would be a fair amount to pursue. Doug never mentioned figures. I'll let it go, so we can concentrate on our work. We'll ask the judge to order him to pay legal fees, though. I'm just glad we've seen the last of this dork. I think it's best to leave Mr. Cooper to his little criminal practice so he can go back to short-changing his clients and chasing that tramp secretary of his around. Did you believe her? She looked about a notch above an East Colfax streetwalker."

Streeter thought about all that. On the one hand, he was glad she was going to drop the claim against Cooper. It showed she wasn't still looking for the easy score she didn't deserve. On the other hand, he felt a strange sense of protectiveness toward Ronnie.

"My, aren't we catty," he said. "She wasn't that bad. Scrape off a little of her eye makeup and she'd be kind of attractive."

"Oh, pull-ease, Streeter." Story rolled her eyes but was surprised that she felt a faint twinge of jealousy. "Attractive? You've *got* to be kidding."

He changed the subject. "At least we've seen the last of Cooper and his friends. I hope. He may not take this beating too well, you know. When Bill McLean goes for the jugular, he can really piss people off. There's something else we have to talk about. I gather you want to keep going with this treasure hunt."

"You're darned right. Look, if you're running out of money, just let me know. I'll get you more."

"No, it's not that. There's still money left."

"Did you hear anything in Boulder to make you want to stop?"

"No. As a matter of fact, the more I hear, the more I think we might be on to something."

He told her about Susanne and the Squirrel handle and how Doug had operated in Boulder. She listened intently to every word.

"And you asked if I wanted to stop now," she said when he finished. "Hell, we're just getting started. We've got the general layout and now we can focus in on specifics. Where do we go from here?"

"From here? Story, before we take another step, I have to tell you that this thing is getting dangerous and it could get even more twisted from now on. Your car and your dog were bad enough, but it's getting worse. Someone fired a couple of rounds into my house last week. At night after our meeting with Cooper."

"My God! Was anyone hurt?"

"No. It was the middle of the night and they just shot out a couple of windows."

"Do you know for sure it was connected to this business?"

"Not for sure. But I don't believe in coincidences, and now someone knows where I live. I hate that, especially if it's someone with a gun who doesn't mind firing it. And even worse, I think that someone has a badge."

She scowled. "A policeman? Where do you get that from?"

"The license number the guy got that night your car was trashed was for an unmarked police car. My hunch is it's the same cop who nailed Doug. I think he's the one that helped the cocaine disappear from the police-evidence room, and now he doesn't want any more attention. I suppose the shots could be Cooper just trying to scare us off the scent of the money, but my hunch is it's a cop."

"So go tell the cop we're not interested in him. Tell him we'll leave him alone."

"Now, why didn't I think of that? You want me to go accuse a cop of vandalism, tampering with evidence, and shooting at me and then tell him, 'Hey, but that's cool. We'll forget it if you will.' He'd blow me away on the spot, and I couldn't blame him."

"Look, Streeter." She stood up and came around the desk. Her face looked like it did that day in the squash court. "I don't care what you do or don't do about this cop or whoever it was that shot at your precious church. But I'm not giving up on this thing. If you want to, fine. I'll get someone else to help me. I'm simply not quitting."

Streeter stood up and faced her.

"You have no idea what you might be getting into, do you? You think this is just some other 'account' you might lose. You could lose a lot more than money if it's what I think it is. Cooper is capable of God knows what, and if it's a rogue cop, he could be worse. What's so damned important about this money?"

"It's mine. That's what's so important." Then she lowered her voice. "I don't want to argue with you. If you want out, I understand. Keep the money I gave you and no hard feelings. But I'm not stopping. If Cooper's behind this, that just makes me more convinced that I'm on the right track. Who knows what Doug may have told him? Or who knows what he told the cop who helped get him off? I'm going to keep looking, with or without you. For what it's worth, I hope it's with you."

Streeter laced his fingers behind his head and stretched back to give himself time to think. After a few seconds he said, "I'm not saying I want out. I'm just letting you know what we're in for. As far as I'm concerned, there's no way I'm going to let this asshole get away with shooting at my house. That's a bad precedent for someone in my line of work. I'm in, Story. I just wanted you to know the kind of people we're dealing with here."

"Okay. I'll consider myself warned."

"Do you own a gun?"

"I have a little thirty-eight. I usually keep it next to my bed."

"Do you know how to use it?"

"An old boyfriend showed me how. He's the one who gave it to me."

"Keep it close, just to be safe. And put it in your glove compartment when you go out. You never know when it might come in handy."

"I assume you have a gun."

"Several. I usually keep a three fifty-seven short-barrel under my car seat."

"Do you have a permit?" she asked.

"All of mine are registered, but I can't get a concealed-weapons permit. Practically no one can anymore. It seems that the cops hate to make the bad guys nervous by allowing honest citizens to carry a hidden piece or two. I doubt if we need them, but someone out there has a gun, and I'll feel better if you do, too."

"So where do we go from here?"

"I want to keep talking to Doug's friends, all the people he worked with. We know this money isn't in any bank, but it might be in a locker at the train station or a place like that. If Doug was as distrustful as I think, he wouldn't have told anyone about it. But maybe he left a spare key with someone for safe keeping without telling them what it's for. Maybe several spare keys, judging by what I heard up in Boulder."

"I'll make a list of anyone I know of who was close to Doug," she said, jotting something down in her Daytimer.

"Include even those people who weren't too close to him. He might have picked someone he wasn't tight with. And I'll want to go over everything he left at the house. We should do that together."

"Why don't you come over tomorrow night? I'll have it all ready and we can plow through it."

"Fine. And I'll want the address and phone number of his family up in wherever he's from. Wyoming, wasn't it?"

She frowned again.

"Some problem with that?"

"I'll have it for you," she said. "It's just that his mother is such a bitch."

"I don't want to move in with the woman. I just want to talk to her."

As Cooper slithered back to his office after court, he felt like he'd just paid a thousand dollars for a hooker and then couldn't perform. On top of that, she'd laughed at him. Why was that courtroom so packed? Rage and humiliation surged through him in giddy waves.

When he got to his office, Ronnie was in the lobby. "How did you make out?" she asked, even though she could tell from his expression.

"How'd Iraq make out in Desert Storm? I got totally hammered, that's how. Get me Soyko on the phone."

"No need to. He's waiting in your office," she said. "He got here about two minutes ago."

"How did he . . . Uh . . . Aw, who gives a shit? Come on. I want you in on this, too, seeing as how you're so interested in Doug Shelton."

Cooper walked into his office and saw Soyko sitting in front of his desk, with Jacky Romp sprawled out over the couch. Both men were smoking cigarettes, and they remained quiet when the attorney entered with Ronnie behind him.

"Do you two have to do that in here?" Cooper yelled as he sat down. He waved his hand like he was swatting invisible flies.

"Just a hunch, court sucked," Soyko said, crushing out his cigarette.

"Brilliant." Cooper looked off to the side. "That fucker had the judge in his hip pocket. Judge my ass. More like some affirmative-action appointment with an attitude. We got totally shot down."

We? Soyko was tempted to remind Cooper that he'd lost on his own. But he let it slide. Bust his chops and the lawyer might just self-destruct on the spot. Instead, he kept looking at Cooper, letting him blow off steam.

"That motherfucker . . ." Cooper muttered, too upset to finish. "And that bitch client of his. Both laughing at me. Rubbing my dick in the dirt. I don't know who I'd like to see dead first. They should both be tortured. Now she even has the option of coming after me for money. Judge José there practically told her to do it. I'd like to burn her for this. Her lawyer, too."

"That can be arranged, you know." Soyko's voice carried no emotion.

"Forget it. I just keep thinking of the stones on that broad. Lying in court under oath."

"Be a shame, someone'd try and get something they don't deserve like that," Soyko deadpanned. "There oughta be a law."

Jacky cackled at the irony.

Cooper looked from one man to the other. "Just keep yukking it up, you two. Big goddamned joke, isn't it? Let's us concentrate on what we have to do to get that money Doug hid. Okay? I don't suppose you have any good news for me on that score. You know, I don't even give a flying fuck about the money so much anymore." He lowered his voice, a thin trail of spit lacing off the side of his mouth. "I just want to stop this Story broad from getting it. What the hell kind of name is that anyway? Story. What is she, some princess from a fairy tale? I want you two to go balls to the wall on this thing. Take no prisoners and spare no expense. Find that money. I want all these bastards to bleed. Whatever it takes to screw them over."

"I hear you, counselor." Soyko got up. His partner got up, too. "We'll get right on it. You should maybe take the day off. Looks like you're about to blow wide open."

"Don't worry about me. Let's just deal with this fast and hard. Find that money, and no more Mr. Nice Guy bullshit."

When the two men left, Cooper leaned back in his swivel chair and began rocking quickly. Ronnie just stared at him for a while.

"You should have calmed down before you talked to them," she said.

"Yeah, why's that?"

"Because they might get the wrong idea about what you wanted. They might think you want them to hurt someone."

"Aw, Christ, Ronnie. Give it a rest. I just told them to find the money, whatever it takes."

"And you don't think they might take that to mean, mess somebody up? Really put the spurs to them?"

"Of course not. I made it perfectly clear. They won't get carried away."

She studied him for some time. Poor dope really didn't get it. Here he was with his coat on fire and he's busy looking for lint.

"Yeah, sure. Why would they?"

15

For someone who supposedly made a lot of money, Douglas Shelton had few belongings. Streeter discovered that the next night, when he and Story sifted through his so-called earthly possessions: clothes, papers, books, desk, golf bag, cabinets, knickknacks, ski equipment, and other items that belonged to the late realtor. They went through virtually every page of every document the man kept. They were at it for over three hours without finding anything the bounty hunter would say vaguely resembled a clue.

"He liked his cars and his clothes, but he never showed any real interest in accumulating much property," Story explained as they worked. "He'd hit the museums from time to time, like I told you before. But he never really collected things, from what I could see. Most of his spending was geared toward looking good. A lot of his money went to restaurants, too. We ate out almost every night. He bought some stuff for the house, but not much."

It was well after nine when Streeter noticed how hungry he was. "I'm starving. You want to call out for something?"

They were standing in the middle of what used to be Doug's study, surrounded by open boxes, open drawers, and stacks of papers. They were both wearing faded jeans, T-shirts, and sneakers. His was a white Broncos shirt, hers powder-blue, touting the name of a perfume he'd never heard of. Streeter appreciated the way her jeans so comfortably snuggled up to the contour of her legs and bottom without appearing like they'd been applied with a paint roller. But she kept her makeup and earrings on, which looked inappropriate to the task and to her clothes. Totally casual was not Story's style.

"I'll get the menu and we can call the Pagoda," she told him. "Great Szechuan, if you like it."

"Fine. I'll eat anything that's got duck in it."

He was sorting through a file marked "Taxes—1990 All." Apparently, Doug was fascinated by detailed and ultimately insignificant paperwork while at the same time he ignored obviously important things. For instance, Streeter found meaningless receipts and obscure reminder notices, yet no copy of Shelton's completed 1990 tax return. There was no discernible pattern to what he kept and what he threw away. It made Streeter's job more difficult. Luckily, Story had come up with a list of thirty-seven people—addresses and phone numbers included—who knew Doug, so he had more leads to explore.

"I don't know if this is doing us any good," he told her when they'd finished. "About all I can figure out is, he has a very strange sense of filing, and he doesn't know the correct name for the mayor of Denver."

"Mayor Webb. What makes you say that?" She came back into the study after calling for the Chinese food.

"There were some notes he kept with his bank slips where he wrote out 'W. Webb Wellington' instead of 'Wellington Webb.' He had to be referring to the mayor. Don't you think?"

"He must have written a check to Webb's reelection campaign. Who knows? Doug never was much on details. I could show you this letter he was writing to his mother. He wrote like a sixth-grader. All this melodramatic crap about how precious his time in Wyoming is. Doug was strange about his family. Especially his mother."

"So I gather. Like I said yesterday, I'm going to have to go up there and talk to her fairly soon."

"I suppose, but it won't be fun. She's really lonely and incredibly judgmental. Apparently, she's second-generation German. Real old-school and totally long-suffering with her religion. She thinks that if you smile too much you're not going to the Kingdom of God. In a strange way, Doug was sort of in awe of her. He'd complain about her, but when she was around he treated her like royalty. She was always criticizing him, yet he still tried to impress her. It was like he thought if he made enough money she would finally approve of him.

"Doug has this brother who's in and out of homes and hospitals. He's mentally and physically disabled. The mother, Gail, blames the world for that. She blames the world for everything miserable in her life. She blamed Doug's father until he died, and then she started blaming Doug. Now she's probably just sitting out there on the old family farm and blaming whoever's nearby."

"Doug was a farm boy?"

"Hell no. They lived on what was left of Gail's family's farm. They never worked the place. Gail was a schoolteacher and his father was a pharmacist."

"That would help explain Doug's interest in pharmaceuticals. You think she might know anything at all about what he left behind?"

"It's unlikely. They didn't see each other more than once a year in all the time I knew him."

Story had ordered a Happy Family combination and a gallon of hot-and-sour soup. They each drank a beer while they waited.

"Didn't you tell me he left you a clock?" Streeter asked.

"Yes he did. I took it to a good friend of mine who's an antique dealer and he knew of a buyer for it. I didn't particularly like the thing myself, but the guy paid twelve thousand five hundred dollars for it. I gave my friend a nice commission and I still kept over ten grand."

"I guess you *can* put a price on memories. That must have made your day. I didn't know there are clocks that expensive."

"Hell yes. My friend was telling me about ones that easily get two or three times that. This one was a Charles Gabrier or something like that. He threw a bunch of names at me. You wouldn't believe how pretentious the world of antique clocks is. I got a crash course on it."

"Twelve thousand's a lot of money. How'd he get such an expensive clock? He doesn't seem to be the type to go for high art."

"I wondered about that, too." Story frowned as she looked at him. "He told me it was given to him by a client once in return for Doug helping get her a great home-loan rate. But that's an awful lot of gratitude. Maybe he waived his commission to get the thing. It could be that all his trips to the museum gave him an idea of how valuable the clock is. Perhaps he had an appreciation for the finer things that he never shared with me. That's possible. Apparently, there was a lot that he didn't share with me, and Doug was no idiot. He had a good mind, when his head wasn't up his butt. That's a pretty conflicted metaphor, isn't it?"

Streeter nodded and said, "I've never had much interest in antiques. By the way, was Doug paranoid?"

"He was cautious but not particularly paranoid. Especially considering the line of work he was in. Why?"

"He has a flyer over there from a company called the Executive Protectors Inc., out in Indiana. It's only four pages, but it's got all this phone-debugging equipment. Scramblers, pen transmitters. All kinds of electronic equipment and home-security products. Did he ever actually buy any of that stuff?"

"Not ever. At least not that I know of. But some guys like to get product information and then never do anything with it. He'd get flyers for all sorts of different equipment and that was it. Doug hated to part with his money."

"Well, I'm not sure how all guys are, but Doug was one very

strange pack rat. Judging by what he kept in his files, he seemed to be a warehouse of useless personal information. Keep an eye out for anything like that. You know, electronic equipment, security stuff."

They both sat in silence for a minute, drinking their beers.

"Frank's been getting a lot of hang-up calls today," Streeter finally said. "That usually doesn't happen. One time the guy said 'Fuck off' and hung up. He said it so fast Frank wasn't sure he heard it right."

"Really? What time was that?"

"About five-thirty or so. Just before I left to come over here. Why?"

"I got a few hang-up calls last night, that's all. I wonder if this is from our friend the paint-spraying cop," she said.

"It sounds too juvenile even for him. Do you usually get many hang-up calls?"

"Once in a while. Never four or five in one night."

"Let me know if it keeps up. The guy didn't use my name, so it may have been just a random call." He tried to sound convincing. "I talked to a detective friend of mine who's on the Denver Police Department. I gave him the name of the cop I think helped Doug. Detective Arthur Kovacs. My friend's going to check him out. Evidently, Kovacs has been in Denver for about five years, and he's due to retire soon. He's got a rep as a world-class bully from back in his days as a Detroit cop."

Story just nodded. Since their discussion the day before, neither of them wanted to think much about possible danger. Streeter was concerned for Frank and Story. Their food came, and they set it out on the dining-room table and dug in. Streeter was famished and Story wasn't far behind, so they ate in near silence. When they were done eating, he started nosing into her past.

"Were you always interested in advertising, Story?"

"Always. Even in high school back in Omaha, I knew I wanted to run an ad agency somewhere. In a good-sized city. Then my family came out here for a vacation when I was a junior and I knew I wanted my agency to be here. I've never doubted my decision and I've never looked back."

"You're pretty headstrong."

"I believe if there's something you want you should go for it with all you've got. And if there's something in your life that doesn't contribute to that goal or holds you back, you get rid of it. No questions asked. Doug was the one sad exception to that rule. There's only one thing I want out of life. Everything. That may sound spoiled, but that's how I feel."

"You're right. It sounds spoiled. But at least you know what you want."

"And what do you want, Streeter?"

"I want to be left alone to do my own life my own way and never have to kiss anyone's ass. I want to know where I stand with people. I want the Broncos back in the Super Bowl, but I want them to win it this time. I want to know who's going to cover the spread for every college football game this fall. I want good food and I want good friends. And when I think about you in your little squash outfit that day, sometimes I even think I want you."

"You think you want me, but you're not sure."

"Not at all sure, is right. You make me nervous. For one thing, you're incredibly materialistic. Money-hungry, one might say." He was enjoying himself. Plain to see Story wasn't used to being spoken to like this. "Also, your whole relationship with Doug was pretty bizarre. You two never really connected. Physically or emotionally. Plus, you don't level with me. You're 'somewhat less than totally candid' way too often. If I can't trust you in our little working agreement, how could I trust you as a lover?"

"Oh yeah? And what fun is it if you trust your lover?"

"That seems terribly sophisticated, but I'm not sure I know what it means. I know I don't like the sound of it."

"About that second thing, I told you how little Doug and I had going for each other. He wasn't much for any kind of contact with me. Emotionally he was quite immature, and physically, let's just say he was self-conscious. Doug was about as well hung as a field mouse, if you get my drift."

Streeter grinned and raised his eyebrows, nodding slightly. "I thought organ size wasn't supposed to matter to you women."

"*Right.* And we women don't care about a man's income, either. Is that what you guys tell each other in the locker room to feel more adequate?"

"I don't usually have to tell myself anything to feel a hell of a lot more than just adequate." He leaned back in his chair. The conversation definitely was drifting into a dangerous area, but he was feeling warm and getting excited. He flashed on how it would be nice to kiss Story right then. "Our discussion's taken an interesting turn here. You want to keep going with it?"

The topic was making her nervous and moderately aroused, two feelings she didn't often experience. She was afraid of blushing, so she shifted back to his earlier comments. "You think I'm money-hungry, superficial, and dishonest. You make me sound terrific." Story stood up and started fussing with empty food containers.

"Actually, you make yourself seem terrific. I just make you sound real."

"I certainly doubt if I come across as pompous as you do."

"Believe me, you have that ability. Look, I don't want to start a fight, but you asked. I'm just trying to be honest."

She put down the food containers and smiled. "You're a real character, you know that? Mr. 'I Gotta Be Me.' That kind of crap's usually just a cover-up for being a loser. Not that Streeter—so much more than adequate as he may be—is a loser. Besides, regarding your crack about maybe wanting me, it's not really your call, is it?"

"Usually it's best if those decisions are mutual."

"I suppose. But for now, I have to get some sleep. I think we're through with our business for tonight, anyway. I've got a staff meeting scheduled for first thing in the morning and I'll need some sleep."

Streeter nodded, a vague trace of a smile on his face. "A Saturday staff meeting. You never let up, do you?"

On the way home, he felt wired and strangely anxious. He had hoped there would be more useful information in Doug's things. Also, he wondered if Story had shown him everything or if she was still holding back. Despite his attraction to her, he couldn't shake his doubts about her. Her bullheadedness troubled him. And what was that I-want-it-all crap? She sounded like a bad Volvo commercial.

When he got home he picked up his phone to check his voice mail. He had one call, a call that would change his mood for a long time. Actually, it would change his life.

"Streeter, it's me." It was Darcy McLean. She was sobbing. "Bill's in the hospital. He's hurt awfully bad. Someone beat him. Please call whenever you get in. I mean, I'm at Swedish Hospital. Please come."

He played it over several times, hoping it would change. When the message finally sank in, he froze for a minute, nauseous. He went to the bathroom, but nothing would come up. Then he got in his car and drove to the hospital.

16
_____

William McLean was still unconscious when Streeter got to the hospital. He had suffered a severe concussion along with several broken ribs and numerous broken facial bones. His left arm, particularly at the elbow, was badly mangled. The doctors didn't know the full extent of his internal bleeding. He was in serious but stable condition, and word was that he would live. No one could tell if there would be any permanent brain damage, but, because of his age, the sooner he regained consciousness, the better.

Darcy was waiting in a television room down the hall from intensive care when Streeter arrived, shortly before three o'clock. She was so pale and tired that he barely recognized her. Stacy, her sister, was with her, and there were two cups of cold coffee sitting on the table coagulating silently in front of them. The television was off, and it seemed so quiet, like the entire hospital was empty. Streeter noticed that the two women didn't look like sisters. Darcy had dark features, ink-black hair streaked modestly with handsome gray, and lively hazel eyes. Her sister had washed-out, brown features and light hair that approached being blonde. The only common threads in their appearance were their height—both about five feet six inches—and their clothes: khaki shorts, sandals, and white polo shirts.

Stacy left to get fresh coffee.

"What happened, Darce?" Streeter asked. "Is he going to be all right?"

She looked up and smiled, but it barely creased the pain and fatigue in her face. "He's going to live, but they're not sure how he's going to come out of it."

Streeter stood there for a minute with his mouth open, vaguely aware of how foolish he must look. That was the best he was able to do: he couldn't focus his thoughts clearly. Finally, he mustered up a weak, "How're you doing?"

Darcy shook her head cautiously, as if it was fragile. "I'm sick to my stomach. My God, I was so scared. When they first called me it sounded like he was dying. I can't even imagine that. I got here about ten last night, while he was still in surgery. This is nothing but pure torture."

"What the hell happened?" Streeter sounded hoarse, as if he had just woken up.

"Somebody beat him. The police don't know who it is yet. They used bats or sticks or something. Can you believe that? It was still light outside. It must have happened last night, about six or so. It's all such a big mess that nobody knows for sure. To be honest, I didn't understand half of what the police told me. I was too upset. I felt like one of those hysterical bimbos from daytime TV. I just kept picturing Bill getting beaten. Maybe dying."

"It's going to be okay, Darce." He sat next to her and put his arm around her shoulder. Despite her fear, she felt solid and wasn't trembling. "Tell me what you can."

Stacy got back just then with the fresh coffee and gave a cup to each of them. "I ran into the floor nurse out there and she told me they don't expect any change for tonight," she said as she stood next to the couch looking down at them. "Are you going to stay here, Darcy? I'll stay with you."

Darcy stared at her for a long time, as though she had difficulty understanding what her sister said. Finally, she nodded.
Then she looked back at Streeter. She took a sip of her coffee,
and that gave her a boost.

"The officers said they found him down on South Santa Fe,
behind one of those little sleazy hotels."

"What was he doing down there?"

"He was supposed to meet a client. Bill got a call about four,
maybe four-thirty. It was from a brother of this man he repre-
sented last summer in a really bitter custody fight. The brother
called and said the man got picked up for stealing—shoplifting,
actually—and he's supposed to get bailed out of jail pretty soon.
He asked if Billy would meet the both of them at his motel in
a couple of hours, because the guy needed legal help. He pleaded,
so Bill went. It turned out that the motel was closed and it was
all a trap. Obviously."

She took another sip of her coffee and was quiet. Streeter felt
a growing sense of guilt, and he couldn't understand why. Darcy's voice brought him back.

"What kind of animal would do this? Tell me, Streeter. You
know all of these low-lifes."

"Thanks a lot." He thought of the most logical answer, but
when he said it he didn't sound too convincing. "It could have
been someone he put away back when he was the DA. Bill nailed
a lot of sickos and made more than his share of enemies. Most
likely this is a revenge deal. Some jailhouse brainstorm."

Darcy nodded solemnly, as if that made a great deal of sense,
and then looked straight ahead. "I hope they catch the bastard
and fry him." Suddenly she looked back up at him. "There's not
much you can do here. Stacy'll stay with me. But I'd like you to
do something for me over the weekend."

"Of course. Anything."

"Talk to the cops. I want to know everything they know, and
I want to know it right away. Ride them hard, Streeter. I want
to keep the pressure on to find this guy. Will you do that?"

"Sure. But I'll hang around here tonight. I can't sleep anyway."

Streeter didn't eat again until late Saturday afternoon. By mid-morning, he started smoking cigarettes. He hadn't smoked more than a couple of packs in the past ten years, but now it was steady Camels, no filters. Pure, high-octane self-punishment. He couldn't shake that guilty feeling. The only thing that made him feel better was hounding the police. McLean regained a shaky consciousness shortly before noon. For the rest of the day he didn't know where he was or much of what happened, but the worst was over. When he heard that, Streeter called Story and filled her in on the beating.

"Thank God he's not going to die," she said, obviously shaken. "This is terrible. You don't think it had anything to do with my suit against Cooper?"

"Could be. Like I told you, I don't believe in coincidences. I'm going to check around, and I'll let you know what I find out."

"When you talk to Bill, give him my love. I'd like to come to the hospital and visit him. Do you think that would be all right?"

"There's a lot of family there today and he's not really thinking too clearly yet," he told her. "Maybe you better wait a day or two, until things settle down."

In the early afternoon, Streeter drove to police headquarters, across the street from the Denver Mint. He went to the assaults division and talked to the sergeant heading the investigation. Because of McLean's high-profile DA career, his beating drew media coverage as well as a high priority with the police. Sergeant Stan Haney, a rubber-faced veteran with an obvious fashion impairment, told the bounty hunter that the beating looked like the work of at least two people.

"The doctors took wood splinters from Bill's skin," Haney said, his voice raspy from years of cigarette smoking. Although he was fifty, he still had the squat, stocky build of an old-time football player. A leather-helmet kind of guy. He was wearing a loud sport coat and a wide tie that indicated he hadn't been to a clothes store in well over a decade. "They found two different types of wood. One came from a baseball bat. The other was from a piece of raw oak. There was a deep cut on his right side, too. Looked like some sort of weird knife. They worked him over pretty hard, but I don't think they wanted to kill him."

"Why do you say that?"

"Well, for one thing, he was obviously still alive when they stopped. If they meant to kill him, they were pretty sloppy. He crawled about a hundred yards from where he was beaten. And it wasn't no robbery, either. They left his wallet and they didn't even bother to go through the car. We figure probably some assholes he sent down to Cañon City who wanted a little payback. Prison-style bullshit."

"Who found him?"

"Some guy that lives next to the motel. Checked out okay. He was working at the time it happened. When we found him, he was scared shitless, too."

"Did they leave anything at the scene that'll help you out?"

"Not much. We found tracks back there that look like they're from a big car. We're checking that out now. The weapons weren't there and, believe me, we scoured the whole place looking for them." Then Haney glanced off, smiling. "I think maybe Bill got in a lick or two himself."

"What makes you say that?"

"The doc told us the knuckles on Bill's right hand were badly bruised. One of them was broken. My guess is, he got a couple a punches in."

Streeter smiled. McLean boxed at Northwestern as an undergraduate. "I'm sure that whoever did this didn't expect the job to be quite as tough as it ended up. Anything else?"

"Nothing really." Haney paused. "We're doing all we can. Bill McLean has a lot of friends on the department. Give me a holler if you need anything else, and tell his missus we're all pulling for him."

When he got back to the church at about eight that night, Streeter went to Frank's apartment to kick around some ideas. The bondsman, who had known McLean longer than Streeter had, was badly shaken by the news. He looked terribly old and almost lost in his thick terry-cloth bathrobe. Frank had seen enough violence in his life to fill a Clint Eastwood film festival and he was sick to death of it.

"Jesus, big guy. I don't know what it's all coming to anymore." Frank grabbed a half-full bottle of Johnny Walker Red from the counter in the kitchen and then nodded for his partner to follow him to his office. That's where the two did most of their drinking together. When they sat down at his desk, Frank poured two tall ones—neat—and proposed a toast.

"To Wild Bill McLean." The bondsman held out his glass for a second and then took a long pull on the Scotch.

"To William." Streeter nodded and took a small sip. He noticed that he still was wearing the same jeans and T-shirt from the night before at Story's. Suddenly he felt grimy and wanted to take a shower. "This has got me thinking, Frank. That gunfire last week, and now this. Between Cooper and whatever cop is running around out there, I can't believe this attack was a con that McLean put away in the old days. I've got to believe it was tied in with Doug Shelton and that whole crew."

"You're probably right. But, hell, Bill won't be blaming you. That's not his style and he knew what he was getting into when he took on Cooper."

"That may be true, but I've got to put an end to all this junk. It's getting way out of hand. Shootings, beatings, vandalism." He lit another Camel and then crushed it out almost immediately. "I just met Carey for a few hoists down at Nalen's. He did some checking today and found out that Kovacs, the cop I think's behind this, was at a seminar Friday afternoon until way after six. Then he went to dinner with some of the boys. He couldn't have done Bill."

"He could have gotten some other cop to do it for him."

"Yeah, but then you have a conspiracy. A police conspiracy,

no less. That's not likely. Plus, that court hearing was just the day before, and Bill kicked the shit out of Cooper. He might want some quick revenge while he's still hurting."

"That makes sense. You find out where Cooper was last night?" Frank held up the bottle to see if Streeter wanted more.

Streeter shook his head. "Cooper didn't do this himself. Carey told me about a guy that works for Cooper. The guy's name is Psycho or something nutty like that. There was talk that Cooper sent him to slit the throat of a witness not long ago. Bill was cut by a knife, too. This nut has a sidekick, and I was told there were two people who beat Bill. Then there were all those hang-up calls last night. That sounds too chicken-shit for a cop but, who knows, a couple of these jerks that Cooper would hire might think it's pretty clever."

"Sounds very possible. Did you discuss all this with Carey?"

"Yeah, we ran over all the options together. For all we know, Cooper and half the police department are in on it together. I'm not sure why a cop would hassle Story or why someone shot at us. And I'm not sure why Bill's in the hospital. Neither is Carey. I tell you, Frank, this makes my little bail jumpers look halfway decent. Very sane and simple. All I know is, I have to do something. I have to talk to all these jerks and see what I can shake out of them. This Psycho and his playmate for starters. Carey said this was a message to Bill. There's been more messages flying around here than at a damned Western Union convention. Maybe it's time I start sending some messages of my own."

"I hear you, but be careful," Frank said with a dismal smile as he struggled to get up from the desk. The Scotch had taken its toll. "You're heading into the low end of nowhere with these people. They're poison, all of them. I don't want to have to break in a new skip tracer and get a new tenant for that loft of yours."

"That's a very warm thought, Frank. I'll hold it close to me in the days ahead."

17

"Will you relax, Ronnie? You don't even know for sure it was them." Cooper kept trying to grab her shoulders to steady her, but she was too agitated to be touched. Ever since they saw the news of McLean's beating on television Saturday night, Ronnie'd been hopping around like her shoes were on fire. She was furious and scared. It was now Sunday afternoon at Cooper's downtown loft, and she'd whipped herself into a state of inconsolable bitchiness that he'd never seen before.

"You had to make all those threats against him after the hearing," she said. "Right in front of those two freaks. I told you they'd see that as the green light for some kind of violent horseshit like this. And what the hell do you mean, you're not sure it was them? Get real, Thomas Hardy."

"Okay, it probably was them," he conceded. "I'll be more careful from now on. But why are you so upset? You didn't even know this damned McLean. And they said on the tube he's going to pull through. It's not like he was actually murdered."

Ronnie glared at him. Then she adjusted the front of her silk bathrobe and looked away. The hell you gonna do with this mutt?

"What a relief! He was only beaten half to death. And here I was starting to worry that you didn't have a conscience. You know, after that Commerce City stunt, we don't need more attention from the cops." Her voice rose as she spoke. "Even they can't be so stupid that they're not going to start putting this together fairly soon. It looks pretty obvious to me that you're the common denominator here. One might think that professional police detectives would notice that, too."

Cooper drew back, his forehead chopped deep in concentration; his words came more slowly now. "But they have nothing on me. Absolutely nothing concrete in nature. You must understand, Rhonda, that what seems 'pretty obvious' to you simply does not convict people in a court of law."

"Oh, right, Thomas Hardy." She spit the words out. "You're always right. For another thing"—she stopped to light a fresh cigarette off the one she was finishing—"these are very dangerous guys. They get an idea in their heads and someone gets hurt. What if they get the idea you're in their way? Or me? We might get something very 'concrete in nature' from those two, in the form of a baseball bat to the skull."

She thought of Soyko's visit to her apartment. She wouldn't tell Cooper about it, but the idea of him coming back for another visit was always with her, like ground glass under her fingernails.

"I'm their boss. They work for me." Cooper's voice was loud and shrill again. "They'll get back in line."

"Aw, Tom, you really don't get it." Her voice softened and she lowered her head a bit. He looked kind of pathetic, standing there in crisp new blue jeans with his pudgy stomach oozing out over his belt. *Pressed* jeans, for Chrissakes. "They work for themselves. You're just the guy that gives them stupid ideas and pays them. You like to have them on the payroll because it gives you a sense of power. Like you're suddenly above the law and you can reach out and hurt people any time you want. But you've got no power with them. No control. That should be obvious by now. Look at that little welder. Dopps. And now this. These two freaks are beyond you. They're beyond everything but their own crazy reality."

With that she walked into the kitchen area and poured herself another cup of coffee. Cooper's loft had twelve-foot ceilings and few interior walls. Ronnie didn't like it: it reminded her of a furniture-store showroom.

Fundamentally, Cooper knew she was right. He had been feeling a growing sense of fear since they heard about McLean. The beating bothered him more than the Dopps hit. At least with Dopps he'd instructed Soyko to go talk to the witness and get him to leave town. McLean was totally free-lance. All their own idea. But he had had enough of Ronnie's lip, and he couldn't bring himself to show her he made a mistake. To let her know she was right and he was powerless. He stalked after her.

"Listen, you." He was spitting lightly as he spoke. "They work for me and so do you. I'm sick of your whining about those guys. An arrogant son of a bitch like this McLean deserved everything he got, and more. So did that worthless punk up in Commerce City. I'm glad they did it and I'm glad I gave them the idea. And you let me worry about the cops. If they get within ten miles of me on this, I'll turn Soyko and that detestable little fuck Romp over to them in a second. I've got this thing under control, but I'm getting sick and tired of the way you talk to me. You were nothing before I met you, and I could turn you out any time. Now I've got to go to the office for a while. Just lighten up. I'll be back about five. In the meantime, why don't you make yourself useful and clean up around here!"

Cooper made a point of keeping hard eye contact with her until Ronnie looked away. He was furious and yet he knew he really didn't want her to leave him. "Look," he said with a gentler voice. "it's going to be all right. I'll have a talk with them when I get down to the office. You just shouldn't keep riding me like that."

Then he nodded and walked out of the condo without trying to touch her again. Anger and fear boiled inside Ronnie, forming a noxious burn in her stomach. I was nothing before I met you? She thought about leaving him, but that was so dramatic and final, not to mention fiscally unsound. First things first. Get those two "investigators" out of the picture. For good. She glanced at the phone, and the thought that had been percolating since she first heard the news about McLean suddenly erupted. She finished her coffee and had four more cigarettes—then she did the deed.

Her hands shook as she dialed the police number she had memorized the night before. It being Sunday, she had a little trouble getting through to the right department. Finally the right officer answered.

"Detective Lesley, may I help you?" The question came quickly through the line, and Ronnie almost hung up. The voice sounded so young.

"Are you working on the McLean case? The beating that I saw on the news last night?"

"Yes ma'am. Sergeant Haney is in charge, but he's not in today. Do you have any information regarding the attack?"

"You bet I do." She rolled her eyes at how loud her voice was.

"May I have your name, ma'am?"

"No, junior. I'll just tell you what I know and I'll tell you once. Try to get it all down. The same two men who did that Dopps guy up in Commerce City, the knife job, did McLean. I'd check out a couple of guys in Aurora. One of them's named Soyko. I think his first name is Leo. The other one is Jacky Romp. They live just east of Havana, near Iliff. They're the ones you're after. They'll give you a ton of crap, but be careful. They're trouble. And nobody asked them to do it. They did it on their own."

"Ma'am, how do you know this?" Lesley's words were coming quickly. "If I could just have your name and phone number."

"I told you, no, sonny boy. Look, just nail those guys. If you don't get them now, there'll be more trouble."

With that she slammed down the receiver. Seconds later, she

The Low End of Nowhere 137

lit a cigarette and tried to remember exactly what she had just told Lesley. Her thoughts were clouded with fright. Soyko and Romp at her house. All anger had left her during the call, and it was replaced with fear.

Sergeant Haney had seen the look a thousand times. The same just-try-me sneer he got from damned near every dime-store hard-on he ever met. But this sneer wasn't forced or shaky like some of them. It was no pose. Haney could tell this guy meant what was carved on his face. His eyes gave up nothing and he smelled like he never showered. Contaminated. And Haney knew he had nothing on Soyko and his buddy, but he just wanted to shake the tree, see if anything fell out. That phone call to Lesley the day before was all he had to go on in McLean's case.

Soyko kept thinking how he could probably slap the hell out of this flabby old man before he could get his gun out. The guy looked like he could have been tough once, but that was about a hundred years ago, when he was young. Still, Soyko had never moved on a cop before, and he knew it would be a mistake. He also thought how Haney had squat to go on except for this one lame tip. He looked over and saw Jacky on the couch, twitching in rage and glaring at the detective.

"You two can have a lawyer if you want one," Haney said. "Course, then we all go downtown and make a big deal over this."

"I suppose we could just do that, but it don't matter," Soyko shot back. "We ain't talking to you about nothing, anyhow. Downtown, here. Don't matter. What's all this about? You come here talking about a guy dying up in Commerce City and some other guy getting beat up. We don't know squat. Last Friday, we were both over to the Drift Inn playing pool. All night. We can probably only get about twenty guys to back us up."

"I bet they're fine citizens, too." Haney was getting mad. "What about the afternoon of June fourth? I suppose you could get another twenty guys to back you up on that one?"

"That's guaranteed, pal. Look, I got no idea what you're talking about. Get my lawyer? Man, I work for lawyers. Jacky and me are private investigators. Like on the television."

Haney took in a deep breath and crushed out his cigarette. He thought how he'd like to kick some respect into this mouthy little punk. For twenty-seven years he'd been listening to all kinds of trash. White trash, black trash, brown trash. Whatever the color, trash was just trash. He had no idea who called with their names, but he was believing it more.

"What lawyers?"

"That's confidential." Soyko leaned back against the dining-room table, smiling. He didn't know if it was confidential or not, but he had heard it on enough lawyer shows and movies to use it.

Lesley had told Haney that the woman said something like no one ordered these two guys to do it either time. He said she sounded nervous about that part. Lesley didn't get a chance to ask her exactly what she meant.

"Could be it was one of your lawyers got you into this." He took a flyer. "The lady tells us you were on your own, but I'm not so sure."

Soyko felt his face flush for just an instant. "Unless you want us downtown, I don't have to say a word." Forty-five minutes is enough with this clown.

"Take it easy, slick." Haney leaned forward, obviously furious. His face looked soft, puffy from overuse, but even Soyko backed up a shade. Haney realized he had hit a nerve. "We've got some more checking to do on both you pukes. Maybe you might want to make sure you can get those twenty guys for the afternoon of the fourth and for Friday night. I'll be seeing you again. You can fucking bank on it."

When he left, Jacky got up and kicked the side of the sofa with a frightening amount of force for a thin man. "Son of a bitch," he screamed at Soyko. "Who did it?" His face was the color of blood.

"Got a pretty good idea. For one thing, he said it was a broad."

"How you know that wasn't a lot of crap?"

"Because that cop ain't ambitious enough to do no home-work. Someone called on us or he would never have been here. If they had anything, they'd be building it into a case right now. To them, this is just an assault that'll blow over and a homicide out of their backyard. They were just squeezing our nuts to see if we'd fold."

Soyko was pulling his fingers individually, deliberately crack-ing each knuckle as he spoke. "When Cooper ordered this thing with McLean, he told us not to let it get back to Ronnie. Then yesterday, when he called, he told us how pissed she was. My bet is, he fed her some shit like it was all our doing. Not that I care. And she would tell the cops that it's our idea. Try and cover for her fat-ass boyfriend. My thinking is, she just got so mad she called the cops sometime yesterday or first thing this morning. Only two people know about us, and there's no way Cooper made that call. If it was him, he'd cut a deal, roll on us, and the first time we see the cops they'd have a warrant."

"That miserable little bitch," Jacky fumed, his jaws not moving.

"We gotta deal with this," Soyko said. "With both of them. And we gotta do it quick and hard. No fucking doubt about that."

18

Ronnie listened to the phone ring at the other end of the line. She had been trying to reach Cooper for well over an hour. He'd left work early that afternoon, and she needed to talk to him. Desperately. Her head pounded from nicotine and nervous fear as she paced her apartment. That call to the cops the day before was, in her own words, "making me mental." The more she thought about it, the more she realized that if they talked to Soyko he'd quickly figure out she dropped the dime on him. She tried to convince herself the police wouldn't move on him and Romp unless they had more evidence to go on. But how could she know that for sure?

She reached for her purse, containing her cigarettes, and glanced at the clock again. Almost seven. Cooper had to be getting home soon. She fumbled around inside the huge bag for a couple of minutes, looking for the pack. "Enough damned junk to fill a suitcase," she said furiously to no one. Inside there was the petite, off-white cellular phone that Cooper had given her for her birthday and an empty box of M&M's. There were nine half-full bottles of nail polish, along with her entire linty candy collection and an assortment of makeup far too extensive to itemize. There was her key chain, complete with attached hot-pepper spray designed to ward off dogs, and several checkbooks. There was a separate key chain for her personal safe-deposit box and a small coupon book. Finally, she found her pack and noticed that she had only one Marlboro left. She stuck the cigarette into her mouth angrily and lit it. Ronnie had a habit of turning fear or anxiety or sadness into anger. It never seemed to hurt as much. At that moment she'd rather be furious than feel the terror inside her.

"Screw it," she mumbled to herself and slipped her shoulder into the long strap from the black leather purse. If she had to sit around to wait for Cooper she'd jump out of her skin. Might as well go get some more smokes from the closest 7-Eleven. She figured he'd have to be home by the time she returned.

As she walked down the hall leading to the outer door, she felt more aggravation. Someone had parked in her usual spot that night, and the entire lot to the east was full. She'd had to park on the street that ran along the side of the building and past the lot. Definitely not my night, she noted.

When she got outside, she was surprised at how bright the sun still was. She put on her pink-rimmed sun glasses—"my hooker shades"—and took a couple steps toward her car, some fifty yards away. That was when she saw Jacky Romp get out of the driver's side of his El Camino. She looked farther and saw Leo Soyko get out of the passenger's side. They had parked the big vehicle between her usual lot and where her car was now parked in the street. Ronnie was absolutely amazed that her first thought was how nice Romp's car looked. Must be a new wax job: Just how the hell *does* my mind work? Her second thought was that she was thoroughly screwed. No chance to get to her car without them seeing her. And they'd be coming her way any second.

"Which one's hers?" Jacky asked his friend as they looked over the long white two-story apartment building.

Soyko lifted his arm and pointed to his left. "Over there. Sort of a basement apartment. Total shithole. I think that's her car on the street there. The maroon Tercel. Betcha Numb Nuts leased it for her. Spoiled bitch. Let's go get her, Jacky. She's done enough damage."

Ronnie saw Soyko point toward her building just before she ducked back into the hallway. She knew if they got her inside she'd be dead. Or wish she was. Instinctively, her right hand shot down into her purse and she grabbed the keys with the pepper spray. Lot of good that'll do, she thought as she fought back the panic. She glanced out the window and saw the two men walking slowly toward her. There was no other way out of the building, and she didn't have time to get to her apartment, way at the other end of the hall. She froze with fear and got ready to scream.

At that exact moment, the door to the nearest apartment swung open and three large men walked out. Two looked Hispanic, the third nondescript. Ronnie smelled a sticky blast of pot smoke trailing them into the hallway. She'd seen two of them before, and one, the shortest but stockiest, had flirted with her in the laundry once. They all were in their early twenties and dressed in Target grunge clothes. They smiled hazily at her.

"Hey, man. It's the blondie," the stocky flirter said. His voice was enthusiastic but syrupy, like he just woke up. Bad-ass pot voice. "Hey, blondie, man. How you doing, baby? You want to come in and party big-time? Party with Hector maybe?" His eyes got dreamy as he spoke but he definitely wasn't joking. His friends awkwardly nodded approval and flashed their stoned, shit-eating grins.

Hector wasn't much taller than Ronnie, but his arms looked thick as logs and his neck was the approximate size of his shoulders. She guessed his weight at well over two hundred pounds. His two friends were thinner and each was almost a foot taller. She instantly knew what she had to do.

"That sounds hot, Hector," she said in a breathy voice usually reserved for Cooper when she wanted something—a voice so laced with promise the lawyer never could turn it down. Her shorts were small and tight, and most of both smooth cheeks of her butt were exposed. The pink halter top added nicely to the effect. "Very hot. I've been wanting to do that ever since we talked that day."

"All right, man! *Amigos!*" Hector couldn't believe his good fortune. His friends shuffled their feet aimlessly and grunted. "Come inside, baby, for a little bong action. What you say?"

Ronnie took a step toward Hector, placed her left hand on his shoulder, and shot him a look that would stiffen a priest. They were eyeball to eyeball, and her words came out in a husky whisper. "One problem, big guy. My old boyfriend, the fucker that used to beat me silly, him and his buddy are right outside. He's pissed because I dumped him. If they get their hands on me, I'm history. Can you boys make them go away? Then we can party our asses off. Can you get rid of them?"

The large man on Hector's left fielded that one. "They beat you, little lady? That's pure horseshit." He sounded much more cowboy than Hispanic. "We're gonna tear both them bastards new assholes. You just watch this."

Hector nodded, his face twisted in concern. "We see who beats who now, baby. You let Hector take care of their shit." He pulled Ronnie around behind him so she was facing the doorway with the three heroes between her and the world outside.

The door swept open a second later and Jacky Romp and Leo Soyko strolled into the hall. The confidence on their faces waffled when they saw the three men waiting for them. They stopped about five feet from the men, and Soyko looked past them to Ronnie. "Hey, Goldilocks. You got bodyguards now?"

"Damned straight she does," the cowboy-sounding guy said as he glared down at the two. "Maybe you two shit buckets want to see how tough you are with men instead of girls. Maybe you come to the right place."

"Damnit," Jacky sputtered in rage. "You stupid cracker fucks don't know what you're doing. Just move on and you don't get hurt."

Hector took a step forward so he was a couple feet away from Soyko. "She stays and you go. Now. We not shittin' around here, man."

End of discussion, Soyko reasoned. His right fist snapped up and shot into Hector's mouth before anyone else could move. It wasn't a full punch, but that was usually more than enough to put someone down. Hector was stunned and he staggered back two steps. But he didn't come close to falling. Soyko knew they were in for a fight. The big cowboy rushed Jacky and threw him against the wall. Jacky screamed and started throwing punches, but he was clearly no match for the big man. The guy on Hector's right then rushed Soyko, and they both fell to the ground clawing each other. By this time Hector had recovered, and he jumped on top of Soyko.

Ronnie wasted no time. She slid along the wall closest to the door, past the fighting bodies, and grabbed the door handle. Then she looked back for just a second. Neither Soyko nor Romp noticed. She opened the door and was in a full run toward her car before she realized that in the excitement she'd squeezed her pepper spray down her leg. She figured the fight would last long enough for her to get to her car and drive at least a few miles. It didn't matter to her which side won. None of the five men would ever see her again.

19

"A lot of this crap seems to be coming back your way, Mr. Cooper." Sergeant Haney's voice was low and smoldering.

The lawyer looked up but didn't actually see the sergeant. He couldn't stop worrying about Ronnie, not to mention himself. She'd called him late last night and wouldn't say where she was staying. She was screaming with rage and crying from fear at the same time. Ronnie was mad because he had gotten them involved with Leo Soyko, and because Cooper hadn't been home for her call earlier in the night. Afraid, obviously, because the two hit men were still on the loose and still looking for her. Ronnie said she was "just outside of town" and she'd call him back this morning so they could make plans for getting together. He knew something drastic had to be done: Soyko and Romp were coming after both of them.

"What are you talking about?" Cooper said automatically. "What's coming back my way? My fiancée, the woman I love, has just been threatened in the most brutal and reprehensible fashion, and you're making it sound like I'm responsible. My God, she could have been killed."

They were standing in the hall outside Cooper's office along with a second detective, a chubby Hispanic man. He had the scarred complexion of a public golf fairway but wore an impeccable herringbone suit. The Hispanic cop didn't speak and Haney didn't introduce him. Cooper had returned to his office from a quick court appearance and found the two of them waiting. Although the sergeant wasn't smoking at the moment, his clothes reeked of tobacco and his breath smelled like a tiny reptile had died inside his mouth sometime ago.

"Oh, you could maybe convince me you didn't do that particular thing," Haney responded. "That brawl. She is your fiancée, like you said. All I'm saying is, a lot of crap seems to be headed your way. That guy up in Commerce City. Bill McLean. Now this."

"And just how am I connected to McLean, for God's sake? Or that witness in Commerce City?"

"We know you were in court against McLean last week and that he kicked the living shit out of you. And we know what happened to the case against your murder client, Borders, when the witness died."

Cooper looked at the detective like he just really noticed him for the first time. Haney had that all-over-bloated look that middle-aged men get from beer, fatty foods, and inactivity. The guy's heart was probably encased in sludge, like a filthy carburetor, and any beat could be its last, Cooper thought. To the attorney, Haney seemed utterly diseased and foul.

"I can account for my whereabouts at all of those times," he told the cop. "Are you really suggesting that I beat up a fellow attorney? You're not even as smart as you look, and *that* hardly seems possible. And what do I get out of attacking and possibly killing Ronnie? I love her."

"Yeah, yeah. I'm sure you do. And she's a real hot number, from what I hear. We got a tip from a woman on Sunday, two days ago. She tells us a guy named Soyko and someone named Romp were involved in McLean and Dopps. Turns out they both know you. So we go talk to those two first thing yesterday morning, and guess what? Your secretary or fiancée gets chased later by two guys matching the descriptions of Soyko and Romp. Several people get beaten like—how'd you put it?—'in the most brutal and reprehensible fashion.' All this happening right outside your fiancée's apartment. Incredible how it shook out like that."

The news about Ronnie talking to the police hit Cooper visibly. He looked away for a moment.

"Seems you didn't know about that call, did you?" Haney, seeing an opening, stepped closer. "I'll tell you the same thing I told that warped motherfucker Soyko. We're going to be looking long and hard at everything. We know those guys work for you. We'll put it all together, counselor. You got my word on that."

Cooper's stomach felt like Greg Norman was practicing his short irons off of it. So Ronnie called the cops on those two and this was their response. She never mentioned that call. Not Sunday or last night. He straightened up and returned Haney's glare.

"Sergeant, I resent this obvious attempt at intimidation. Believe me, your superiors will be hearing about how you have conducted yourself here. And I do not choose to continue this conversation without my lawyer present."

"That's probably not the dumbest idea you ever had." Haney nodded and looked at his partner. "Or will have."

When they left, Cooper stood in the hallway for several minutes considering what Haney had said. Then he went inside and told his receptionist to hold his calls unless it was Ronnie. He went into his office and sat down. He was sucking air in shallow blasts and his exhales sounded like a crippled accordion. Everything seemed beyond his control. He thought of how he wanted to call Ronnie into his office but couldn't. He opened his bottom drawer and pulled out the shiny Colt Python. He shifted it from one hand to the other, but the gun didn't give him any clarity. And it was options and clarity that he desperately needed. His life was unraveling laboriously around him. Soyko and Romp on a rampage, probably gunning for him. Ronnie terrified and in danger. And, hell, it would be just a matter of time before Haney would be back with a search warrant and then an arrest warrant.

He was pretty sure his investigators wouldn't roll on him. Certainly not out of loyalty, but they'd both rather get bone-marrow cancer than cooperate with the police. Still, they almost certainly would come after him themselves. They'd probably think he put Ronnie up to that call. They were so far out of control, who knew what they'd do next? What was it Ronnie had said? "They work for themselves. You're just the guy that gives them stupid ideas and pays them."

He thought of her. That woman always was far more perceptive than any three of his classmates in law school. Damn, she was right about a lot of things, but she must have been out of her mind to call the cops.

Got to do something, he told himself. If he went to the cops, he could finger the two men for Dopps and McLean. He could say he never asked them to do it but just paid them to go have a talk. Ronnie'd back him on all of that. It was almost true, and he knew Haney was drooling to clear those cases. He could say that, when he heard about what they did, he was too scared to call the police. But after the attack on his secretary, he knew they had to be locked up.

"Think again," he muttered to himself. How could he explain why he hired them to talk to McLean after he knew they killed Dopps? He was sure to get nailed for conspiracy, among other charges. Plus, he reasoned, as long as those two were alive, either in prison with him or on the street, eventually his sorry ass would get whacked. They'd have to be stopped with no chance of getting started again. Only one way to do that. He looked at the revolver for a long time.

Who was he kidding? He knew he could never shoot anyone.

He shifted to his next option. It was his only real option and he knew it: get far away and fast. Hook up with Ronnie and get them both out of Colorado by the next afternoon. It would take him that long to pull his money out of his accounts and sell his second car, the old Corvette, to that dealer on South Broadway who always was so hot to buy it. His quick calculations told him he could get maybe sixty-five or seventy thousand together that soon. Enough for a new start somewhere else. It would probably mean the end of his legal career. That certainly wasn't what he had in mind when he left law school, but it was better than getting shredded by Soyko, or spending the next fifteen years playing house with a three-hundred-pound ape in Cañon City. He'd like to do something to avenge the assault on Ronnie, but getting himself killed was in no way suitable. Better he should live, preferably out of jail, to keep her happy, he told himself. Leave all that Chuck Norris nonsense to those better suited for it.

"Someone here to see you, Mr. Cooper," the receptionist barked through the intercom. Her voice was drenched in satisfaction. "A police detective."

Cooper frowned. What did Haney want now? As he was reaching for the intercom button to tell her he'd be ready in a minute, his door swung open and in walked a man he hadn't seen since Doug Shelton's preliminary hearing.

"Looks like this ain't your week, counselor." Art Kovacs shut the door behind him and approached. "And here it is, only Tuesday."

"Well, come right in and make yourself comfortable," Cooper said with mock indignation. He paused. "You look familiar."

"We met on that Doug Shelton bust." Kovacs now stood at the desk.

"You're Korchak. No, wait. Kovacs, right? Arthur Kovacs, wasn't it?"

"It still is." The detective smiled quickly at his own cleverness. He dropped into the chair across from Cooper like he hadn't sat down in months. "I think we should have us a talk here. You look like you could use help. And I mean help from someone that's got a little pull."

"Let me guess. You just happen to have a little pull." Cooper was confused.

"Bingo." Kovacs pointed a finger at him like a pistol. "I don't want to waste a lot of time, so I'll just lay it all out. You'd be very mistaken to consider this a suggestion. We'll call it a mandate. That's a new buzzword we hear downtown. Now, I know for a fact that you're basically fucked with the department. It's just a matter of a day or two before that birdbrain Haney'll have something to go to the DA with. That means you'll be charged and they'll come down your throat with a meat cleaver, believe me. When Haney gets a hard-on for someone, he don't let up."

"I figured that one out for myself."

"I'll bet you did." Kovacs loosened his light-tan tie and rolled his neck like it was stiff. He was wearing a short-sleeved shirt the approximate color of prune juice, and his forearms were so hairy there was practically no skin visible. "Here's where your new friend could come in handy. I'm working on this investigation, too. I can make sure it drags out for a while, and I can give them enough troubles that maybe you don't burn. Maybe. They got a circumstantial case on this McLean thing, and that guy up in Commerce City—forget it. They got very little unless Soyko flips you. Is that possible?"

"Not likely."

"Well, then, with my help you might not be in such big trouble, after all. At the very least I can let you know what's coming down, and when and where. Think that might be helpful to you?"

"It might at that," Cooper acknowledged. "I just wonder what it is you want in return for all this magnanimous assistance?"

"I want you to stop chasing after Doug Shelton's estate. I want you to forget that guy ever existed."

"How did you know I'm chasing anything?" Cooper sat up straight in his chair.

"This coke whore what used to play with Shelton told me Soyko was trying to scare information out of her. He did a good job of it. I'll level with you, partner. That estate was located a long time ago. By me. Mr. Shelton told me a lot of interesting things about himself and his business ventures right after he was arrested."

"I gather that would have been about when you two hatched up a deal to steal the evidence against him."

"Basically. He took a fair amount of persuading, but he finally opened up."

Cooper broke into a smile of recognition. "So that explains who beat the snot out of him right after his arrest. How much did he leave?"

"There was some snot beating, all right." Kovacs grinned. "Dougy left enough to make me happy but not enough so's I'd want to share it with you or this Story what's-her-name. I don't need no interference from anyone. I'll deal with Story and her big, bad bounty hunter on my own. You just deal with those two jerkoffs that work for you. Pull them off the hunt. That sound like something you can handle?"

"It certainly does." Cooper sat back for a minute. He knew that if he told Kovacs how out of control Soyko was he'd get no help. "I'll be glad to do all that's within my power to keep my associates from making further inquiries into Mr. Shelton's estate."

"I don't give a shit what's within your power. Just call off those two mutts."

Cooper nodded. However, he had no intention of coming away from this Shelton search empty-handed now that he knew who had the money.

"You know, Kovacs, I put a lot of time and effort into looking for this money. If I were to suddenly cease my efforts, I feel as though I should be compensated in some fashion."

"No fuckin' way!" Kovacs yelled. He could feel his stomach churning. He'd been popping Pepto Bismol tablets like they were breath mints and still his intestines complained. No one ever cooperates. Everyone's always got their own angle. "You maybe keep from getting skinned alive on this thing. That should be compensation enough."

"I am not certain that it is." Cooper frowned thoughtfully. "But for, say, twenty thousand, my comfort level would increase dramatically."

"Oh, would it now?" The cop calmed down and studied the

attorney. "Let me get back to you on that one. I'd hate to do anything to disturb your fuckin' comfort level."

"Fair enough. Can I ask you one more question?"

"Would it matter if I said no?"

"How much did Douglas pay you for your help with his evidence?"

Kovacs stood up in disgust. His stomach was burning fiercely now, and he wondered where the restrooms were.

"Go to hell. Just get those two nut cases off my ass and away from my money and I'll let you know what's going on from our end."

He walked out of the office in determined search of the nearest "facilities." When the detective planted himself in the toilet stall on Cooper's floor, he was sweating from a gastric burn that gripped him like an enormous swamp slug. His insides were getting worse every day. His so-called partner had suggested this stupid talk with Cooper. Plain to see that the lawyer was more trouble than he was worth. No way he could control Soyko and Romp. Kovacs knew he'd have to do that himself. Turned out he had to do everything himself. And his partner was becoming as useless as Cooper. The stress of all these decisions was turning his stomach into a mini-Chernobyl. He just wanted to end the anguish, and it was becoming clear that that meant he was going to have to end several lives.

Streeter got information on Soyko from Cooper's receptionist on Monday. Without hesitation, she gave his and Romp's phone number and address. The bounty hunter had gone to their apartment a couple of times that day, but no one was home. Finally, about ten o'clock Tuesday night, he went back and saw a light in the window. Walking up to the third-floor unit, he could feel his nine-millimeter tucked into the small of his back. It was there strictly for self-defense.

From the outside walkway leading to the apartment, Streeter could see the shaky blue glow of Soyko's television dance off the curtains. He tried to look in the window, but the drapes were drawn too tight to give him much of a view. He rang the buzzer several times. No one answered. Then he pounded on the door. Still no answer. He rattled the handle, and was surprised to find it unlocked.

"Anybody here?" he asked calmly as he opened the door a couple of inches. Nothing. He pushed harder and repeated the question. "Anybody here?"

When he pushed the door open and stepped into the living room, he got his answer. There—draped over the couch, half on the floor—was the process server who had given Story her papers at Cooper's. The left side of his head was matted with blood, and there was a large spray of red over the couch and wall a few feet from him. This must be that Jacky Romp that Carey mentioned.

Streeter took out his handkerchief and covered his right hand. He walked to the couch and checked Romp for a pulse. There was none, but the skin was still mildly warm, indicating that he hadn't been dead for long. Streeter noticed that both of the man's wrists were cut and the marks looked fresh. Romp's face was twisted in rage, like he had died giving someone serious verbal grief. Judging by where the blood spray ended up on the wall, Streeter guessed that he was shot kneeling down and then sort of thrown onto the couch after he was dead. Streeter backed away from the body. He wiped his prints off the doorknob and left.

When he got back to the church, he went to Frank's room. Once again, the bondsman automatically grabbed his Scotch and they headed to his office.

"It's getting way out of hand, Street," Frank said when they sat down at his desk. Then he nodded to the Scotch bottle. "This is getting to be a regular event around here. You got to go to the police."

"I called 911 from a phone booth on the way back here."

"I assumed that. I mean you got to sit down with them and fill them in on all of this stuff."

"That would be nice, except that I think it's the police who's doing most of it. This Jacky business wasn't Cooper's work. And Soyko wouldn't do Romp. No motive, and Carey tells me these two guys were closer than brothers."

"You think Kovacs did it?"

"Romp had cuts on his wrists. My guess is handcuffs. Kovacs doesn't want anyone messing into Doug's business. This is his way of telling Cooper to back off. He probably figured he'd have to be a little more forceful with Cooper than he was with Story."

"So where's Soyko now?"   .

"I wouldn't mind knowing that myself. I'm meeting Carey tomorrow afternoon to see what I can find out. I also got a call today from Cooper's secretary. Seems she was attacked last night and she wants to get together with me tomorrow and talk about it. Ronnie Taggert. I may have mentioned her."

Frank was puzzled. "Why'd she call you?"

"I gather she can't go to the cops, because she's in over her head. And she doesn't think Cooper'll be much help." Streeter smiled. "I think maybe she's got a thing for me, too. For whatever reason, she trusts me."

"Great. You need to get messed up with someone like that. You got a real knack for hitching up with trouble all of a sudden."

"I'm not hitching up with anything," he said, dropping the smile, "but I'm dying to find out what she knows about all this. We're meeting first thing in the morning for breakfast."

Frank shook his head like he had a stiff neck and poured another drink. "Let me know if you need anything. And watch your ass, huh?"

20

Jacky Romp was one of the most dead-looking bodies Soyko had ever seen, and he'd seen maybe a dozen guys in that precise condition. He'd been standing in the middle of the living room smoking and looking down at Jacky for almost half an hour. It didn't take an orthopedic surgeon to figure out that Romp's condition wasn't brought on by natural causes. One side of his head looked like he'd stuck it in a blender. It had lolled off to his left and rested on the couch back. His legs shot straight out, like he was a puppet thrown down hard. It looked to Soyko like someone had used a cannon on his partner.

He had known Jacky for nearly ten years and roomed with him for most of that time. Jacky was not only Soyko's closest friend, he was the only real friend he ever had. But Soyko wasn't so much sad as puzzled about what to do next. Not about what to do with the killer. That was a definite no-brainer. No, he wondered about what to do in general without Jacky around.

Suddenly he turned to face the wall, let out a dull wail, and ran his fist through the cheap plaster. He did it twice more, then felt better. Jacky was history, but someone had to pay. Soyko would still leave town tomorrow, as they had planned, but he would be by himself. He knew he'd have to be careful until then. If the cops weren't on his tail before, this would certainly get them there.

Life could be very strange at times, he decided sadly.

He walked into his bedroom and stuffed his clothes into two suitcases. Exactly what happened to Jacky? It wasn't a burglary, because nothing was missing. It didn't seem likely the cops did it, either. The name Tom Cooper waltzed slowly through Soyko's noxious, if sparse, mind. So did the term "payback." The attack on Ronnie Taggert had to be avenged, so Cooper must have hired a couple of goons to turn Jacky out like that. Easy enough to find out. Go to his office in the morning and don't leave until you get some answers.

Forget Doug Shelton's money and that Moffatt broad, Soyko thought. He could feel pain and uncertainty sprouting around him. Time to take the two actions that always brought him relief: he had to lash out and then he had to split. This McLean beating had turned into one monumentally bad idea. He could see that now. Also taking Ronnie on brought too much heat, and maybe cost Jacky his life. Tomorrow, dealing with Cooper, that had to be done.

Then he would leave town.

He went back to the living room. When he reached in and cleaned out Jacky's wallet he noticed a foul odor. Jacky must have soiled himself as he died. He wondered how many guys Cooper had hired. Tiny Fred, maybe. He'd find out tomorrow. When he got Jacky's money, he left without saying a word. If Leo Soyko knew one thing for absolute certain, it was that there was no point in talking to a dead man.

He and Jacky lived in a wood-stained condo project, strictly low-end. It was the kind of prefab place where, when the real estate market goes sour like it did in the early eighties, fore-closure notices sprout on the windows like Christmas wreaths. Their unit opened directly into an outside stairwell that emptied into the parking lot.

Soyko had just gotten down one flight of stairs when the

woman from the unit below came staggering out. She was pushing fifty, which seemed ancient to him, and usually she was either asleep or in the process of drinking herself to sleep. She
smelled like the Dumpsters out back and slurred her words into
barely recognizable, choppy strings of syllables. And, clearly, she
was hot for the two men who lived above her. Just my luck, Leo
thought.

"How we tonight?" she asked. "Taking a little trip, are we?"

"*We* ain't doing nothing, you and me." He set his bags down
and looked at her.

She made a bitter face and drew her head back. "Why you
gotta talk to me like that? All the time. And where's your
roomie?"

"He's asleep."

"Your other friend leave? Where is he?"

Soyko perked up. "What friend is that?"

"The big guy in the Buick."

"Who you talking about? I was gone for a while."

The drunk, he never did know her name, could see that she
had his interest, so she played it to the hilt. "Maybe you could
come in and we can talk about it."

He didn't have the time or the patience for that. Even if he
had, the idea made him moderately sick. Instead, he reached out
with a gnarled right hand and grabbed her by the throat. Then
he squeezed hard. Her eyes widened in pain and terror and she
let out a thunderous, involuntary belch.

"Maybe not," he said. "Maybe I don't have time for your crap.
Now, what big guy you talking about?"

"Yuh, yech," escaped from her mouth.

He loosened his grip slightly. He noticed a series of dried
brown stains on the front of her flowered bathrobe, and for a
second he felt like gagging. "What did this big guy look like?"
He loosened his grip even further.

"Good-looking. Late thirties maybe." Her voice was tiny.
"Brown hair combed back some. Shoulders a mile wide."

He let the woman go. Then he thought of that muscle-head

boyfriend of Moffatt's. Streeter was the name Cooper mentioned. The bounty hunter who was with her that day at Cooper's. Against Soyko's advice, Jacky had made a bunch of hang-up calls to him last week. The guy was supposed to be tight with McLean, Cooper said. Had to be this Streeter that did Jacky, Soyko concluded.

"What kind of shit is this?" The drunk was rubbing her throat, which was turning red and felt like she'd swallowed a frozen tennis ball. "You're a regular asshole, you know that?"

"Relax. You'll live." Then, as an afterthought, "If you call what you do living."

He picked up his suitcases and headed toward the car. No need to squeeze Cooper about who did Jacky. It was that Streeter. To hell with Cooper. Soyko decided to follow Streeter for a while. Maybe he'd get lucky and the big guy would lead him to Moffatt, so he could take care of both of them. A two-for-one payback. Jacky deserved that much.

By the time he drove out of the lot, he was in a much better mood.

The drunk just stood out in front of her door for a long time after Soyko left. Her breathing was starting to get normal again. "Bastard," she mumbled to no one. She was glad she hadn't told Soyko about the other guy that went up there, before the big guy. That first visitor was not so nice-looking. He looked sick and ugly. And he had the look of a bully, just like Soyko. He had knocked on her door by mistake, looking for the men upstairs. The guy had to be a cop. Even a drunk could see that. She stood outside her door seething. Then she went inside and made a phone call, to 911.

21

Streeter was never much for breakfast. Particularly the cooked, restaurant kind. So he just ordered a large milk and looked out onto the half-full parking lot of Rudy's Ranch Buffet, the diner where he was to meet Ronnie in about ten minutes. The name notwithstanding, Rudy's was about as country as a subway. It was generic corporate schlock, with the grimly sterile atmosphere of a school cafeteria and Dwight Yokum softly piped in. Streeter figured they named it Ranch Buffet to sucker people into thinking they'd get a huge farm meal and then maybe not notice the glorified airplane food they were actually served.

Rudy's was located in the hideous maze of culs-de-sac, shoppettes, and rambling streets with names like Briarwood Lane in Littleton, a far-south Denver suburb. With Ronnie staying at a trucker's motel out in rural Douglas County, about five miles farther south, she suggested Rudy's to Streeter because it was roughly halfway between her and the church. Also because Soyko would never think of looking for her there.

"Here's your milk," the waitress said, stating the obvious as she stood over his booth.

"Do you have a nonsmoking section somewhere?" Streeter had just noticed the swirl of cigarette smoke around him.

"Sure." The waitress clearly was bored. "Over there. Just sit anywhere you want." She threw her head listlessly toward a far wall and walked away.

Streeter worked his way into a booth on the back wall. He could no longer see the parking lot but now had a clear view of the entire restaurant and would be better able to see Ronnie come through the door. He still had a few minutes before she was set to arrive, so he sipped his milk and patiently looked around the room.

As Ronnie drove north toward Rudy's, she thought how all her plans of settling down with Cooper in Denver and leading a "normal" life with the attorney were dead. When she escaped Soyko on Monday, she'd headed south and checked into the motel. She finally called Cooper about midnight and told him what happened. The little worm uttered a few cursory words of concern and then went into a selfish tirade about her not caring about him.

"Did it ever occur to you, Rhonda, that I should have been apprised of this situation?" he'd sputtered indignantly into the phone. She could almost picture the wad of spit forming at each side of his mouth as he worked up his usual head of self-absorbed fear. "All this time with those guys running around out there. It's just fortunate I'm still in one piece. No thanks to you. What if they had come after me?"

"You lousy chicken shit," she'd screamed back. "I almost get killed and all you think about is what *might* have happened to you. How typical."

She wouldn't tell him where she was. Instead, they decided to meet in a couple of days at a motel just outside of Colorado Springs and leave for Mexico together. They'd get their hands on as much cash as they could before then. Most of that would come from Cooper selling his 'Vette and closing his bank accounts, with another portion from Ronnie taking out "ready cash" from their joint safe-deposit box.

But the more she thought about it the less thrilled she was. His reaction to her attack and his general inability to protect her made Ronnie reluctant to stay with the man. He wouldn't have that much money, and his earning power as an attorney probably was shot. And let's face it, she reasoned, his practical judgment grossly sucks. Look at how he misread that situation with Romp and Soyko. So she picked up just over twenty thousand dollars from their box. Now she had the Tercel, a fair amount of cash, plastic credit, and most of her clothes, which she'd retrieved from her apartment. The police would be after her as a witness against Cooper, and she could be facing charges. Leaving town definitely was the best move. By herself. Before then she wanted to straighten out a few things, and Streeter might help. He had a confidence that drew her to him. Not really showy, but a nice hint of cockiness. And he seemed trustworthy.

The bounty hunter was about half done with his milk when Ronnie came through Rudy's front door.

"I'm glad you made it," Ronnie said as she approached his booth.

"I said I'd be here." He liked the pale-pink summer sweater she had on. Short sleeves, like something a bratty teenage girl would have worn in a 1950s movie. "Eight-thirty Wednesday at Rudy's. You hungry?"

"I don't usually eat before noon. Coffee'll be fine."

The waitress came and took her order and they sat in silence until it came. Streeter spoke first. "This can't be easy on you. Are you all right?"

She nodded and stared directly at him. "You know the name Leo Soyko?"

"Cooper's flunky? I've heard rumors."

"Jacky Romp. You ever hear of him?"

Streeter flashed on Jacky's body on the couch. "Yeah. He's dead. Have you seen the morning papers?"

Ronnie looked stunned. "How? Yesterday?"

"The *Post* said his body was found about midnight at his apartment. Shot twice in the head at close range."

Ronnie didn't appear to be experiencing anything close to grief. "Maybe there is a God." She smiled quickly. "He and Soyko were the two boners that attacked me Monday night. If Romp had his way I'd be dead. Do they have any idea at all who did it?"

"No arrests, according to the paper. Do you think Soyko might have killed him?"

"I can't imagine why."

"Did they have any other enemies?"

Ronnie smiled and her head jerked in a knowing nod. "Only anyone who ever met either of them. But I can't think of anyone in particular. Tell me, Mr. Bounty Hunter, what's your hunch?"

Streeter's eyebrows shot up and he took a sip of his milk. "I have someone in mind but I doubt if you know him. Did Cooper have any friends or associates in the Denver Police Department?"

"Honey, you're looking at all the friends Thomas Cooper has in the world."

Again there was a brief silence.

"So, Ronnie," he said deliberately. "Why'd you call this meeting?"

"A couple of reasons. I'm leaving town soon and I hoped you could help me handle a little unfinished business. This news about Jacky takes care of part of it. Soyko's another part. Those two were scum and I'd like to see them both buried. Soyko's looking for that money Doug Shelton supposedly left behind. Cooper's looking, too, but I have a feeling he's out of the picture from now on. If you and that Story Moffatt chick are still going after it, you better be careful. I don't suppose you'd do me one little favor and shoot Soyko?"

Streeter could see she wasn't entirely joking. "You don't suppose right."

"Just a thought. If you won't shoot him, maybe you can help put him away. He killed a witness in a murder case up in Commerce City named Grundy Dopps. Tell the police that. Tell them Cooper paid Soyko to try and get Dopps out of town and then

Soyko decided to kill him instead. I've been involved with Tom
Cooper for more than three years now and I know that whole
bunch of jerks. I'm finished with all of them, but I'd hate to see
Soyko get Doug's money. The thought of Leo Soyko getting any
reward out of this makes me sick."

"Me, too."

"I'll bet 'you, too.' If I was a gambler I'd say you're the kind
of guy who doesn't like to lose."

"Who does?"

"Right. Anyhow, I want to tell you what I know before I leave
town. What you do with it is up to you."

"I'm listening." Streeter leaned forward.

"If it was me still looking for that money, I'd head over to
wherever they're keeping what's left of Doug's Porsche. I used
to date a guy who works at an import garage on South Downing.
I ran into Bobby not too long ago and we went out for a few
beers. As it turns out, he'd worked on Doug's car a couple years
ago. Bobby told me it was customized special somehow."

"I thought the insurance people and Story did that."

"They might have, but Bobby led me to believe the car was
very special. He was vague about it, but my instincts say check
out the car."

Streeter nodded. "I was going to do that anyhow. But if my
hunch is right, I don't think what Doug left could be stored in
any car."

"Do what you want, Streeter. Just so you beat Soyko on this.
Another thing. There was some cop that busted Doug on his last
coke deal. I can't remember the guy's name anymore, but Doug
was terrified of him. He beat almost the entire shit out of Doug
right after the arrest. You ever come across the cop?"

Streeter nodded. "I've talked to him once." He paused briefly.
"I think he might of had something to do with Jacky's situation."

"Then he can't be all bad," Ronnie said quickly. "I just wanted
to warn you about him. Another hunch of mine is that this cop's
looking for Doug's money, too. Doug said he was a real macho

pig. Of course, so's everyone involved in this mess. Except for Tom Cooper. He isn't quite that evolved. He's what I'd call a macho pig wannabe. It's what he strives for."

"Yeah? Is that how he got hooked up with Soyko and Romp?"

"You got that right. Tom has this incredibly screwed-up notion of what's manly and cool. He's pretty insecure, and when he saw Soyko he saw a lot of the things he wanted to be. Lean, tough, decisive, always able to back up the talk with action. Tom could talk the talk but he could never walk the walk. Anyhow, between the cop on Doug's case and Soyko, this ain't going to be fun from now on."

"Like it's been a regular party up to now?"

"True."

"Look, Ronnie, I appreciate all this, but if you really want to stop these guys, why don't you go to the police?"

She rolled her eyes wildly and sat back in the booth. "I tried that once and it almost got me killed."

"How?"

"I blew the whistle on Soyko and Romp for beating up the lawyer. McLean. They damned near killed me for it."

"Are you sure they were the ones who went after Bill?"

Ronnie nodded. "For sure. You had some doubts?"

"Not really." He pulled out one of Frank's business cards and a pen and began writing on the blank backside. "Listen, Ronnie, here's the name of a cop. A friend of mine. Carey. A detective. Give him a call before you leave town and tell him what you know. Tell him about this conversation and that you know me. You can trust Carey." He finished writing and handed it to her. "At least think about it, okay?"

She took the card and studied both sides. "All right."

"Someone's been giving me and Story problems lately," he continued. "A few shots were fired at my house, and her car got vandalized. Could that have been Soyko and Romp?"

Ronnie frowned and thought for a few seconds. "Not that I know of. Moffatt mentioned something like that at the meeting with Tom and I asked him about it later. He didn't know what the hell she was talking about."

He nodded. That meant Kovacs did it.

Then her voice softened and she smiled. "So. Are you and this Moffatt an item, Streeter?"

"An item? No. I work for her. Why?"

"Just curious. Dougy used to talk about her a little. She sounds like a real live wire. Doug said she was so cold he thought maybe she had Freon sprayed all over her libido. You ever get that feeling about her?"

"I never gave it much thought," he said, hoping he sounded convincing. "Story can come across as somewhat shy of blood, and there's times I'd like to wring her neck. But Freon sprayed in that area sounds a little overstated." Ronnie was as catty about Story as the ad woman had sounded about *her*. "What difference is it to you whether she and I are an item or what's sprayed where on her?"

"I'm just curious, Streeter. I think you're an interesting man." She studied him with a scant smile on her face. "You're probably better than she deserves. That's all I was thinking."

There was a genuine sincerity to the remark that touched him. "Thanks. Listen, Ronnie, if I find whatever Doug left behind, maybe I can cut you in on a slice of it. For your help. In the meantime, you be careful, and think about calling Carey. He'll level with you, and we both know Soyko and Cooper belong in prison. Plus, that way maybe you could clear yourself from any trouble with the police."

"I might just do that. I'm curious. How are you going to find me to give me my 'slice'?"

"Where are you headed?"

"I haven't given it much thought. Maybe I'll find you some day and you can tell me how it all turned out."

22

"You look a little peaked there, kid." Detective Bob Carey was pouring cream into his coffee at the Newsstand Cafe, a coffee/magazine shop on 6th Avenue, near the governor's mansion. He stared hard into Streeter's eyes while stirring his coffee. "You wouldn't happen to know anything about this peckerhead Jacky Romp, would you?"

As he stood there, Streeter felt his own coffee spilling on his hand, so he set it down. Then he pulled up a tall stool next to Carey at the long counter and sat down. It was sunny outside, and the post-lunch-hour traffic was heavy heading east on the one-way 6th Avenue.

"Not really. That's why I called you."

The detective nodded and said, "That's very good, because, like I told you, a person can get into a lot of trouble dancing around with people like attorney Thomas Cooper and his friends."

"It would seem so. Look, I'm just curious because of Bill and all. I met Cooper once. I don't really know any of the rest of them."

Streeter liked and trusted Carey, but he was a cop. No way he wanted any cop knowing he had been at Soyko's apartment the night before. Not yet, anyway. He also wondered if Ronnie Taggert would call Carey. That question was answered before he could settle into his seat.

"It's starting to look as though the whole situation is taking care of itself," Carey said. "These guys are like a bunch of inbred rats turning on each other. The rumble downtown is that Soyko must have flipped out yesterday, judging by the way they found Romp. Some woman who lived below them called in and said she saw Soyko leave about eleven last night and he was really steamed up. Everybody's out looking for Soyko today. I'm sure they'll get him pretty soon.

"It seems for sure these characters were in on the McLean thing and some other pretty heavy garbage. Over the weekend, one of the guys investigating McLean got a call from a lady saying Soyko and Romp did everything but shoot JFK. We sent someone out to talk to those two and, before you know it, Cooper's secretary nearly gets attacked by two guys exactly matching the descriptions of his two investigators. A woman named Ronnie Taggert. We figure she must have been the one who made the call.

"Then, just before lunch today, none other than Ms. Taggert herself—who's disappeared since her assault—calls me and asks if we can sit down and have a talk in the not-too-distant future. Seems there's this absolutely splendid bounty hunter exactly matching *your* description who gave her my name and number. She's got all sorts of information for me about this entire mess. I'm meeting her tomorrow morning—that is, assuming she's not dead or out of the state by then. I tried to get it sooner, but she wants to wait another day for some reason of her own. So now Romp's dead and his partner and Cooper should be in custody before long. With Ms. Taggert's help, we should be able to nail these two pricks to the wall and wrap up a whole lotta stuff."

Streeter smiled when he thought about Ronnie. "Listen to that lady, Robert. I had a good feeling about her from the time I met her at Cooper's. She's all right. One tough ball breaker, but my read is that she's honest. Do you really think Soyko turned on

Romp? And why would Cooper want to hurt Ronnie? Those two were dating. Or whatever it is that people like Cooper do."

"We got to sort all that out. The first thing we want to do is bring everybody in for questioning, especially Cooper. He had to be in the middle of all of it, but we're not sure how he fits. I heard he took that Ronnie thing pretty hard, so maybe that was just the two other guys playing around on their own.

"Anyhow, when we sent some people out to their apartment last night, we find old Jacky Romp laying on the carpet looking like he went bungee jumping off a fifty-foot bridge with a sixty-foot cord. Half his head was blown away. The woman who lives below them said she heard the two men fighting shortly before eleven and then Soyko went charging out like the place was on fire. We went through the El Camino that belonged to Romp and found a bat that they traced to McLean's beating. They got an arrest warrant for Soyko for assault on McLean and homicide for his friend. Or should I say ex-friend. Trouble is, no one knows what he's driving, and he could be halfway to Mexico or Canada or someplace like that by now. Do you think this fits in with what you're doing with Shelton's widow?"

"Hard to tell." Streeter didn't want to share much with Carey. "Who knows about that?"

Carey just looked at him for a few seconds. "I'd suggest that you lay low for a while. Just go back to chasing your bail jumpers until we sort out all the crap on this shooting and until we get Soyko and Cooper." Carey drained his coffee. "Will you do that simple thing for me?"

"I'll certainly give it some thought. Will you keep me posted on everything from your end of it?"

Carey grinned. "I'll certainly give it some thought."

When he left the Newsstand, Streeter got into his Buick and grabbed his cellular phone to call Story. He had resisted buying one for a long time, but finally he decided that since he spent so much time in his car he should have one. To someone in his line of work a car is like a portable office. Maps, phone, handcuffs, gun, camera, spare film, a change of clothes, and assorted surveillance and work tools, even a cup to urinate in, Streeter's Buick had them all.

He planned to spend the rest of the afternoon interviewing people on the list Story had given him. It would take his mind off Soyko. Let the cops deal with him from now on. When he got her on the phone, Story wanted to hear all about the unraveling of Cooper's empire. He told her most of what was happening, but not about his being at Romp's apartment or his meeting with Ronnie.

"It looks like things are coming together pretty well for us," she told him. "Your friend Bill's out of trouble, and Cooper and his crew should be way out of the picture before long. If that cop you think shot at your church leaves us alone for a while, that will free us up to work on Doug."

She had a way of saying "us" that always let him know she meant him.

"I'll let you know if *we* find anything," he said evenly. Then he hung up without saying goodbye.

He went to the church to talk to Frank and see if he had any messages. The bondsman was out, and there was nothing on the voice mail. Streeter glanced at the mail on Frank's desk. There always seemed to be a stack of junk solicitations and catalogues. One eight-and-a-half-by-eleven, two-color brochure caught his eye. It looked familiar. It was from the Executive Protectors Inc., the same company whose flyer was in Doug's files. Streeter leafed through it, wondering what Shelton wanted from the company. In the middle of page eight he found the answer. Not only did he find what Doug had bought from the Protectors, but if he was right, Streeter was one big step closer to finding whatever was hidden.

What he saw on page eight was called "The Movable Bank," a fireproof, bulletproof, solid-steel strongbox. "Ideal for keeping the things you value close to you at all times," the ad copy gloated. A photograph at the bottom of the page showed the twelve-by-twelve-inch-square box being inserted under the back seat of a nondescript car.

"Fits easily under car seats, in car trunks, engine compartments, or a thousand other places. Also good for home and office security. Regularly $179.95, now only $159.95. Locks extra."

Streeter reread the ad copy several times. He studied the picture, the box designed for small spaces in a car or truck. Story was adamant on how fussy Doug was about his Porsche: he wouldn't even let people in the back seat. That was probably where he'd kept the strongbox. Ronnie's mechanic friend said the car was customized, and this must have been what he meant.

And what was the common denominator in all his trips to get money and drugs, both in Boulder and Denver? The Porsche. A 1988 red 928. A nice car, but not valuable enough to deserve all the attention he gave it. Doug never was without cash or cocaine, because he never went anywhere without his car and the strongbox. Streeter had just been thinking about what a portable office his own car was. Doug's car was a portable safe and merchandise showroom: a drug dealer's portable office. Story said they'd looked through the car but then had given up because so much of it was burned or demolished. This "Movable Bank" could survive that. For the past few days, Streeter had been thinking that Doug had left valuable artwork hidden. Obviously, you can't store much of that in the back of a Porsche. So it must be money or something like money that he'd left behind when he headed off to the great unknown.

He picked up the phone and dialed Story's office number. "I'm coming over," he said. "I know where Doug left his money."

There was a long silence on her end of the phone. Finally, "Are you sure?" He couldn't decide if she sounded frightened or threatening.

"I'm not positive, but it'll be easy enough to find out. I want to move on this—now. I mean right now. I'm coming over."

"Please do."

With that, he hung up, grabbed the brochure, and went to his car. When he got there he looked inside his trunk to make sure he had all his tools, especially his crowbar. He slammed the trunk shut and got in the driver's seat. As he pulled away from the curb, he was driving much faster than usual. At Broadway, he turned south and zipped toward Capitol Hill.

Soyko wondered what all the hurry was about as he pulled out into traffic, about a block behind Streeter. The bounty hunter had been driving so slow and cautious all day. And what was so interesting in the trunk?

23

Story was pacing—marching, actually—in the downstairs foyer of her office building when Streeter arrived. She was wearing shorts, a plain white blouse, and flats. More casual than he had ever seen, but there was nothing casual about her demeanor. Her shoulders were rigid, her frown deep, like her squash pose that day at the gym. She'd had time to work up a good head of skepticism while he drove over. Story Moffatt was not the kind of woman who suffered false hopes or fools easily. Her pinched-up attitude instantly put him off.

"You know, Story, this is supposed to be good news," he said as he walked slowly toward her.

"Let's go upstairs and talk." Her voice was low and she didn't smile.

"Hello to you, too." He followed her up the stairs, the Executive Protectors brochure rolled up in his hand like a club.

When they got to her office, she nodded for him to go in and then told her secretary they were not to be disturbed. That finished, she came inside and closed the door. Streeter was standing in the middle of the room, watching her closely.

"Do you know for sure, Streeter?" There was a whiff of pleading in her voice. "I don't mean to act like a bitch, but I don't think I could stand it if you're wrong. Not after all that we've been through with this thing."

He nodded, his eyes nailed to hers. "It's the car. Doug left whatever we're looking for in his car." He held up his hand, palm toward her, as she grimaced. "I know you said you looked through part of it and that it was destroyed and all. But it's in there. Look at this."

He opened the brochure and held it out for her. She stared at it but wouldn't touch it.

"Does this look familiar?" he asked.

"I . . . Should it?" The bitchy edge returned.

"Read the name."

Story looked back to the catalogue and studied it. Her frown deepened.

"It's that booklet from Doug's stuff. I didn't know you took it with you."

"I didn't. Frank got this in the mail. He gets this kind of flyer all the time. We never read them very closely. I've never had much need for all these James Bond gadgets. But when I saw this today, and read the name of the company, the same one as Doug's flyer, I looked through every page to find out what he wanted from these guys."

He turned the booklet back to face him and stared at it for a moment. Then he flipped it open and went to page eight.

"I thought he was after the phone-sweeping equipment," he told her. "You know, home-security garbage, something like that. But this is what Doug wanted. I'll bet my life on it."

He turned the book around and gave it to her. This time she took it and read the open pages closely. Suddenly her head shot up and she looked at him.

"Fireproof. That's it, Streeter. We didn't look inside the Porsche because everything was burned. I figured that anything inside had to have been destroyed. But this"—she looked back at page eight—"this would take care of a fire. If he got one of these boxes it's in that precious back seat. No wonder he was so touchy about letting people back there. We have to get to that car."

"No kidding. Plus, I got some information this morning that Doug customized the damned thing. Almost from the start, I was thinking that if he left anything it was probably not cash. I assumed he invested in something like artwork or cars. Things that you can buy and they'll appreciate with time and then you can sell them without Uncle Sam finding out. But if this box is our answer, we're probably looking at cash. Do you know where the Porsche is kept?"

"When I saw it, they were keeping it at the police impound. They told me it would be there for a few days and then they'd ship it off to a junkyard. Oh, God, Streeter. You don't suppose they would have crushed it? We'll never get anything out of it."

"Relax, Story. Was there anything left intact? Any parts to salvage?"

"The back end was okay, I guess."

"Then they probably kept it for parts. Give me the phone book and I'll call the police yard to find out where they took it."

Streeter had dealt with the Denver police-impound people dozens of times in the past. Working for various lawyers suing insurance companies, he'd had to take photos of cars after they'd been in accidents. Luckily, the police had an excellent system of storing and disposing of vehicles, so if Doug's Porsche hadn't been crushed, the bounty hunter didn't anticipate any trouble finding it.

Story went behind her desk, fished out a phone book from her credenza, and handed it to him. He looked up the number for the police-impound lot and called. The clerk told him that all the cars shipped out last year would have gone to one of two lots. She gave the names and telephone numbers of both. Streeter hit paydirt at the second one, All-American Auto Salvage, just north of I-70 and northwest of the old Stapleton International Airport. That part of town is a run-down patchwork of tool shops, rusty salvage yards, ratty open fields, and an occasional convenience store or saloon.

"How late are you open?" he asked the man at All-American, who verified they had the Porsche. "Seven? We'll be out there before then. As a matter of fact, we're heading up now. What's that? Row thirty, slot twelve? Thanks. No, we're just going to take some pictures for the insurance claim. That's right."

When he hung up, Story asked, "What was all that about insurance-claim pictures?"

"This guy owns the car now. If I told them what we're after, he'd have it pulled apart by the time we got downstairs. This way, he'll leave us alone. Junkyard owners are used to people like me taking pictures of cars. He won't even watch us."

They had to fight rush-hour traffic, so they didn't make it to All-American until just before six. The sun was still high in the early-summer sky, and the view of Denver to the south and the Rockies to the west was spectacular, even if their immediate surroundings were not. The lot owner, an obese man with an apparent bathing dysfunction, steered them toward the Porsche.

"See that shed by those trucks there?" he asked without getting up from a filthy couch next to the office. "Car you want'll be right up next to it. How long you think you'll be?"

"Half hour, tops," Streeter answered.

The owner just nodded. Streeter kept his eye on the shabby wooden shed as he drove toward it. When they got into the main aisle, along the back row, Story suddenly got excited and jabbed an index finger toward the windshield.

"There it is. That black thing over there. You can see the red toward the back, where it wasn't burned."

Streeter pulled off to one side, so his Buick would sit between the Porsche and the office. The Porsche's burned front tires were curled up under the body like a begging dog's paws. All its windows were broken and he could see that the door on the passenger's side was badly buckled. There was a layer of hard black soot over everything but several feet in the rear. The car looked like it had been dipped in licorice. Streeter got out of his Buick and went to the trunk. He pulled out his camera and handed it to Story, who was beside him.

"Keep an eye on the office. If that tub of lard comes out here, pretend you're taking pictures."

He put on some work gloves and grabbed the crowbar. Then he walked to the driver's side. The Porsche was nestled between an old Celica on that side and the wooden shed on the other. Streeter had to step carefully over broken glass that was scattered in the aisle.

"I'll start here. It looks easier to get into, and he might have been more likely to put the box right behind him."

The driver's door was buckled almost as badly as the passenger's, but it was cracked open a few inches near the top. Streeter grabbed the edge firmly and gave it a hard pull. It groaned open. Inside, it still smelled freshly burned in the warm air. When he bent in, he could see why no one would bother looking too closely. The seats were charred stretches of soot, and it was hard to tell where anything started or stopped. He came back out and looked at Story.

"Nothing destroys like fire," he said. "I'm going to just start pulling everything apart and see what I find."

She walked over next to him and looked inside the car. "Can you imagine dying in there?"

Streeter frowned and then bent back inside. He knew that his chinos would be ruined by the soot. He pushed the front seat forward and kneeled in, his knee resting on the transmission hump in the back. The car was a liftback, and he had to push the seat back upright. Then he took the straight end of the crowbar and poked around the front edge of the back seat. Horizontally, at about the point it touched the passengers' calves, there was a slight lip where the top of the seat came over. He slipped the crowbar under that and lifted. The seat came up, and he could see that there was nothing but springs under it. He lifted it higher, so that the crack ran partially to the seat on the other side of the transmission hump. He poked around under that side, and the crowbar clanked into something solid. No springs under there. He got out and walked around the car to where Story was waiting.

"I think it's on the other side," he said.

"Just hurry."

"Why? This isn't going anywhere."

He walked out onto the main aisle, behind the Porsche, and then around to the passenger's side, next to the shed. This time he had to use the crowbar to coax the door open. He bent inside. Then he put the claw of the crowbar under the seat opening he had created and gave a hard pull back. That forced the opening to smile all the way to the door and let him see the dusty, but highly functional, Portable Bank under the seat.

"Yes sir," he said quietly to himself. Now he could feel the beads of sweat rolling freely down his forehead. With the crowbar he reached under the seat and tapped the box. Then he leaned back and looked at Story. "I knew it was here."

She bent into the car like she was going to confession. "Bring it out."

Streeter bent down again and jiggled the strongbox. It was in tight, maybe even welded down. Then he looked more closely and he couldn't believe what he saw. There was a single eyehole-and-flap arrangement for a padlock, but no lock. Doug must have thought just having the box hidden like that was security enough.

"No need to. It's not locked."

"You're kidding. Open it."

Streeter slipped his gloves off and flipped the box top up. He looked inside and was mildly disappointed that it wasn't even full. On top was an eight-and-a-half-by-eleven manila envelope. He picked it up, squeezed it, and handed it to Story. It felt like money inside, but unless the bills all were thousands, there couldn't have been too much. Under the envelope were two other items. One was a plastic baggie with what appeared to be a chunk of white powder. Streeter quickly estimated it to be something just over ten ounces of cocaine. He left it there.

"There's a few ounces of coke in here, too," he said without looking up.

"Anything else?" Her voice was still expectant.

"There's another envelope. A smaller one." He picked it up as he spoke. It was white and unsealed. Before he could look inside, Story jabbed her hand back into the car, her palm up.

"That would be mine." Her voice left little doubt that she meant it.

Streeter looked up at her and then back down at the envelope. He handed it to her without a word. As he sifted through the strongbox one more time, he lifted out the cocaine. He got out of the car, stood up, tossed the baggie into the air a few inches, caught it, and studied it.

"You can keep that if you want," Story said as she stuffed the smaller envelope into her purse, with the larger, money envelope jammed in her armpit. She was looking at her purse as she spoke. "We'll call it a tip."

Streeter tossed the baggie in the air one more time and then bent back into the car. He replaced it in the box, shut it, and looked around. He pulled the seat over the box again. When he was done, he got out and brushed himself off.

"Let's go before the owner comes out."

A strange sadness fell over both of them. Here they were, standing in the middle of a wretched junkyard with these packets of drugs and paper. Bill McLean was in the hospital, Ronnie Taggert almost killed. Doug Shelton and Shannon Mays had died, probably trashed out on the cocaine from the back seat. The sun moved closer to the mountains and the air was still. Nothing seemed very important.

"Hardly appears to be worth it, does it?" he asked.

"It'll be more worthwhile when we find out what's inside. Don't you want to know how much money there is?" she asked as she pulled the big envelope out of her armpit. "A third of it's yours."

Streeter kicked the car door shut. "You can tell me on the way back to town. All I really want now is a shower."

Story turned and moved first. She walked with her head down. When she got to the back end of the car, she turned right, toward the Buick, and looked up. Streeter had the nagging feeling he was forgetting something, so he took one more look inside the car, through the window. Then he walked out to where Story had gone. He had just turned into the main aisle when he heard her scream. He looked first at her and then toward his car, the direction of whatever scared her.

There, leaning with his butt up on the trunk of the Buick and his legs crossed casually in front of him, was Leo Soyko. His face shivered in brutality but his voice was under control.

"Old Ronnie Taggert was right, after all," he said. "She told me to check out the car." Then he straightened up and gracefully shook the lethal belt buckle loose from his pants. The blade looked almost black in his shadow. He looked at Story as he moved toward her. "I believe you got something of mine there, darlin'. I'd strongly suggest you hand it over."

She was frozen, not sure who the man with the knife was but vaguely recalling his face from somewhere. The knife and his bloodshot eyes let her know she could easily lose everything.

"Let's have it, little lady." Soyko took another step.

"Streeter," Story yelled as she looked back for him over her shoulder.

The bounty hunter had been slowly coming forward as Soyko spoke. He was now at the back edge of the Porsche, just behind her, in the main aisle. "Back up, Story. Just back up." Then he directed his voice sharply at Soyko. "And you, hold it right there."

His words caused Soyko to stop and look at the man who spoke them. With that hesitation, Streeter repeated his instructions. "Back up, Story."

She started moving automatically heading in the direction of his voice. When she got to him, he reached out and grabbed her shoulder, gently but firmly. He pulled her back a few steps so she was behind him and he was between Soyko and her. All the while he kept steady eye contact with the man holding the knife.

"Just keep on going, Story. Get out of here." His voice stayed even; then suddenly he yelled to Soyko, "And you stay put!"

"I been waiting for this all day, shithead," Soyko responded. "I owe you big-time for Jacky. Getting whatever you found is gonna be a nice bonus. That and cutting up you and the lady." He was advancing as he spoke and there were only a few feet between them by now.

The blade looked short but thick. Soyko's hands looked equally thick around the base of the knife, and his shoulders quivered in anticipation. A sick feeling came over Streeter as he remembered what he'd forgotten inside of the Porsche—the crowbar. He wished he had either it or the gun he kept under his car seat.

"I had nothing to do with Jacky. I was at your place for a minute last night but he was dead when I got there. I'm pretty sure it was a cop named Kovacs who did it."

"Oh, a cop. Definitely. They run around killing people all the time. The lady below us made you for the guy."

"She's full of crap. She made you for the guy when she called the cops. They're looking for you right now."

"The cops, huh? The same ones that killed Jacky, I suppose. Shut up."

Soyko lashed out with the knife, shooting his right hand out at the bigger man like he was throwing a punch. Streeter quickly backpedaled and avoided the blade. Soyko lunged again and Streeter backpedaled again, the blade hitting only air. Trouble was, Streeter was stepping back into the space between the Porsche and the shed. It was a narrow space with no exit. Soyko could keep coming until there was no more room to back up. Streeter took a quick half-step forward to see if his attacker would give any ground. He didn't budge.

"Nowhere to run?"

At that Soyko made two more quick swipes with the blade. Both times Streeter had to give ground, forcing him closer to the back wall. He could hear Story yell something, but he couldn't make out the words.

He yelled back, "Get out of here. Get to the office."

Soyko straightened up, a smile crossing his face. "Saving the lady, huh? Now, that's sweet."

He then went back into his attack crouch, lifted the blade to shoulder level, growled, and moved forward. He intended this to be his last charge. It was.

Streeter saw it coming and, in the time it took Soyko to travel the last three feet, he turned slightly to his left, so he was facing the shed. As Soyko came, he deflected the blade hand by striking Soyko's wrist with his left forearm while, at the same time, grabbing him behind the head. He squeezed hard at a patch of hair and held Soyko upright for an instant. Then he turned the smaller man's head so that he was facing the shed from about two feet away.

He tried to ram Soyko's head into the shed to knock him unconscious. Instead, he rammed the head into the vacant cavity where a window used to be. All that was left was the jagged row of broken glass along the bottom of the ledge, which now smiled up like a row of uneven teeth. As Streeter shoved Soyko's head toward the building, his exposed neck was forced into the glass. The jagged edge cut through Soyko's throat like it was paper, and he died instantly. He died on his feet, leaning into the shed. Streeter held the head in place as Soyko gave one monumental kick back with both legs. When his feet again hit the ground, his whole body slumped.

Panting furiously, Streeter let go and took a step back. Out of the corner of his eye he could see Story walking toward him. She was pale and her mouth formed a gaping circle. Still, her voice was calm.

"Is he dead?"

Streeter kept staring at Soyko, breathing hard, his pulse racing. "No. I think he's just resting." Then he backed up and looked squarely at her. "Of course he's dead."

"Who the hell is that?" She was bent forward, and her breath seemed labored. "I've seen him before."

"His name is Leo Soyko. Cooper's muscle."

"His what?"

"His enforcer. He's one of the guys who beat up McLean for Cooper. He's also one of the guys who tried to attack Ronnie Taggert, Cooper's girl. He's killed people, too. The cops are looking for him right now."

Story stared at him, still breathing through her mouth. "I didn't know about this Ronnie thing. Why didn't you tell me?"

Streeter walked out from between the car and the shed. He was still shaking but starting to calm down. He looked at his pants and saw a trace of Soyko's blood painted on the side like a design. "I didn't have all the details until this morning."

"How did he find us?"

"I don't have a clue."

They were standing close now. Streeter could hear someone yell from the front of the lot. He looked toward the sound and saw the enormous lot-owner walking toward them. Actually, the guy looked like he was trying to run, but it came off absurdly slow and he appeared to be quivering as he moved.

"Who is Jacky and what did Kovacs do to him?" Story pressed on, much of her composure regained.

Streeter looked at her again. "It seems that Kovacs is getting more violent. Look, we better go call the police. I'll fill you in later."

"I've got my cellular in my purse."

As she called 911, Streeter went back for another look at Soyko. He appeared almost comical now, bent over the shed window, his body draped limply down the side. It was like he had been kneeling, looking inside, and he fell asleep. But there was nothing comical about the blood drooling down the side of the shed.

"They'll be here in a few minutes." Her voice brought him back. "What do we tell them about what we were doing?"

He thought for a minute. "Tell them we were going to take pictures and I started looking around inside and found the box."

"We're not giving them the money." She hugged her purse closer to her body.

"No need to. Hand them the coke and they'll be plenty happy."

That satisfied her. They could see the yard owner coming closer down the aisle, but they still couldn't make out what he was saying.

"Streeter, are you all right?"

"I'm not sure." His breath was getting back to normal, his thoughts were clearing. "I guess this had to be done. Like taking out the garbage."

The thick sadness they'd felt when they first found the money returned to both of them now, but much more pronounced this time.

24

"Jesus Christ, big guy. You must be eating your Wheaties." Sergeant Haney shook his head as the paramedics pulled the wilting body of Leo Soyko off the shed and placed it carefully on the gurney. "You just saved the taxpayers a ton of money. A trial, and then keeping that bug at Cañon City for the next hundred years or so, woulda cost a fortune."

Streeter said nothing as he watched them zip Soyko up in the body bag. He had had to defend himself, but he still felt a little sick watching the body being wheeled away. This should end the killings. Story was standing about twenty feet away talking to a young black uniformed officer. Streeter had difficulty making them out in the growing darkness. Haney crushed a cigarette with his shoe and squinted at the cocaine baggie in his hand. With a nod, he signaled to another uniformed officer. The officer walked over, took the baggie, and listened to the sergeant for a minute. He smiled at Haney like they were sharing a private joke and then he walked away with the cocaine.

Haney turned to Streeter again. "You sure that's all the flake you found in there?" His tone was more resigned than accusatory.

Streeter nodded. "I can tell you in all honesty that that's all the drugs I found in the car."

"The guy that runs this place is pretty pissed off at you for lying about what you were doing out here. He wants us to check out your car, to see if you found anything else. Says that whatever you found in the Porsche belongs to him and you should turn it over."

"You want to look in the Porsche, you don't need my permission. You want to check out my car, be my guest. And if you want to give that slob all the cocaine, that's entirely up to you."

Haney grinned and thought for a moment. Then he continued, "No need for that. You say that's all you found, then that's all you found."

Just then, the black officer and Story walked up to them. "All done with her, Sarge," he said.

"Give her a ride home," Haney responded.

"I came with Mr. Streeter. I'd prefer to go home with him." Story's voice was even, but she was anxious to leave.

"He's going downtown with us," Haney said without looking at her. "We'll need to get a statement from him, and that could take quite a while."

She nodded and looked at Streeter. He was standing with his shoulders slouched like he was tired. "I need to talk to you before I leave. Is that all right with you, Sergeant?"

"Fine by me." Haney was still looking at the shed.

Streeter walked her to the police patrol car. It was new and white, one of those nondescript, aerodynamic makes. It looked like a giant bullet in an unribbed condom. He hated its utter lack of style.

"You're not in any trouble, are you?" she asked.

"Probably not. They have to make out a report, is all."

"Give me a call when you get home tonight," she said. "I'll let you know how much money you have coming."

"There didn't seem to be that much cash in the envelope. I can't believe there's enough there to make all this killing worthwhile."

"Believe me, Streeter, I had no idea it was going to be this dangerous. But it'll be worth it. This cash is just the tip of the iceberg. There's a lot of money yet to be found, and now I think I know how to get it. I promised you a big payoff if we got what we're after. With what we found today, that payoff's getting very close. I know where the real money is."

"Something in that other envelope?"

"Exactly."

"Did you know all along that there were two parts to our little hunt?"

"Not really. I hope you believe me about this. I've leveled with you for the most part all along. I didn't tell you everything all the time but I didn't really lie to you." She reached out with her right hand and gently brushed at some soot that was smeared on his arm. "I know you must think I lack strong values. Or any values. But believe me, Streeter, I didn't want all the pain, and I never wanted to see you get hurt. I certainly never expected you'd have to do something like that." She nodded toward the shed.

"This gets more bizarre all the time," he said as he rubbed the bridge of his nose. "Knowing you has been . . . How would I put it? Let's just say it's been a very high-concept relationship, Story."

"We're close, believe me. If we're on to what I think we are, you'll feel better about all this. Just give me a call when you get home. Are you okay with not being there when I count out the money?"

"What choice do I have? These guys'll need me for a couple of hours and you'll be alone with the envelope. I doubt that you'll wait until I get there to open it. I have no choice but to trust you now. Just try not to be somewhat less than totally candid, okay?"

"I will. Call me later. We have to get together tomorrow. Good luck."

"I could be really late with them. If I am, I'll call first thing in the morning."

"Whatever you think is best." With that she turned and got into the police car. Streeter walked back to Haney.

"Nice-looking woman," the sergeant observed. "You two going at it?"

"Going at it? What the hell is that to you?"

"Just curious." Haney smiled. "Lighten up, for Chrissakes. By tomorrow morning, you'll be a local hero. You're the guy who took out the big bad man. Did it unarmed, no less. When word of this gets around town, you'll be handling more ass than a proctologist."

"Haney, I had no idea you're such a romantic."

25

By the time Max Herman had pulled in front of Cooper's building that afternoon, he'd reached a state of delirious equilibrium. He was toxic to the bone after drinking and pounding cocaine up his nose for three days straight. He hadn't slept for more than a couple of fitful hours since he started. Nor had he eaten much other than an occasional handful from the giant Fritos bag—large, dipping size—on his back seat. He hadn't bathed or brushed his teeth in nearly seventy hours. From time to time he went to the bathroom, and he smelled of queasy perspiration and warm malt liquor. He was wearing the same crumpled blue jeans, red-and-orange Hawaiian shirt, and sandals that he'd slipped into the previous Sunday afternoon. His hair was pulled back in a filthy ponytail, and a pair of expensive aviators hid two runny and narrowing eyes that looked more like fleshy little bags.

Still, despite the three days of ferocious abuse, he felt in control, coherent, and focused. He used to call it drinking himself sober during those vicious all-nighters with the bowling team, when he'd go right from the bars to his plumbing shop in the morning.

"I know what I got to do," he'd told one of his burned-out drug buddies as they sat drinking in a downtown bar earlier that afternoon. "No doubt about that. I got me a thirty-eight-caliber Smith Lady. Nice little five-shot number. That prick Cooper's got to pay. Ruined my life, is all he did."

Max's battered mind drifted back over the events of the last couple of weeks.

"I spent so much time and money paying this asshole that my business went down the tubes," he continued bitterly. "You know the drill. Fucking suppliers won't give me no more credit. No credit, no product. No product, obviously, no cash flow. Next thing you know, no girlfriend. Bitch left me Monday. Back to her husband, of all things.

"And then, to really make it worse, I find out that this shit-bucket attorney is holding out a truly fine plea bargain on me just so he can run up his bills. I can see doing a deuce or so in Cañon City if I can hop to it and get it over with. Maybe give up a couple customers to the cops and get just probation, for Chrissake. But thanks to this lawyer my case is all dragged out and costing me a ton. I figure I spent nearly fifty-five large just to get hosed by this cocksucker."

"It ain't fair," his friend said, shaking his head in painful wisdom. "I'd take care a his shit. Right quick."

"Fuckin' A. My life is crumbling around me and I got to watch this douche bag sitting comfortable in his cushy office with that little fuck-puppet secretary taking care of him. And using my money to foot the bill." Then he lowered his voice. "I bought me the Smith and some bullets from this jive ass at a spade joint up in Five Points. I plan to settle this guy's hash today."

Indeed, Max had scraped together what cash he could, loaded up a couple of grams of coke and his clothes into the ratty old Porsche, and made his decision. He would visit Cooper at home, shove the gun down his throat, rob the place, and then . . . And then what? Max had no qualms about stomping on the state's drug laws, and he even threatened people from time to time.

But he'd never physically hurt anyone and he certainly wasn't a killer.

He'd improvise, he told himself in the car. The word came to him from deep in his foggy stupor. He liked the sound of it. Make it up as you go along. That suited him just fine, and he smiled idiotically. Yes sir, hang loose and improvise. Once he had the little schmuck begging for his life, Max figured, he'd automatically know what to do. With that, he took one last pull from a warm can of Colt .45 Malt Liquor, tossed it on the floor in front of him, and belched triumphantly at his steering wheel. He shoved the gun into his belt, the handle resting between his sweating gut and his shirt.

It took him nearly a minute to find and properly activate the door handle. When he stepped out of the car, his left foot caught on the floorboard and he stumbled forward. He landed hard on the street on both palms and both knees, cutting the former and bruising the latter.

"Mothafucka!" he yelled at the pavement. He staggered to his feet, looked back at the car door, and kicked it shut. "Cock, suck-fuck!" he screamed at the offending equipment. Both palms ached as he brushed tiny bits of sharp gravel from each. "Motha," he mumbled in conclusion.

Denver Police Detectives Petronilo Padilla and Art Kovacs watched the pathetic show from their unmarked car across the street. They both laughed.

"Is he ever fucked up or what?" said Padilla, the driver, with the horrible complexion and the expensive clothes. "I'd like to have me a little talk with that guy. Bet he'd blow a point three on the Breathalyzer."

"I'll get his plate number," Kovacs said. "You keep an eye on where he goes. He takes off again, we'll call it in to Traffic. We ain't got no time now to nurse that moron, Petro."

"You ever see a Porsche with that much primer on it?" Padilla asked. "That tub of shit can't be worth as much as my Nissan."

"That sounds about right. Look, he's heading into our guy's building. What the fuck?"

"Maybe he's the man's driver." Padilla smiled at the thought. "Be some fun following those two coconuts around, huh?"

"Yeah. Some fun."

The two detectives had been sitting on Tom Cooper's remodeled loft building for the past six hours. The attorney had been holed up there for the past couple of hours, and Padilla and Kovacs were instructed to "ride his tail like bikini underwear" if he tried to leave. Sergeant Haney would be bringing the arrest warrants sometime around six or seven, and they would all go up to pop Cooper together. That was the official plan. It was now almost five, and Kovacs instantly didn't like the intrusion from the drunk.

Kovacs had had to scramble to get on the detail with Padilla. He had no idea Haney was so close to an arrest, and the news caused him to drastically change his plans. He called Cooper early that morning and told him part of his revised plan. He said the bust was going to hit tonight, so Cooper better move up his travel arrangements. The lawyer better have his cash and clothes all packed and ready that day. Then he instructed him to meet him in the basement garage of his building at precisely five.

Finally, Kovacs told Cooper, purely as a safety precaution, to be sure and bring his gun with him. That was where the plan shifted, and Mr. Cooper wouldn't find out about it until about four minutes past five, when the detective would put a couple slugs from his service revolver into the attorney's head. No way Artie Kovacs was going to let Thomas Cooper get hauled in and use what he knew about Jacky Romp and Doug Shelton against him as a plea-bargain chit. And he just couldn't take the chance that Cooper would successfully escape. Kovacs would wait until a couple of minutes before five, tell Padilla to go and check the upper floors, and then slip down to the garage to meet Cooper. With the lawyer bringing his own gun, it would be easy enough for Kovacs to claim the shooting was self-defense.

"Maybe you should hop up there and see if this goof's going after our guy," Kovacs suggested.

Padilla thought for a minute. "Naw. I mean, why? If they're going to leave together, we'll see it. They have to come out this way. And if he's going up there to cause the man some trouble, let him. This lawyer's one major-league asshole, from what Haney tells me."

As Kovacs looked off, he felt his stomach churn laboriously. A hot lick of heartburn bubbled up behind his sternum. He reached into his shirt pocket and pulled out another antacid. Placing it carefully on his tongue, he decided to wait a few minutes and then order Padilla to go check the floor. His whole plan still could easily unravel.

Thomas Hardy Cooper kept the front pages of both the Rocky Mountain *News* and the Denver *Post* with him that entire day. The headlines and stories about Jacky Romp were the best news he'd received in weeks. His world may have turned utterly sour, but he was still better off than that punk Jacky Romp. At least he was breathing, and as long as that continued, Cooper knew he had a shot at making things right. Now, he thought, if only Leo Soyko would meet the same fate, he'd be a happy man. The attorney assumed it was Kovacs who'd disposed of Romp. He further assumed that the brutal cop would now be looking for Soyko. Now, *that* would be a battle he'd pay to see.

Cooper had spent the morning closing out all three bank accounts, including the one for his corporation. Then he sold his Corvette to that dealership on South Broadway. He even managed to unload some stereo equipment and a new set of Pings, although he wondered if he might not miss the high-line golf clubs when he hit Mexico.

Now he was finishing up his packing and he had almost fifty-five thousand in cash for the trip south. He had hoped for more but he was in no position to bargain, especially after that call from Kovacs first thing in the morning. He figured that amount, plus the cash Ronnie brought, would give them a running start on a new life. He only hoped she would make their rendezvous. She was furious on the phone Monday night, an anger he couldn't understand. Then, when she called the next morning, she still wouldn't tell him where she was staying. She sounded remote and indifferent to their plans. When she didn't call today, Wednesday, he started to worry.

Cooper had barely slept the night before and he had been stuffing his nose with blow all day. Normally, he never touched the stuff, but he needed it to stay alert, and he knew he would need more to get him through the next couple days of driving. He had just over nine grams of cocaine left. That should do the trick, unless Ronnie got greedy in the car. Once they were safely to Guadalajara, he would sell his BMW and they'd set up a new life. He'd chosen Guadalajara because it is an inland, mid-sized capital of a Mexican state. He figured it was populated enough to get lost in and yet would not be as obvious a hiding place as the seaside resort towns.

At precisely four-forty-seven, he was ready to load up the car, check in with Kovacs downstairs, and split. Kovacs said he'd have a few bucks for Cooper from Doug's stash. Nowhere near the twenty grand he'd hoped for, but enough to make meeting the obnoxious police detective worthwhile. He grabbed his two suitcases and the metal briefcase with his life savings.

As he closed his loft door, a winded Max Herman, bleeding palms and all, was tromping up the stairs. When Cooper turned from his door and reached for his bags, Max wheezed around a hallway corner and into view. At first, Cooper didn't recognize him: Max was the last person he expected to see, and he still had on his dark aviators. But the lawyer recovered quickly.

"Maxwell. What, may I ask, are you doing here?" Cooper stood there with his bags in hand, about six feet from his visitor.

Max paused for a second, surprised to see the attorney before him. "Where are you going, may I ask, Mr. Shit Bird?" The sentence seemed to puzzle him for a second: he frowned deeply from behind his shades. Then he remembered his gun and struggled to pull it from his belt.

Cooper saw the small revolver and, understanding the gravity of the situation, took a step back. He realized that his Colt Python was in the trunk of his car, where it did him no good.

"Hold it right there, Mr. Bird Shit," Max yelled. Then, in a quieter voice, he added, "It's judgment day. Time to pay the piper." He had no idea what that meant, but it was the best he could do.

Cooper watched the gun wobble in Herman's hands. He calculated his options. He could try to talk some sense into the man, talk him out of the gun. Or he could try to verbally bully him into surrendering the weapon. Or, if Max was as far gone as he appeared, he could simply walk past him. He decided to invest a couple of minutes in conversation.

"What seems to be bothering you, Maxwell?"

Max took a minute to gather his thoughts. He suddenly felt nauseous and disoriented.

"The fuck you think is bothering me?" Actually, by now he was curious himself. All he could remember for sure was that Cooper had done something bad to him. He must have, or else why would Max be standing out there in the hallway with a gun on the man?

"I'm certain I have no idea." Cooper sensed that Max was running out of steam. He assumed that somehow the idiot had found out about what little work he'd put into the case. However, it might be no more complicated than that the imbecile was so wasted he was beyond all logic and was simply lashing out.

"You're certain," Max repeated as if he were considering a language foreign to him. He noticed his gun was pointing to a spot just in front of Cooper's feet, so he pulled it back up to aim at his chest. Random thoughts from the car came back to him. "Improvise," he shouted. "You sold me out. I'll improvise."

Cooper now felt relatively safe. He thought that the only real danger was if the gun went off by accident. He decided to wait until the barrel sagged down again and then walk past Max.

"I would suggest that you go home and get some sleep," Cooper said in his most soothing voice. "Then come see me at my office first thing in the morning. I'm certain we can straighten out whatever it is that's troubling you."

Armed or not, Cooper believed that Max Herman by now was manageable.

Max considered what Cooper said. His legs twitched briefly. He was dying to take a leak. He felt he had lost control of the situation and he feared he would soon lose control of his bladder. He took a deep breath and yelled, "Not good enough, Mr. Screw-Over. We settle this now." Settle what? He struggled to remember.

This is nonsense, Cooper thought. "Maxwell, please lower your weapon and go home. We'll iron this all out in the morning."

At first, there was silence. Then, as the gun barrel slowly lowered again, the clotted, nasal sound of a snore came from Max's open mouth. He was, literally, asleep on his feet.

Cooper rolled his eyes and in an even tone inquired, "Maxwell?"

The snoring sound only grew, and by now the gun was pointed almost directly at Max's own feet. Cooper had wasted enough time. He adjusted the bags in his hands and took two steps forward. He was about three feet away and just off to the right when Max jolted awake. Instinctively, he lifted the gun. All he saw for certain was the gleam of light from Cooper's brushed-metal briefcase. He still was almost asleep when he actually squeezed the trigger. Twice. The gun went off like a little cannon in the narrow hallway. Cooper's face looked stunned as the two slugs burned into his upper chest. His tongue shot out and his eyes froze wide open as his head shot back. He fell dead to the floor with his bags still firmly in his grip.

Max looked down at the lawyer and slowly realized what he'd done. That realization sobered him up plenty. Immediately. He looked down the hall in both directions but he was unable to move. He could hear footsteps pounding up the open stairwell.

Even that couldn't prompt him to move. As the sounds came to the top of the stairs, he finally started to backpedal away from Cooper. By the time Kovacs and Padilla came off the stairs and got a full view of what happened, Max had turned and was running away.

"Freeze," Kovacs screamed.

Both he and Padilla had their guns aimed at the fleeing figure. Automatically, Max turned back toward them and squeezed off a quick round. The bullet landed harmlessly in the ceiling, almost immediately over his own head, but it caused both detectives to drop to their knees. They opened fire from about fifty feet away. Miraculously, Max was able to run a few more steps, to where the hallway took a sharp right. He was gone before the officers got back on their feet.

"Follow him," Kovacs commanded Padilla. "I'll go back to the lobby and cut him off when he gets there."

"Right," his partner yelled as he ran down the hall. When he got to the corner where Max had just disappeared, he stopped and leaned his back against the wall, his gun clutched immediately in front of him with both hands. He inched his head around the corner. When he didn't see anyone, he ran down that hall.

Kovacs leaned over and glanced at Cooper for a second. He bent down to verify what he already knew—that the lawyer was dead. Next, he picked up the metal briefcase and opened it. When he saw the cash, he whistled lightly to himself and smiled. He closed it and glanced around the hall. Then he spotted a utility closet and went to it. He opened it and put the case inside, under a small bench. He'd be back for it later. As he shut off the closet light and closed the door, he heard three shots being fired from the downstairs lobby. He ran down the stairwell to verify something else he already knew—namely, that Padilla had killed the drunk.

Kovacs couldn't believe his good fortune. First the wino takes care of Cooper, and now Padilla takes care of the wino. For the first time in weeks, his stomach didn't feel like it was about to explode.

When Streeter walked into his apartment that night, it was almost twelve-thirty. Too late to call Story, and he was too tired to care about what was in the envelopes he'd pulled from the Porsche. He had given his oral statement to three different detectives at police headquarters and then went through a long written statement. All the while he kept picturing Soyko's body slumped over the shed and hearing the grunt from the man's death kick. The bounty hunter thought he'd feel deeply guilty and make all sorts of connections between this death and the one at Western Michigan all those years ago. But, strangely, he didn't. Soyko was one useless piece of garbage who had hurt a lot of people. A little bit of death didn't look half bad on the guy.

Streeter almost was too tired to check his voice mail, but he grabbed the phone in Frank's office right before he headed upstairs. There was one message. It was from Ronnie Taggert.

"I was watching the news and it looks like you've had a busy day." Her voice sounded soft, and Streeter could picture her in her hotel bed getting ready to fall asleep. "My hero. You did a good job on Soyko.

"But you weren't the lead story tonight," she continued, sounding more tired. "I don't know if you saw it, but Tom Cooper's dead. They said on the television that it was a pissed-off client who shot him to death. Then a Mexican cop killed the client. There's been so much going on the last few days. Unbelievable. It happened late this afternoon, about the same time I gather you were taking care of Leo Soyko. I was supposed to meet your friend Carey tomorrow but I don't think that's necessary now. Everyone he wanted to talk about is dead. So I'm going to bed, and then I'm leaving Colorado first thing in the morning. I've got serious thinking to do. This is goodbye. Thanks for the help and—who knows?—maybe we'll run into each other somewhere down the road. I might end up coming back here eventually."

Streeter sat there and stared at the phone for a long time. Then he stood up and walked upstairs to his loft. So much to think about, and he was so damned tired. As far as Cooper was concerned, it didn't shock him. The only surprise was that it wasn't Kovacs who pulled the trigger. He'd sort it all out after he got some sleep.

26

"What in the hell were you doing this morning?" Frank asked Streeter as the two stood out on the front stoop of the church that Thursday afternoon. "It sounded like you were throwing them damn weights against the garage door."

Streeter only nodded. He woke up early and he felt so jazzed that he went to the weight room and pumped serious iron for almost two hours. Later, he called Story and they agreed to meet at the church at four o'clock. She told him that there was just over thirty-one thousand in the envelope but said not to worry. "Then we'll be taking a little drive this afternoon and get the real payoff," was how she put it.

"I didn't sleep all that terrifically well last night," Streeter explained to Frank as they waited for her.

"I don't doubt that." Frank shook his head. "I'm surprised you slept at all, for crying out loud, after that business yesterday at the junkyard. It was me, I'd still be smashed. You feeling any better?"

"It was no picnic. But maybe now it's all finally over. I talked to Carey a little while ago and he filled me in on that shootout at Cooper's apartment. This town's turning into another Tombstone. And I don't mean the pizza. It sounded like the damned O.K. Corral over at Cooper's yesterday. Enough's enough."

"You got that right. I see by the paper your friend Kovacs was involved. Another coincidence?"

"I can't figure that one out. Carey told me that Art Kovacs didn't fire a shot. And there's no way he could have set it up like that, to have the other guy, the client, do it. I don't know what to think. Carey said that the second cop, Padilla, killed the guy that shot Cooper. He said Kovacs is clear on the whole thing. But I still can't believe I've been barking up the wrong tree with him. Coincidence, my ass. I have a feeling we haven't seen the last of Artie boy."

"For your sake, I hope you're wrong. What's next between you and the little lady with the money?"

"That's what I'll find out when she gets here. She said we have one more stop and we're home free, whatever that means. We found a little bit of money in the car but she said there's a lot more waiting for us."

"This is her now." Frank nodded toward the street.

Story's Audi pulled up in front of the church. She parked and got out, wearing a flower-print dress and sunglasses. Streeter had never seen her look better. Or happier. She smiled at both of them as she approached. "Gentlemen. Out getting a little sun, are we? How're you feeling, Streeter?"

"Better than our old friend Tom Cooper."

"Isn't that something? It looks like yesterday took care of a lot of things. I hate to see anyone get hurt, but Cooper died like ne lived. So did his two associates."

"That they did," Streeter said.

"I hope to hell you kids are finally out of the line of fire," Frank said.

"It looks that way," Story said. "Can we go inside and talk?"

Streeter nodded toward the door. "Mind if Frank sits in?"

"That's fine with me," she said.

"This place is turning into a damned war room," Frank said

as they settled into his office. He took his usual spot in the big chair behind the desk.

Story sat in front of the desk, next to Streeter, and pulled an envelope from her purse. It was the smaller package they took from the Porsche. She also pulled out a thick wad of cash and handed it to the bounty hunter.

"There's about ten thousand there. Your third of what we found."

"Not a bad day's work," Frank said.

Streeter set it on the table, barely looking at it. "What else do you have?" He nodded to the package in Story's hand.

"This is what we've been after all along. Maybe I should have guessed it, but that's hindsight. We've been looking for clocks."

"Great," Streeter said. "Another couple of clocks. Now, that definitely makes everything worthwhile. You're telling me Doug left a few more clocks?"

"A lot more. These are receipts for thirty-seven of the stupid things. They're all worth about the same as the one he left in the townhouse. Or more. If they're in good shape, I place the total value at close to half a million dollars."

Frank let out a loud whistle. "Holy moly. That much for some clocks? What are they made out of? Gold?"

She turned to face him across the desk. "You'd think so. When I sold that other one, I got a short course on how valuable these things are. I had a hunch Doug may have bought more, but I had no idea he bought this many or that some of them would be so valuable. A couple of them go for almost thirty thousand each.

"Judging from the receipts, he bought all but a couple of them when he lived in Boulder. Before I met him. Some of these purchases are ten years old. Clocks." She shook her head. "That would explain his interest in the art museum. They've had clock exhibits there. It also fits in with his interest in mechanical things. He may even have tried to repair or restore some of them. God, I hope not. Not with his mechanical abilities. But at least he would be able to tell what kind of shape they were in when he bought them."

She pulled out some of the receipts. "They're all named after clockmakers and such. Look, Streeter. Here's one that's a William Webb Wellington. That must have been that reference to Webb in his checkbook. We thought it was the mayor. This is where all Doug's extra cash must have gone. Judging from what he paid for them and what they're worth now, that man knew his clocks. I talked to my dealer friend this morning and ran some of these by him. He told me what they're worth now, and I'll tell you, Doug made out all right. The good part is that we can sell them through my friend, and even with his commission, we'll still end up with over four hundred thousand. Maybe more."

Streeter looked at the receipts in silence. Then he said, "I thought it was artwork. Collectibles like paintings and antiques are the perfect investment for a drug dealer. A great way to hide assets. Everything is cash and there's practically no way to trace it for taxes or by the police. That is, if you buy at the right price, tuck them safely away, and then know when to sell them. Clocks make sense."

"We've got it made," Story said.

"Yeah, right," Streeter interrupted. "I take it you have them in your trunk?"

"Of course I don't have them." Then her voice softened. "Not yet, anyhow."

"My next question is fairly obvious."

"Yes, it is. And the answer is, Wyoming. They're up in Wyoming."

"What the hell they doing up there?" Frank shot in.

Streeter sat up. "They're with his mother. I wanted to talk to her all along and you kept saying no."

"I didn't say no." Story narrowed her eyes. "I just said I didn't think she would have anything. But now that I know what we're after, it makes sense. Assuming Doug trusted her, which he must have, her farm would be the perfect place to keep them. She probably had them under her homeowner's insurance. No one would think of looking up there."

"You know for sure she has them?" Streeter asked.

"There were a couple of letters from her in with the receipts. She talked about the whole situation. She's been keeping them in her basement and in the barn. The last one was bought about four years ago, and the clocks were all safe and sound at that time."

"So now what?" Streeter asked. "We call her and let her know we're coming and then rent a U-Haul and go get them? You think she'll just hand them over like that?"

"Hardly. Gail Shelton is one tough, self-centered old broad. Like I told you, Doug was kind of afraid of her. When you meet her, you'll see why. Plus, she can't stand me. But I talked to my attorney this morning and she said that I have every legal right to them. Doug's will says I get everything he had. My guess is, it's his way of telling the old lady what he really thought of her—otherwise she would be a beneficiary. I've got the will in my car, and I figure with a big guy like you along she'll have no choice but to turn them over."

"Right." Streeter frowned at Frank. "She gives me any grief, I kick the hell out of her. I hate to be negative, but what if she's already sold them? That could leave us basically fornicated, if you pardon my language. She's had months to do it, and that would be the smart move."

"Then we've got problems. If they're gone, we'll have to take her to court for the money. That could drag on forever. Let's just keep our fingers crossed."

"And you want to go now?"

"No point in waiting."

"You two think it's safe?" Frank asked. "I mean, the way this thing is going, who knows what's waiting for you up there. Kovacs may not be the one, but someone spray-painted your little puppy and shot at this place."

Story stood up impatiently. "I can't worry about that now. That's my inheritance and I intend to go get it. I have every right to it and I'm not going to let anyone stop me. I'm going now. With or without you, Streeter."

He stood up, too. He took the cash she gave him and slid it across the desk at Frank. "Put that in a safe place for me." Then he turned to Story. "We'll take your car, but I'm going to bring my thirty-eight along, just in case. I don't know if we're out of danger yet or not, but I don't want to get caught without a gun ever again."

27

Detective Arthur Ernest Kovacs certainly had done more than his share of twisted and degrading things for money over the years. But he figured sleeping with Gail Shelton easily had to have been the worst. Just the thought of it made him blink as he drove. Gail might be only nine years older than him, but she always seemed more like a maiden aunt. Too much of that Lutheran Bible guilt, he reasoned, made her look ancient in the morning. Like a stack of dry firewood next to him in bed.

Every trip up Wyoming State Highway 211, just north of Cheyenne, felt more like a forced death march to Kovacs. Thank God, this is the last one. Payday, and then no more dealing with the farm hag. Since he first met her, at Doug's funeral, Kovacs had been sucking up to Gail and turning on what he passed off as charm. Between that and laying on plenty of the old baloney about how he'd see to it that no one grabbed her precious clocks, he was able to talk her into a nice chunk of the revenue from them.

Now Gail finally had received her last check for the clock sales from a broker in Salt Lake City. Kovacs figured his half to be about a quarter of a million. Throw in the fifty or sixty thousand from Cooper's metal briefcase, next to him on the car seat, and his pension, and the officer figured to hit retirement in the approximate vicinity of solid comfort. God knows, he had never saved more than a couple hundred bucks on his own.

After tonight, no more worrying about Moffatt, either. Once he got the cash in hand no one could touch it. The sun was sitting low in the west as he pulled up the driveway to Gail Shelton's ancient house. The dump always reminded him of Ma and Pa Kettle's farm. No more of her endless ramblings about how she grew up in this pile of bricks and boards, he thought. No more bullshit flattery. And maybe, finally, no more eruptions and fiery spasms from his tortured insides. With the money in hand, Kovacs figured, it was young broads and solid food from here on out.

"Gracious, Arthur, you look like you've been sleeping in a Dumpster for the past few weeks," Gail greeted him when he walked into the kitchen. "I suppose you'll want a drink. You always do. Well, you know where it's located." She nodded toward the cabinet over the sink. "You better make it a strong one. You and I have to talk about a few things."

Gail had been pacing the decrepit kitchen when Kovacs entered. The room hadn't been remodeled in over thirty years, and it always smelled stale, with a hint of cooked onions. Heavy black metal pots hung ominously on the wall like medieval bondage equipment.

Gail was grim this evening. She knew that the upcoming confrontation was going to take all of her resolve. But it had to be done. She desperately wanted this mulish, sadistic cop out of her life, and she had no intention of parting with the kind of money she knew he expected.

"Who shit in your oatmeal?" Kovacs saw no need to hide his thoughts. "Can't you try and be pleasant? Just once? We should be celebrating."

"Please, just get your drink. I think it's time we both cut all the malarkey and leveled with each other. What's in the briefcase?" she asked, pointing to Cooper's metal case, which he'd lugged in with him.

"This is something I picked up from Doug's attorney. It's a long story, but the bottom line is, I got a little something extra for my efforts down there to Denver. There's cash in here, but there's still enough room for what you owe me."

"That's what we have to talk about."

With that, she turned and headed into the adjoining living room to sit on the old couch. That room wasn't much more pleasant than the kitchen, but at least the onion smell was less pronounced.

Kovacs reached over the sink and grabbed the lone bottle of discount bourbon stored there. As he poured a double, neat, into a glass advertising a local gas station in loud colors, he wondered why Gail was in such an angry mood. She was never what you'd call cheerful, but this was the first time she'd actually insulted him. He took a long pull on his drink and then headed to the living room, where he sat down in a stuffed chair facing the couch.

"There some problem with your guy in Salt Lake?" he asked. "That what got you in this mood? Didn't you get the checks this week?"

"The checks are in and the transaction is complete," she answered formally. Gail ran a hand through her wiry gray hair and frowned. "But we have to talk about the finances. You see, Arthur, it's not going to be the way we decided originally. I've made some changes."

"You made changes, huh? I don't remember you asking me about that. What might those changes be?"

She looked at him for a moment and then reached over to the end table and grabbed a rumpled brown paper bag. After studying it, she tossed it to him. Kovacs caught it and looked inside. There were rolls of twenties and fifties, but it didn't look like it amounted to any two hundred fifty thousand dollars' worth.

"This looks a little light, Gail. How much did you get for the clocks? The final grand total, I mean."

"To be honest, something just under five hundred twenty thousand."

"So I should be looking at what in here? Maybe two hundred sixty. Is that what I'm looking at, Gail?"

"No, it is not. There is exactly one hundred and twenty-five thousand in there. And that's the change I referred to." She sat back as if to indicate that was the end of the discussion.

"You got any more bags around here for me, or is this your idea of being clever?" He shifted impatiently in his seat.

"Don't act like a child. That is a lot of money."

Kovacs put his drink down on the floor between his legs and set the money bag next to it. Then he got up and took a step toward Gail.

"Enough of the crap, you old cow. I put up with a lot from you these past few months, but I did it for half of what those clocks were worth. That was our agreement. I had to deal with a ton of shit down there in Denver to keep people away from this money and keep your saggy ass safe. I did things that you don't need to know about but I kept my word. And, as ugly as it got down there, it was nowhere near as bad as what I had to do up here. Sex with you, hell, it was like doing it with a pile of old newspapers."

"I'll just bet you know what that's like, too," she shot back. "Look who's complaining about sex, will you? I deserve a medal for getting a rise out of that alcoholic roll of blubber you call a body."

His eyes widened in rage, and he drew his hand back a few inches like he was going to hit her.

"That's just great," she screamed. "Go ahead and hit me. Is that how you prove you're a man? I can't believe I ever saw anything in you. Your little act about caring for me was so obviously false. Such a lie. And all that garbage about keeping our affair a secret. Like it was our own little world we were building here. You were ashamed of me, is all."

She was crying by the time she finished.

"You got that right!"

"Now that I've got the money"—she looked up—"I don't need your 'protection' anymore. So I'm cutting your commission in half to compensate me for all the humiliation you've caused. Men have never been much more than trouble in my life. First that useless husband of mine, and then those two sons. Philip, poor child of God, will need to be in a home for the rest of his life. And the other one was nothing more than some kind of homo drug dealer.

"But at least his money will pay for Philip's care. Poor Philip, he's so lost. God knows, he's so bad off. This is my chance to make sure he'll be taken care of, and I am certainly not about to give that money up to some broken-down booze hound. You can stand there and yell all you want to, but that money's in a trust for Philip, and there's no way on earth you'll touch a penny of it. Just take what's in the bag, guzzle your drink, and then leave. And if you ever come back on my property, I'll have you arrested for trespassing and assault. Don't think I can't do it, either. I've lived up here all my life and I've got plenty of clout with the local law."

Kovacs took a step back, stunned by what she said. Trust funds, no more money. He couldn't believe it.

"You gotta be shittin' me. That money's around here somewhere and you better produce roughly a hundred thirty-five thousand, right now, or you'll regret it. Believe me. I ain't screwing around here."

"You 'ain't screwing around here.' What utter intelligence," Gail said as she rose from the couch to face him. "You're so coarse, Arthur. So dumb, too. Do I have to use puppets or something to get through to you? There is no more money. It's gone. It's in a fund in Laramie. That's where Philip is. You can't get at it, I can't get at it. Now, take this money and leave. You're not making out so poorly. I'm sure it'll keep you in bourbon and pornography for the few miserable years you have left."

Rage gnawed at Kovacs' innards like a starving rat. He felt

wildly nauseous, and the burn in his chest seemed as though he was having a heart attack. He shot both hands out and caught Gail squarely on her shoulders. The push knocked her backward hard into the couch, and the momentum of that caused her to almost bounce back to her feet.

"You bitch," he hissed. "You spent my money on that retarded kid. Who the fuck do you think you're dealing with?"

There was genuine terror in Gail's eyes when he drew his forty-four from its shoulder holster under his sport coat. Before she could say another word, the detective balled up the heavy gun in his fist and drove it into her face. He did it three more times, smashing the left side of her head and face. As she lay there, Kovacs thought for sure she was dead. Not that he cared.

Slowly, he wiped the bloody gun on the couch next to Gail. Then he went into the bathroom and cleaned it off better. When he was finished he scrubbed his hands. Back in the living room, he grabbed the bag with the money. Gail moaned and turned slightly on the couch, but the policeman barely noticed. Instead, he went to the kitchen and put the bag on top of Cooper's briefcase on the table. He took a long pull straight from the bourbon bottle and decided to go through the entire house. That bitch had to have part of the money around here somewhere, he reasoned. Kovacs wasn't leaving until he found it. Then he would make sure the old lady never told the local law what happened.

28

"So, Streeter, how is it that a stallion like you never got married?" Story asked as they drove up State Highway 211 toward Gail Shelton's house.

He smiled. "Stallion? Never been married? If only you knew. You're looking at one of the most frequently married men in Colorado. I've made the trip down the aisle on numerous occasions, with a couple of near misses."

"Really?" She glanced at him for a second. "How many trips are we talking about?"

"More than I care to admit."

"Why not tell me?"

"We'll be at the farmhouse in less than fifteen minutes and it would take a lot longer than that to run down my matrimonial history. We'd need a cross-country trip." Then, after a short pause, "Okay, I've been married four times and I've been engaged twice, make that three more times."

"Very impressive. You could practically have your own segment on *Oprah* with that kind of numbers. I trust they weren't all as cheap as that blonde working for Tom Cooper you were so interested in. Honestly, what do men see in something like that, Streeter?"

He shrugged. "She had a lot of appeal, Story. I think there was more there than you realize. And that's the second time you've acted jealous of her. I'm going to start thinking you're interested in me if you're not careful."

"Eat your heart out, big boy." She was quiet for about a mile and then, "One question. How come you couldn't make it work with any of those women? It certainly couldn't have been the woman's fault every time."

"You're right about that. It wasn't always their fault. I'm not sure if there was one reason they all failed. Let's just say that I'm not particularly good at long-term projects. I'm better at starting the fire than at keeping it going. That and my selection process tends to be flawed."

"Does that bother you? I mean, wouldn't you like to go the distance with a woman eventually?"

"I don't give it too much thought anymore." After a pause, he added, "Yeah, it would be nice to make it work." He studied her profile. "Now I have one question for you. Why do you always have to run things and have everything your way?"

"Technically, that's two questions.'

"I'm not particularly good at math, either. Look, I don't want to pick a fight, but at times you take being headstrong to a new level. Why?"

Story seemed to be genuinely considering his words. "I have a friend who's a psychologist and she thinks that being aggressive is my way of keeping people off balance and at a distance. She thinks I'm afraid that, if I give up even a little bit of control, then I feel like I won't have any control at all. She said that, deep underneath, I'm not very secure."

Streeter continued to study her face as she spoke. Sometimes, he noticed, when she wasn't giving orders, she had a soft vulnerability that gave him an excited little twitch in the pit of his stomach.

"What do you think about that?" he asked.

"It's more probable than I care to admit. I've always been like that. When I was little, I used to order everyone around so much that my dad would call me 'sir.' Just to tease me. He told me a while ago that he still doesn't like when I do that. Parents." She shrugged. "How do you get along with your parents?"

He didn't say anything at first. "They've both been dead for years. My mother died when I was a senior in high school. Cancer. My father died a couple of years later. Cancer, too, although he had other health problems. He was a heavy drinker. Very heavy. I never knew either of them when I was an adult."

"Look, here's the ancestral home of Douglas Shelton," Story said. "We're here. Time to meet the dragon lady."

Gail's house stood off to the right, about one hundred yards ahead, quietly drooping in the sunset.

"I take it Doug wasn't much for home improvements."

"He didn't do a thing up here since he moved out after high school."

As they pulled into the drive, they noticed a tan Ford station wagon, circa late 1970s, with Colorado plates, nestled up near the side of the building. There was also a new white pickup truck with Wyoming plates off to the left, away from the house. They pulled up behind the Ford and parked.

"Looks like she's got company," Streeter said as he pulled his thirty-eight out of the glove compartment. "I'll just take this in with us in case it's someone who doesn't like me."

"Do you think it could be Kovacs?"

"That would be a coincidence and you know I don't believe in coincidences. Probably just a friend or something like that. But I lugged this thing all the way up from Denver. I might as well take it another twenty feet."

Kovacs was digging through Gail's bedroom closet when he heard the back doorbell ring. The bedroom was the last room he had to check. It was becoming clear that Gail had meant it when she said there was no money around. At first, he thought of just ignoring the doorbell, but then he figured, if it was one of Gail's loopy farmer friends, they would know the old lady was home, and be suspicious if no one answered.

As he walked through the living room, he noticed that Gail had shifted on the couch. Still, she seemed to be asleep. Walking through the kitchen, he gave his forty-four Magnum a quick pat in its shoulder holster. He moved quietly to the back door. Through the thin lace curtains he could see at least one figure standing out in the near darkness of the enclosed sun porch. Then he saw another, larger figure next to the first.

The detective put one hand inside his jacket on his gun as he pressed the light switch. When the yellowish overhead light hit Streeter and Story, Kovacs didn't immediately recognize them. But as he opened the back door, he remembered who they were and pulled out his gun.

It was at about that moment that Streeter made out the detective as well. He automatically reached around to the small of his back, where he had jammed his pistol under his shirt, between his skin and his pants.

Kovacs pushed open the heavy metal screen door and stepped quickly out and down the one step onto the porch. His gun was drawn and aimed at Story, who was the closer of the two visitors. By now, Streeter had his gun out, and he focused the barrel squarely at the cop's profile. Both men were close enough to their targets—five feet away at the most—that they couldn't miss.

Story let out a crisp scream when she saw the gun aimed at her. She spoke first. "Put that damned thing down," she yelled at the man coming out of the house. Then, almost as an afterthought, she added, "Shoot him, Streeter. Do something."

"You shoot me, I shoot her," Kovacs said without taking his eyes off of Story.

"Just take it easy, Kovacs. Put the gun down. Don't even think of shooting. Put it down or you're dead."

"If I'm dead, so is she. I swear it."

The three of them stood under the dingy light in utter silence for a moment. Kovacs was directly in front of the screen door, holding his gun at about shoulder level, with both hands. Story was in front of the door as well but about six feet from it, and Streeter stood off to the right side, a few feet away. He was in the same firing stance as the detective. The porch had an organic smell to it, part old apples and part litter box. There didn't seem to be enough air for all three of them.

"Looks like we got us your basic Mexican standoff out here," Kovacs said with a fair amount of crude irony. His voice had that trained cop control in it. "There's got to be some way we can work this out without two people getting killed."

"What the hell are you doing here?" Streeter asked. "Where's the woman who lives in this house?"

"You mean Gail? Oh, she's taking a nap. I think it'll be a long one, too. So what the fuck are you doing here?"

"We're here to pick up something that belongs to her," Streeter nodded to Story, although Kovacs wasn't watching him.

"If you're looking for them old clocks, I'm afraid you're too late. They're all gone. Sold. Every one of them."

Story, who until now had remained pale and quiet, suddenly stiffened.

"You sold my clocks?" she demanded. "You can't do that. That was my inheritance. Shoot him, Streeter."

"Relax, sweetie." Kovacs smiled at her outburst. "You're quite a little firecracker, aren't you? The old lady sold them, I didn't."

"How'd you get into all this?" Streeter asked. He could feel his shoulders tiring from holding the big gun with both hands.

"None of your business." Kovacs thought he heard a faint rustle from the kitchen behind him and he shifted his eyes quickly. He wanted to turn around, but he knew if he did that he would lose his bead on Story, and Streeter could shoot him. "The real problem for you is, how are you going to get out of all this?"

The question hung in the thick night air for a just a few seconds. No one actually heard anything before the back door exploded open. But when it did, the door's heavy, sharp edge hit

Kovacs squarely in the middle of the back of his head. It pushed him forward, toward Story a couple of steps, and stunned him. Disoriented, he looked back at the door and saw Gail Shelton stalking out of it. The caked blood on the side of her head made her look like a zombie, but she was moving fast and spitting anger. One of the black cast-iron skillets from the kitchen wall was in her hands, and she was lifting it over her head and off to one side. Kovacs looked down at his gun in confusion, and before he could completely reorient himself Gail let out a scream.

"You rotten slime," she hollered as she brought the enormous skillet across the front of her, driving the edge of it deeply into the perplexed cop's cheek and crushing the bone. "You lousy son of a bitch."

Immediately after that, the stunned and by now badly bleeding detective felt Story's fist land on the left side of his head. She had walked around to that side, between him and Streeter, when Gail came flying out the door. Story let out a curse as she swung and landed another punch in almost the identical spot.

Because Story was in his line of fire, Streeter couldn't shoot. From somewhere in his fog, Kovacs knew that he was in trouble. Again, he looked down at the huge gun he was holding with his right hand at about waist level. He brought it up a few inches and when the barrel was aimed in Gail's general direction he pulled the trigger. Fortunately for her, she was just lifting the skillet across her chest for another swipe at the man in front of her. The gun went off like a rocket and a shrill flash of sparks exploded on the skillet as the bullet ricocheted off of it and out into the night air.

Gail's eyes narrowed in further rage at the effrontery of the shot and she lowered the skillet to waist level. She and Kovacs stared at each other for just an instant, and then the farm woman, with both hands firmly on the handle, brought the utensil up and out squarely at him. It struck the forty-four just as the detective was about to squeeze the trigger again. The momentum of the skillet forced the gun upward and eventually back, till the barrel was quickly moving toward Kovacs' chin.

Sadly for him, that was when he fired off another round. The gun was still moving up and back when the flash of the bullet hit Kovacs just below his lower lip. The simmering lead kept flying upward, through his brain and out the top of his head, taking a surprisingly large chunk of his balding scalp with it.

He fell into a fast heap at the feet of both Gail and Story. Streeter had moved forward by now, and he kept his gun on Kovacs even though half his head was blown away. Streeter then kicked the forty-four away from the body. Story instinctively backed off a step or two, but Gail held her ground.

"That man never gave me credit for nothing," Gail said as she stared at the body. "He tried to kill me in there. He always underestimated me."

"He'll never make that mistake again." Streeter looked up at her on the porch step. "Neither will we."

29

"He seems more sad than anything." Story finally defined Kovacs' gaze to no one in particular. "The top of his head's nearly blown off. You'd think he'd be more surprised or pained or something, wouldn't you? You'd think he'd look different than just sad."

Tears flowing down her checks, she turned to Streeter with the question. He grabbed her gently by her shoulder with one hand and pulled her toward him. Then he looked down at Gail Shelton, who had sat on the stoop immediately after dropping the skillet.

"Are you okay?" he asked. "What happened to your head?"

"Oh, don't worry about me. Just take care of that delicate little thing. After all, she's crying. I'm only bleeding." Gail turned away, obviously disgusted.

"I'll call for help in a minute," Streeter answered.

"That would be a good idea," Gail said. "I've got the headache of the century."

"What *was* he doing here?" Streeter nodded down to Kovacs. Story wiped at her cheeks with the back of one hand and looked over to Gail as well. Her tears had stopped.

"Prince Charming? He was my knight in shining armor." She looked down at the detective and said no more.

"What do you mean?" Story asked.

Gail looked up at her like she'd just asked for a handout. She still said nothing. Finally, Streeter repeated the question. "What you mean by Prince Charming?"

Gail shrugged. "He got to me right after the funeral and told me how he and Doug had become good friends. He told me so many things about Doug, personal things, that I believed him. He knew Doug left stuff with me that was valuable and that there could be people coming after it. He said they would want to take the things away from me. He said he would see to it that that didn't happen. I bought it all. Hook, line, and the whole enchilada."

"You mean people like me?" Story insisted. "The people who own the clocks? People who Doug left everything to in his will? People like that?"

Gail looked back at her and actually spoke to her this time. "I didn't know he had a will. I just assumed he didn't have anything much but the clocks. If they were yours, why didn't you come up for them sooner?"

Story blushed, and it was Streeter who answered. "We had no idea where they were until recently. Or even what they were. Listen, can we go inside and call the police? I wouldn't mind a drink of water, either."

Gail got up and took one last look at the dead cop. Then she nodded for them to follow her into the kitchen. When they got inside, Streeter went to the sink for a drink of water and the two women sat down at the kitchen table without looking at each other. Tension was as thick in the air as the cooked-onion smell.

"That fella out on the porch isn't going anywhere, and my little headache can keep," Gail said when Streeter sat down. "We should really have us a talk before any police get out here."

"That's a good idea," Story said. "Kovacs said that you already sold my clocks. Is that true?"

"Yes. They're all gone, and there's no way to get them back.

Sold to collectors here and all the way to England, I'm told."

"Then it would appear you owe me money." Story was look-ing directly into Gail's eyes, but the older woman didn't flinch. "A great deal of money. I've got receipts for thirty-seven of those precious clocks of his, and they showed Doug Shelton is the owner. And I have a will that gives me everything that belonged to him. That means those clocks. According to my calculations, you had better come up with several hundred thousand dollars or prepare to spend your twilight years in court."

Gail considered that for a moment and then leaned across the table toward Story. "Sweetie, you can take me to court or you can grab that gun of his out there and put it to my head. But I don't have anywhere near the kind of money you're looking for. It's come and gone and that's all there is to it."

Story practically jumped out of her chair. "How dare you? Those didn't belong to you. You know how Doug felt about you. He couldn't stand you. He never said a kind word about you."

"I sure as hell didn't know any of them belonged to you. I was his mother. His family needed that money and that's where it went. To take care of Philip. That poor child's treatment is more important than you getting new clothes and a few new toys. Besides, judging from those last few letters I got from him, he wasn't too fond of you, either."

Story's mouth was just opening in response when Streeter stood up himself, holding out his open hand.

"Enough. This guy didn't seem too nuts about either of you, and I can't say as I really blame him. Standing around here screaming at each other like a couple of spoiled kids isn't going to get us anywhere. And we've got to call somebody about Prince Charming out there pretty soon." He shook his head. "Maybe we can settle this fast and first." He turned to Gail. "Exactly where is the money now? Have you spent all of it?"

"In a manner of speaking. I set up a blind trust for Doug's brother, Philip, over in Laramie. He'll be in a home for the rest of his life. He can't take care of himself. The rest of it, just under thirty-five grand, well, I've ordered some remodeling for this old barn. I put most of it in a down payment to the contractor. I plan on fixing this place up and then selling. That takes care of all of it except for his share." She nodded toward the back sun porch.

Both of her guests looked in that direction in unison.

"His share?" Story asked.

"We had an agreement," Gail said. "He wasn't too thrilled with the payment. That's how I got this." She nodded the side of her head with the blood. "He wasn't much for negotiating and, like so many men, he hated changes."

"You had money for him? How much are we talking about?" Story sat down again.

Gail considered the questions for a long time. "If I give you a hundred and twenty-five thousand dollars cash money, will you go away and never come back? I was willing to pay that for him to disappear. It'd be worth that much—easy—never to see you again. And that would sure beat wrestling each other in court for the next few years with no one getting rich but the lawyers."

"How long would it take you to get it for me?"

"You could have it today."

Streeter and Story looked at each other.

"Sounds like that might be the way to go," he said.

Story looked back at Gail, while brushing some hair from her face. Then, slowly, "If I can have it today and you can prove that the money's in a trust, I'm willing to forget the rest. I don't want to take money from Doug's brother. But if I thought you were keeping it for yourself, I'd fight you in court forever."

"We'll call it Philip's reward," Gail said. She reached on top of the metal briefcase, off to the side of the table, and grabbed the ratty paper bag. "Here you go. Now, after the police are done here, our business is finished."

Story took the bag and looked inside. "Fair enough. After I count it."

"You can have this, too, if you want." Gail pulled the briefcase toward her and opened it. She turned it around so they could see the cash inside.

"What the hell is that?" Streeter bent forward.

"Mr. Kovacs brought that to show me, for some reason. He said he took it from Doug's attorney. He said he earned it, but I imagine that means he stole it. Or maybe worse."

"He probably took it off Cooper yesterday," Streeter speculated. "I knew he was dirty on that deal, too." He picked up a stack of fifties and fanned through it. "There must be—what? —forty, fifty thousand in here."

Story looked at the money and then took the stack out of Streeter's hands and threw it back in the case.

"This isn't ours." Then she turned to Gail. "And it's not yours, either. This goes to the police. Let them decide what to do with it. You better call."

Gail took one more quick look at the money and then closed the case. "You're right. Let them deal with it. I've seen enough money for one day."

Gail called the sheriff's office. As the three of them waited, Story actually went to the bathroom with the older woman and helped clean out her head injury. Streeter sat on the back-porch step and watched Kovacs. Detroit cop, he thought. Those FBI agents had it right.

When the paramedics and deputies finally arrived, they spent little time questioning everyone and gathering evidence. This may have been the first shooting death they'd seen in over a year, but they all knew Gail Shelton so well that they pretty much took her word for everything.

It was nearly ten-thirty when Story's Audi finally pulled out of the farm driveway and headed back south toward Cheyenne.

"I have to ask you something," Streeter said after a couple of miles. "When you said the money in the briefcase isn't ours and that the police should have it, isn't that a little out of character for you? I mean, we could have taken it and no one would have known."

"Don't think that hasn't crossed my mind. But I keep remembering when you asked me how much class it takes to try and screw an insurance company with a bogus neck injury. I feel bad about that little stunt. This is one way I can help make up for it."

They drove on in silence until they got to the outskirts of Cheyenne.

"I'll buy you a drink once we get to Denver," Streeter told her. "We deserve it after the last couple of days. Unless you want to hurry home and put that bag in a trunk under your bed for the night."

"I'm so drained, I'm not sure I can make it all the way back to Denver. And I know I can't get that far without a drink."

"You want me to drive?"

"I'm okay for now. They've got a decent little bar at the Marriott in Cheyenne. How does that sound?"

"A hotel bar." He looked at her face in the dashboard light. Her features seemed tired, which relaxed them nicely. He was glad their business arrangement was over, and he noticed that he still had the urge to kiss her. To hold her. Maybe more. "I'm game if you are. Look, if you just want to crash for the night, we can each get a room and then head back to Denver in the morning."

Story didn't say anything for a long time. Then she glanced at him. "Why don't we get that drink and you can tell me about those fires you're so good at starting. Who knows, maybe all we'll need is one room."

Now it was Streeter's turn to be quiet. Finally, he said, "It sure can't hurt to talk about it."

A Long Reach

A Streeter Mystery

Michael Stone

From the creator of the funniest, grittiest private eye to hit Denver's mean streets, comes another mystery starring ex-linebacker, ex-bouncer, ex-husband four times over, Streeter. Yeah, just Streeter. Now, still working out of a renovated church in Denver, Streeter must face his toughest challenge when he gets a call from an ex-fiancée and attorney-with-an-attitude who fears she's on the hit list of a former client. With his characteristic cool, Streeter hits the gumshoe trail again to find hairpin turns in a dark, humorous plot full of nonstop action.

FOR THE BEST IN PAPERBACKS, LOOK FOR THE

In every corner of the world, on every subject under the sun, Penguin represents quality and variety—the very best in publishing today.

For complete information about books available from Penguin—including Puffins, Penguin Classics, and Arkana—and how to order them, write to us at the appropriate address below. Please note that for copyright reasons the selection of books varies from country to country.

In the United Kingdom: Please write to *Dept. JC, Penguin Books Ltd, FREEPOST, West Drayton, Middlesex UB7 0BR*.

If you have any difficulty in obtaining a title, please send your order with the correct money, plus ten percent for postage and packaging, to *P.O. Box No. 11, West Drayton, Middlesex UB7 0BR*

In the United States: Please write to *Consumer Sales, Penguin USA, P.O. Box 999, Dept. 17109, Bergenfield, New Jersey 07621-0120*. VISA and MasterCard holders call 1-800-253-6476 to order all Penguin titles

In Canada: Please write to *Penguin Books Canada Ltd, 10 Alcorn Avenue, Suite 300, Toronto, Ontario M4V 3B2*

In Australia: Please write to *Penguin Books Australia Ltd, P.O. Box 257, Ringwood, Victoria 3134*

In New Zealand: Please write to *Penguin Books (NZ) Ltd, Private Bag 102902, North Shore Mail Centre, Auckland 10*

In India: Please write to *Penguin Books India Pvt Ltd, 706 Eros Apartments, 56 Nehru Place, New Delhi 110 019*

In the Netherlands: Please write to *Penguin Books Netherlands bv, Postbus 3507, NL-1001 AH Amsterdam*

In Germany: Please write to *Penguin Books Deutschland GmbH, Metzlerstrasse 26, 60594 Frankfurt am Main*

In Spain: Please write to *Penguin Books S.A., Bravo Murillo 19, 1° B, 28015 Madrid*

In Italy: Please write to *Penguin Italia s.r.l., Via Felice Casati 20, I-20124 Milano*

In France: Please write to *Penguin France S.A., 17 rue Lejeune, F–31000 Toulouse*

In Japan: Please write to *Penguin Books Japan, Ishikiribashi Building, 2–5–4, Suido, Bunkyo-ku, Tokyo 112*

In Greece: Please write to *Penguin Hellas Ltd, Dimocritou 3, GR–106 71 Athens*

In South Africa: Please write to *Longman Penguin Southern Africa (Pty) Ltd, Private Bag X08, Bertsham 2013*